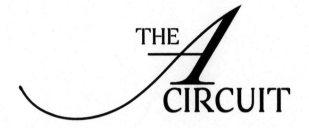

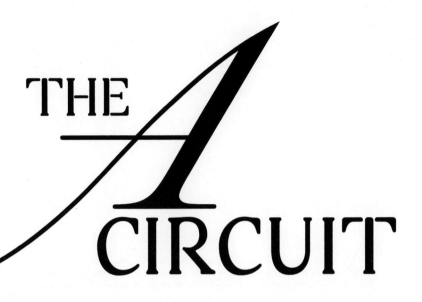

THE A CIRCUIT

GEORGINA BLOOMBERG
& CATHERINE HAPKA

BLOOMSBURY

NEW YORK   BERLIN   LONDON   SYDNEY

First published in the United States of America in May 2011
by Bloomsbury Books for Young Readers
www.bloomsburyteens.com

For information about permission to reproduce selections from this book, write to
Permissions, Bloomsbury BFYR, 175 Fifth Avenue, New York, New York 10010

Library of Congress Cataloging-in-Publication Data
Bloomberg, Georgina.
The A circuit / by Georgina Bloomberg & Catherine Hapka. — 1st U.S. ed.
p.   cm.
Summary: A billionaire heiress, a working student, and the daughter of a famous rock
star compete on horseback riding's elite A circuit.
ISBN 978-1-59990-634-8 (paperback) • ISBN 978-1-59990-641-6 (hardcover)
[1. Horse shows—Fiction.   2. Horsemanship—Fiction.   3. Friendship—Fiction.
4. Wealth—Fiction.]   I. Hapka, Catherine.   II. Title.
PZ7.B62345Aam 2011   [E]—dc22   2011000562

Book design by Danielle Delaney
Typeset by Westchester Book Composition
Printed in the U.S.A. by Quad/Graphics, Fairfield, Pennsylvania
2 4 6 8 10 9 7 5 3   (hardcover)
2 4 6 8 10 9 7 5 3   (paperback)

To my mother, Susan,
for always supporting me,
through the good and the bad
—G. B.

For the people who helped make this happen:
Caroline Abbey, Michelle Nagler,
Frank Weimann, and Elyse Tanzillo
—C. H.

ONE

──── ──── ──── ──── ────

"Stalker alert," Zara muttered in disgust as she saw a fat, sweaty guy with a camera zero in on her father. If she'd thought the paparazzi would be any less annoying here than in LA, she'd thought wrong. Same manure, different coast.

Her father dropped his cigarette and ground it out with the toe of his Tres Outlaws custom cowboy boot. "Chill out, Little Z," he said without looking at her. He leaned casually on the post-and-board fence of the ring, pretending to watch some random panicky-looking pony rider steer a phlegmatic pinto over a tiny pre-beginner-wannabe-hunter course.

Zara rolled her eyes. "Nice pose," she told her father. "Very Zac Trask."

His green eyes flicked toward her, but he didn't answer. The photographer was upon them, the stench of stale BO announcing his arrival. Zac's publicist and a couple of body-guards moved closer. Just in case the guy turned out to be psycho, Zara knew, though she doubted many psychos would waste their time hanging around some sleepy small-time horse show in the middle of New Jersey.

She glanced around, still not quite believing she was here. The showgrounds were dusty and hot under the early summer sun, the humidity making her chin-length dark hair frizz out like some mall chick's. June in New Jersey. It sounded like the title of one of Zac's songs.

The reporter was spouting eager questions at the Rock God, the same ones as always. Zara was already bored. Then again, this wasn't exactly the place to seek any major excitement.

Or was it? She perked up as she spotted a guy wandering past. He had a big nose and a smattering of zits on his chin but was otherwise passable looking, clean and preppy in full Abercrombie regalia, though his demeanor was awkward and his expression vaguely uncomfortable. Probably because he knew he was the only straight guy in a half-mile radius, Zara figured.

She sidled away from her father's entourage, undoing the last button on her Ralph Lauren skinny-fit polo to reveal a little more of her two best features. The ones her mother openly envied, often wondering aloud how her daughter had come by naturally what she'd had to pay a pricey plastic surgeon for upon first arriving in Hollywood.

"Is this place boring or what?" Zara said when she reached the guy.

He blinked, looking startled. "What? Uh, I mean, hi."

"Hey." Zara slouched against the wall. She let her eyes, the same mossy green as her father's, wander up and down the guy. "So you're not a rider, are you? Least you're not dressed for it."

He blinked a few more times, looking nervous. "Me? No. I'm just here to, you know, watch my girlfriend do her thing."

A girlfriend, huh? She should have guessed. Not that a minor detail like that was going to stop her from getting her flirt on. It wasn't as if she had anything better to do until her appointment.

"Really?" she said. "Your girlfriend any good?"

She tilted her head and leaned a little closer, going hard for the double entendre. But the guy wasn't even looking at her anymore. His eyes had just gone all wide and excited.

"Whoa!" he said. "Check it out—isn't that, like, *Zac Trask* over there? Oh my God!"

Zara let her eyes drift shut. Of freaking course. She knew what would happen next. Either this guy would rush off without even remembering she was there, or—worse—he'd figure out who she was and go all weird and fanboy on her. Either way, she wasn't in the mood to deal with it.

"Gotta go," she muttered, hurrying off before the guy could respond.

It was almost time for her to go find that horse she was supposed to try, anyway. She thought about getting Mickey or Saul or someone to go fetch her boots and helmet from the golf cart where she'd left them. But a glance back at the circus surrounding her father made her decide to go get them herself instead. Maybe putting on her gear would help her blend in and look like just another rider rather than the Rock Star's Daughter.

"Easy, boy," Tommi murmured as she felt the horse's body tense beneath her. After his usual easy lead change in the corner, Toccata had just spotted the first jump in the next line. The course decorators had gone all out with this one, creating a freakish mélange of daffodils, fern fronds, and potted lemon trees. Toccata's ears were pricked toward the jump, and Tommi could feel him sucking back against her leg.

She gave him a firm squeeze, allowing a touch of spur to help push the big bay gelding forward while she kept her upper body as quiet and relaxed as a kid on a pony ride. She'd been moving more into the jumpers lately, but had grown up in the hunters and still knew the cardinal rules as well as she knew her own name. Always make the horse look good. Always make the ride look easy. Make it look like a blind, drunken monkey could find eight spots on this thing, eight perfect jumps.

Their takeoff spot was there, staring her in the face. Tommi clucked softly to make sure Toccata had the impulsion to get there. Four, three, two . . .

She felt it coming, that sudden surge of nervous energy through the horse's body. Toccata's stride opened slightly, sending him spurting forward right past the perfect distance. *Damn.*

Sinking down into her thighs, Tommi quickly half-halted, trying to salvage the fence. Normally this was her thing, her skill. Staying cool. Making it work. Getting through to a horse that was losing its mind without giving it away to the judge.

But this time it wasn't happening. Toccata was spooky—that was what made him so careful and round over fences. He was honest enough to keep going when asked despite his fear. But it wasn't going to look easy. Not this time.

Tommi's mouth twisted into a small grimace as they chipped in, taking off way too close to the fence. She had to roach her back and throw her hands forward to stay with the awkward jump. The trip had started so well, but that one bad fence meant it had all been for nothing. Not even Toccata's spectacular style could salvage the round now.

As the horse landed, Tommi pushed the negative thoughts away hard and fast. So their shot at pinning was gone. That didn't mean they had to embarrass themselves. Even if she was only competing for twentieth place at this point, Tommi wasn't going to give up and accept less than that. Why come to the game at all if you weren't there to play?

With another cluck, she sent the gelding forward, staying out of the tack and letting him gather his wits back around him. That was what worked for Toccata. Staying patient, letting him know she was there without pushing too hard and sending him over the edge into panic. She'd had to learn that the hard way, getting impatient with him a few times when she was younger and stupider and ending up on her ass in the dirt more than once as a result.

The next fence, an airy oxer, was coming up fast. But Tommi stayed cool, waiting. Just waiting. Toccata's canter rhythm hadn't wavered despite the chip, and all it took was the tiniest nudge to get him to the sweet spot. He flew over the oxer in a perfect arc, and Tommi smiled.

"Nice recovery," Jamie Vos said as Tommi came out of the ring and dismounted. He was leaning against the rail, his whip-thin body relaxed but buzzing with barely contained energy, like a sports car running in neutral.

Tommi unbuckled the chin strap of her GPA helmet. "Shouldn't have happened in the first place. I knew he doesn't like yellow flowers."

"Okay." Jamie never argued with Tommi when she was hard on herself. He knew there was no point. His blue eyes wandered past her to the short, weatherbeaten man hurrying toward them. "Let Miguel take the Tokester, and get yourself back to the barn, then to the south schooling ring. I need you to ride Ellie for me—someone's coming to see her at three."

"Really? Who?"

But Jamie was already gone, sprinting across the crowded showgrounds in the direction of the pony ring. He never stopped moving for long on show days, even at a smallish local A like this one.

"Ready for me to take him, señorita?" the groom prompted.

Tommi reached into her pocket for a peppermint, which Toccata lipped off the palm of her deerskin glove, leaving behind a trail of foamy slobber. She gave the horse a pat, then handed over his reins.

"Thanks, Miguel," she said. "Don't forget to let him graze a little on the way back to the barn."

The groom's heavy jowls and drooping brows gave his face a perpetually sleepy look, but his dark eyes danced with amusement. "How could I forget?" he said. "He almost knocks me down to get a single bite."

Tommi laughed. Toccata was a character, that was for sure. He wasn't always easy to manage, but they'd been together for a long time, and he was the one horse in her string who would never be for sale.

She was still smiling as she and Miguel parted ways. The groom wandered off toward a patch of grass, chatting companionably to the big warmblood in Spanish, while Tommi headed for the colony of blue-and-white-striped tents that housed the temporary show stalls. On her way back past the main hunter ring she noticed a couple of younger junior riders she vaguely recognized from one of the big Virginia barns. They were leaning on the rail, unbuckled Charles Owens perched atop their perfectly sculpted hunter hair, watching her go by. Tommi didn't remember their names, but she guessed that they probably knew hers. That was the trouble with being in her family. Everyone knew who you were whether you liked it or not.

"Hi," Tommi said with a polite half smile as she passed them.

"Hi," the taller one said, while the other just nodded.

As Tommi rounded the corner of the announcer's booth, she glanced down and saw that one of her field boots had come untied. She bent to fix it. Force of habit. Jamie ran a tight ship when it came to turnout, which suited Tommi's perfectionist nature just fine. Her friends from school were always giving her a hard time about her habit of straightening the merchandise on the shelves while browsing through Upper East Side boutiques.

"I don't know what she's looking so happy about." The sarcastic voice drifted around the corner as Tommi straightened up again. It was one of the girls she'd just passed. "If I chipped in like that, I'd be using some of Daddy's money to take a long trip somewhere far away."

"Yeah. Especially riding a packer like Toccata. That horse could win with my grandma on his back."

Tommi stiffened and her heart started pounding, though she was careful not to allow her expression to change one iota. No matter how many times she heard that kind of crap, it never got any easier to take. *Who needs to learn to ride when her father owns half of New York? If I could afford horses like hers, I'd win all the time, too.*

If they only knew how fresh Toccata could be on a cool morning after a few days off, or had ever tried to stay with one of his big panicky spook-and-bolts when someone's car backfired out in the parking lot. If they could only see Tommi wrestling with one of Jamie's young, green sales horses when it decided it would rather be a rodeo bronc than a jumper. Maybe then they wouldn't assume that she'd bought her way to the top.

Tommi did her best to push the thoughts aside and swallow down the bitterness. She couldn't waste time worrying about what people thought of her. Right now, she had a job to do.

🐎

"Thanks, Miss Nilsen."

"Kate," Kate corrected with a smile. "I keep telling you, Javier. You should call me Kate."

The young guy smiled back tentatively. He was the newest groom on the staff, and while he was a whiz with the horses, he didn't seem completely comfortable dealing with the customers yet. Or even Kate, who was really more coworker than customer.

"Okay," he said. "See you later."

He hurried out of the barn leading the big, flea-bitten gray gelding that Kate had just finished grooming and tacking. As they disappeared out the end of the aisle, Kate checked her watch. Javier and the horse should make it up to the hunter ring in plenty of time to meet Jamie, who was probably going over the Adult Amateur Hunter course with the horse's owner right now. Not that that should be necessary. Most hunter courses were so simple that the horses probably knew them by heart. Outside, diagonal, outside, diagonal. It was amazing how many of Jamie's clients had trouble remembering that, making Kate wonder how they managed to hold down their mentally demanding jobs as attorneys or surgeons or research scientists or whatever.

Kate tightened the band on her blond ponytail as she looked around for her next task. Jamie liked to tell everyone that Kate put the *working* in working student. He counted on her to help him and the grooms keep things running according to his exacting standards, both at home at Pelham Lane Stables, his top Westchester County show barn, and at the A circuit shows he and his clients attended up and down the East Coast.

But as far as Kate was concerned, she could never work hard enough to pay Jamie back for all he'd given her. He was the best trainer and mentor she could ever hope for. No, more than that—he'd changed her life.

Kate had loved horses since she knew what one was, but

her dad's modest salary as a local cop meant that her parents hadn't been able to afford to do much about it. That hadn't stopped her. She'd saved up her tiny allowance, along with birthday cash from relatives, to pay for her first few rides at a local up-down lesson mill. After that she'd been hooked. She'd paid for extra saddle time with odd jobs and mucking stalls and babysitting, and was always first to offer to ride anything with four legs. But even back then, stinking of manure and banged up from schooling the latest half-broke auction-special-cum-lesson pony, she was always dreaming of more.

Then at age fourteen a friend's parents had invited her to come along to spectate at the Hampton Classic. It was by far the biggest, fanciest horse show Kate had ever attended, and she'd been awed by the gleaming, gorgeous horses and perfectly turned out riders—just like the ones in the books and magazines she devoured at the school library. Her friend's family had been more interested in shopping and eating than actually watching the horses, and Kate had ended up wandering off by herself.

She'd recognized Jamie from seeing his picture in all the horse-showing magazines. He was standing at one of the schooling rings watching his riders warm up. It had taken every ounce of courage she had, but she'd walked up to him, introduced herself, and asked for the chance to prove to him that she could ride. He'd looked her over for a long, silent minute with those keen blue eyes of his, then tossed her up on a horse to see what she could do. She'd been at his barn ever since, trading hours and hours (and hours) of hard work, early mornings and late nights and no social life, for the chance to ride and train with the best.

And Jamie *was* the best—everyone said so. Sometimes Kate wanted to pinch herself to see if she was really here, showing under Pelham Lane's colors. Except that stopping to pinch herself would take up valuable time that could be spent lungeing a frisky horse or scrubbing water buckets or cleaning tack or . . .

As much as Kate loved every aspect of her job, it sometimes seemed there was no end to what needed to be done. Especially on show days. To her surprise, though, Javier's departure had left the shed row deserted, the only sounds the distant crackle of the loudspeaker and the horses chewing hay in their stalls.

Kate's stomach grumbled, and she realized she hadn't eaten a thing since the dry toast she'd grabbed on her way out of the hotel at o'dark-thirty that morning. She headed into the tack stall, which was draped in Jamie's clean and classic hunter green and tan barn colors. Matching tack trunks lined up neatly beneath tidy saddle racks; ribbons won by Jamie's clients hung on the back wall. One of the longtime grooms, Elliot, had a real green thumb, and an array of lush ferns and other potted plants finished off the tack stall's elegant look.

Noticing that the wood chips covering the floor were uneven from people walking in and out, Kate grabbed a rake and smoothed out the rough spots until it was perfect again. Only then did she dig a granola bar out of her bag, which she'd stowed in the bottom of the staff trunk.

She sank down onto one of the leather director's chairs in the middle of the stall. A moment later she heard a soft grunt and glanced up just in time to see Jamie's elderly English bulldog, Chaucer, lumber in. Jamie always had several dogs roaming around at home, but Chaucer was the only one of the pack who came to all the shows.

"How you doing, buddy?" Kate said with a smile, leaning down to give the bulldog a pat on his broad head. "Let me guess, you're sniffing around to see if the horses dropped any food in the aisle, right?"

At the word "food," Chaucer's mouth dropped open in a doggie grin, allowing a trail of drool to escape. He wagged his stubby tail, his round haunches wriggling back and forth.

Kate laughed. "How can I resist that face?" She broke off part of her granola bar and leaned down so he could slime it off her palm.

"Hello? Anyone around?" a familiar voice called from out in the aisle.

"Tommi? In here!" Kate took a quick bite, then tossed the rest of the granola bar into Chaucer's eager, drooling mouth. She hurried outside, brushing her hands off on her breeches.

Tommi was a few stalls down, clipping a lead rope onto the halter of a bay mare. Her chin strap was loose and her jacket unbuttoned, but her brown hair was still tidily smoothed over her ears and under her helmet and she looked picture-perfect as always. Kate wasn't sure how her friend did it. She herself always seemed to end up with hay in her hair and horse slobber on her shirt the second she stepped into the barn.

Tommi glanced over when she heard Kate emerge. "Hi," she said. "Where is everybody?"

"Javier just took Mrs. Walsh's horse to the ring, and I'm not sure about the rest," Kate said. "How'd it go with Toccata?"

Tommi grimaced. "Could have been better."

Kate nodded, not asking any questions. Tommi came across as pretty laid-back most of the time, but she was the most competitive person Kate had ever met. That was one of the reasons they were such good friends despite their wildly different backgrounds. They both expected a lot of themselves.

"Did Jamie say anything to you about someone looking at Ellie today?" Tommi asked. "He wants me to ride her."

"Yeah, he said someone might be coming by," Kate said. "But why's he making you ride her? I figured he'd have me do it. Don't you need to start warming up for the High Juniors pretty soon?"

Tommi shrugged. "You know Jamie. He didn't stick around to give me all the details."

Kate nodded. "Bring her out," she said. "I'll help you get her ready."

TWO

Ellie's show name was Eleganz, and it suited her. The mare's graceful neck was arched and she was on her toes as Tommi led her out of the stall. Even her jigging looked smooth and stylish; it was no wonder she'd won nearly every hack she'd ever entered. Tommi murmured to her to keep her calm—Ellie was sensitive and still a little green—and soon had her in the nearest set of cross-ties.

Kate had vanished, but soon reappeared with her arms full of tack and a grooming bucket dangling from one wrist. The mare was nearly spotless already, but Tommi knew Jamie would expect perfection.

"Hand me a rag," she said. "I'll do this side."

Soon both girls were busy knocking every speck of dust off the mare's already-gleaming bay coat. "I wonder who's looking at Ellie," Kate said as she worked. "I thought Jamie wanted to put a few more miles on her before he sold her."

"I'm not surprised people noticed her after Devon," Tommi said. "She was amazing there."

She heard a sharp bark from the end of the aisle. Glancing over her shoulder, she saw Summer Campbell strolling toward them with her obnoxious Jack Russell terrier, Whiskey, cradled in her arms and nipping at the sleeve of her Joules polo shirt. Great. Summer was exactly what they *didn't* need when they were already in a hurry. She was fifteen, just a year younger than Kate and two years younger than Tommi, but somehow dealing with her always felt like babysitting.

"Hi, Tommi," Summer said with a saccharine-sweet smile. "I like your jacket. That color looks sensational on you. It must be one of the new Grand Prixes, right?"

"Yeah, I guess." Summer annoyed Tommi for many reasons, not least because the modest fortune her parents had made in the textile business seemed to make her think she needed to live up to every single snobby-hunter-princess stereotype out there. She spent more time arranging her picture-perfect hunter hair than she did warming up her horses, and cared much more about the labels on her fellow competitors' breeches and show shirts than how well they rode.

Summer turned her milky blue eyes toward Ellie, who had settled down once she was in the ties, seeming to enjoy the extra pampering. "What are you guys doing?" Summer asked. "Who's riding Ellie today? Is Jamie letting you show her, Tommi? Are you going to buy her?"

Tommi didn't bother to point out that while she rode the mare at home sometimes, she'd never shown her. In fact, the only one who had besides Jamie himself was Kate—but it would never even occur to Summer to ask if *she* was showing the mare. She always seemed surprised when Kate turned up in the ring showing a horse for Jamie or one of his clients, as if she couldn't possibly be good enough without owning her own horse or even the full rainbow of the latest Essex show shirt colors.

"Someone's trying her out to buy," Kate told Summer as she undid Ellie's tail wrap.

"Oh." Summer stood there watching her work. After a moment Whiskey started wriggling and yipping, so she set him down.

"Hey, watch it," Tommi warned as the dog immediately dashed toward Ellie. "He'll get stepped on."

"Oh, he's fine. Horses love him." Summer ignored her dog as the little beast scampered beneath the mare's legs to reach the grooming bucket. He bit at a sweat scraper that was poking out, growling and yanking at it so hard that he tipped over the whole bucket.

Ellie jumped at the noise, even though she'd been ignoring the dog so far, and started dancing in the ties. Tommi cursed softly, grabbing a bottle of hoof dressing a split second before the mare would have stepped on it, while Kate went to Ellie's head, talking to her softly to calm her down.

"Aren't you going to finish her tail?" Summer asked, seeming completely unaware of the chaos her dog was causing. "It looks kind of weird—you need to brush it out."

Tommi glanced around for Whiskey, but he'd disappeared—probably into the tack stall to nose around for food or poop in the wood chips. She had no idea why Jamie didn't put his foot down about the ill-behaved little beast. Summer was supposed to keep the dog on a leash if she brought him to shows, but she never bothered unless Jamie himself said something to her—and even then, the leash came off again as soon as the trainer was out of sight.

"I'll get the tail," Tommi said to Kate, ignoring Summer. "We'd better hurry—I want to have time for a good warm-up. You know how Ellie is."

"Yeah." Kate had already finished picking up the spilled grooming supplies. She turned and grabbed a freshly laundered fleece pad from the pile of tack.

"That looks crooked," Summer spoke up as Kate set the pad on the mare's back. "It needs to come this way a little."

"Thanks," Kate said, tweaking the pad slightly.

Tommi rolled her eyes. It wasn't as if Kate wouldn't have straightened the pad when she put the saddle on.

"There's a stain on that saddle," Summer commented as Kate swung Tommi's spare County saddle onto Ellie. "Haven't you cleaned it lately, Kate?"

"It's not a stain, it's a stirrup rub," Tommi said. "It won't show when I'm riding."

"Oh! That's good." Summer smiled. "Is that your saddle, Tommi? It's really nice. If I decide to sell my Butet I might get one just like it." Then she glanced at Kate, who was getting ready to put on the girth. "Be careful not to tighten her girth too fast," she said. "Mares can be touchy about that, you know."

"Hmm," Kate said noncommittally.

Tommi gritted her teeth. Kate was pretty good at ignoring people like Summer—she had to be, to work for Jamie. But while Tommi had endless patience for horses, she didn't have nearly as much for people. It was tempting to tell Summer off when she started criticizing Kate, who knew more about cleaning tack—and everything else about riding—than Summer ever would.

But she didn't do it. For one thing, she doubted Summer would pay any attention. More importantly, she knew Kate wouldn't like it. She preferred to keep a low profile, to the point that Tommi sometimes worried that she was turning herself into a doormat, especially where some of Jamie's bossier and lazier clients were concerned. Tommi just didn't get that. How could Kate be gutsy enough to ride the hottest, rankest, greenest horses that came through the barn, but not be willing to stand up for herself with her fellow humans?

A sudden bark from the next aisle broke Tommi out of her thoughts. It was immediately followed by a torrent of loud swearing, including some particularly colorful phrases that Tommi hadn't heard before.

"Sounds like Whiskey found Margie," she murmured to Kate.

A moment later a woman came storming around the corner. She was in her thirties, dressed in show breeches, purple Crocs, and a stained New York Mets T-shirt.

She pointed straight at Summer. "You!" she said in a voice that probably carried halfway to Connecticut. "That obnoxious little rat you call a dog is trying to get squashed by my horse, and I really don't want to have to clean him out of her hooves. Go get him. Now!"

Margie O'Donnell was one of Jamie's adult clients. She was also the youngest partner in one of the biggest law firms in New York. She had a mouth like a sailor and the self-confidence of a pit bull. Nobody messed with her. Not even Summer.

"Sorry!" Summer squeaked out, rushing down the aisle. "I guess he, um, got away from me."

"Uh-oh," Tommi said as the other girl disappeared around the corner. "Now who's going to tell us how to tack up?"

Margie snorted and rolled her eyes before stalking off after Summer. Kate giggled as she tightened Ellie's girth another hole.

"I think we're almost ready," she said, giving the mare a pat.

"I'll grab the bridle." Tommi was already moving toward the tack room. "We'd better get going."

"Looks like Jamie's not here yet," Tommi said as she, Kate, and Ellie reached the schooling ring.

Kate nodded, hardly hearing her. This was the smallest and most out-of-the-way ring at this particular facility, which was probably why Jamie had chosen it. At the moment it had only two occupants. One was a regal-looking woman in her fifties, who was warming up a handsome Roman-nosed chestnut gelding while the assistant trainer from another local barn perched on the rail and watched.

But Kate hardly saw them. She had eyes only for the second rider, a lanky seventeen-year-old guy on a huge gray horse. The shock of reddish-blond hair sticking out from beneath his helmet gave away his identity, but Kate would have recognized him just by the way he rode. All fearlessness and raw grace. There were several schooling jumps set up in the ring, and she caught her breath as the rider kicked the horse into a gallop and aimed him at a 3'9" vertical at a sharp angle. The horse threw its head up and tried to veer around the jump, but the rider held him on the line and they leaped over, clearing the fence by several inches. When the horse landed, it threw in a dramatic buck and snort, but the rider just laughed, riding through the buck effortlessly and then giving his horse a pat.

"Yo, Fitz!" Tommi called as the gray loped past. "You hoping a little extra schooling might actually help you beat me in the Junior Jumpers today?"

The guy brought the horse to a walk and rode over to the rail. "Keep up the trash talk, Aaronson," he said with a grin. "Maybe someday you'll be able to back it up in the ring." Then he caught Kate staring at him. "Hey, gorgeous," he added. "How'd you like my form?"

Kate blushed. "Chipotle is looking good," she muttered, a little flustered by the way his amused hazel eyes grabbed her own.

Still, she knew better than to take his flirting seriously. Fitzmartin Hall, better known as Fitz, was the only male junior rider at Jamie's barn these days, which made him a hot commodity among the female juniors. It helped that he was tall and charmingly sardonic and that his family had more money than God. Fitz could have just about any girl he wanted, and based on barn gossip, he did. Frequently. Kate knew a guy like that was way more than she could handle. She'd barely ever even had a boyfriend—she'd always been too busy with horses to have much time left over for guys.

"Have you heard how our division's going?" Tommi asked Fitz.

"Yeah, just got a text from Marissa. A bunch of people scratched when they got a look at the course, I guess, so things are actually running almost on time."

"Really?" Tommi checked her watch, then glanced at Kate. "Wow, I wonder if Jamie knew that when he asked me to ride Ellie. I guess he can always switch me around in the order of go."

Kate was a little distracted by watching Fitz swing down out of the saddle. Most guys looked kind of dorky in breeches, but somehow they worked on him. Really well, actually.

"Um, what?" she said, suddenly catching up.

"Or maybe you should hop on and warm her up." Tommi gave a tug on the reins as Ellie jigged in place. "That's probably what Jamie would tell us to do, right? I mean, you've ridden Ellie way more than I have anyway."

Kate glanced down at herself. She hadn't had time to change out of her show breeches after her last class earlier, but had taken off her jacket and shirt collar and traded her tall boots for well-worn paddock boots. "Yeah, except I'm not really dressed to ride for a customer," she pointed out.

"Are you kidding? The casual look is totally sexy on you, Kate," Fitz told her. "Like you're not trying too hard to impress anyone because you know you're hot shit."

"Give it a rest already, Fitz." Tommi shrugged off her show jacket and held it out to Kate. "Here, put this on. The sleeves'll be a little short, but it'll do."

Kate took the jacket gingerly, suddenly way too aware that it had probably cost more than her car. *Literally.*

"Are you sure you don't mind?" she asked. She and Tommi

were close, but they didn't normally share clothes. Why would they? They were both slim, but Kate was a good five inches taller. Besides, Kate didn't own anything that someone like Tommi would ever want to wear. Slumming it in Walmart couture wasn't exactly her style.

"Don't be stupid. It's a lot easier than running back to the barn for yours," Tommi said.

Still hesitant, Kate pulled on the jacket. The expensive fabric slipped over her shirt and draped into place. The sleeves were indeed too short, but the rest fit reasonably well.

"Much better." Tommi smiled as she looked her over. "And nobody will care that much about your boots. They're here to see Ellie."

"But you'll probably need to leave for the ring before I'm done."

Tommi waved a hand. "No biggie. I've got an extra jacket."

Of course. Kate should have known better than to ask. She was probably the only rider at the entire show who owned only a single, well-worn show jacket, a nice quality but not particularly trendy plain navy one she'd bought secondhand.

"Thanks," she told Tommi, feeling a little awkward.

Tommi nodded. "You ready to go?"

Kate glanced over at Ellie, who clearly knew something was up. The sensitive mare was practically breathing fire as she pranced at the end of her reins.

By now Fitz had led his horse out of the ring. "Looks like Ellie's ready, too," he commented. "Like, ready to enter the starting gate at Churchill Downs."

"Yeah. Not exactly the best look for a show hunter," Tommi

said. "Better work your magic before Jamie gets here with the buyer, Kate. Want a leg up?"

"Thanks." Kate pulled down her stirrups and checked the girth, then lifted her left knee.

"Wait, allow me." Fitz tossed his horse's reins to Tommi and stepped forward. "This is a job for a man."

"Really? See any around here?" Tommi quipped.

Kate hardly heard her. She was totally focused on Fitz as he grabbed her knee, his hands squeezing her leg through the thin fabric of her breeches. For a second she sort of spaced out, just standing there with him holding her leg, not sure what to do.

"One, two, three," Fitz counted.

Kate spaced back in at the critical moment, springing upward as Fitz hoisted her toward the saddle. She landed a little awkwardly, which made Ellie spurt forward and almost crash into the fence. But Kate recovered quickly, getting the mare back under control and riding toward the gate as Tommi swung it open.

Yeah, real smooth, Kate thought, trying to ignore the way her knee still felt warm where Fitz's hand had held it.

She was all too aware that he was still standing there watching her, along with Tommi. But she pushed that aside as best she could as Ellie immediately spotted the warm-up jumps in the center of the ring and tried to jump into a canter. When Kate stopped her, the mare objected by squealing like a pig and spinning around in place, humping her back.

"Easy . . . ," Kate murmured.

She sat quietly, letting the mare get her objections out.

Then she set her to work, cutting across the ring as often as needed to avoid passing too close to the adult rider on the Roman-nosed gelding. After a couple of laps she could feel the tenseness seep out of Ellie's body, and by the time the adult rider had finished her warm-up and left the ring, Ellie was trotting around as steadily as an old pro. Finally Kate brought her back to a walk and dropped the reins to the buckle, leaning forward to give the mare a pat.

"Looking good, Kate!" Fitz called.

Kate glanced over and saw him wave, then amble off toward their show stalls with his horse trailing behind him. Whew! It would definitely be easier to stay focused without him watching.

Tommi shot her a thumbs-up. Kate flashed her a smile, then gathered up the reins again, asking for a canter this time. Once again, Ellie started out a little excited, a little too speedy and uneven for a hunter. But Kate soon worked her down into a nice, easy hunter lope.

As she did, she found herself thinking about how the horse she was riding right now—the horse the potential buyer would see and possibly ride—wasn't really the same horse that she'd been at the start. Kate was doing what everyone tried to do in the hunter ring—make the horse look stylish, relaxed, and easy. But in truth, Ellie was anything but easy when she was fresh. At moments like this, Kate sometimes found herself wondering just how fair it was to the potential buyer to get all the kinks out before he or she ever even saw the mare, let alone tried her.

She knew what Tommi would say, or Jamie. They would

say that there was no point in showing a sales horse at less than its best.

And that made sense, it really did. Still, Kate couldn't help wondering what would happen if a buyer fell in love with the perfect, easy horse and then wasn't ready to deal with the not-quite-so-perfect reality . . .

She cut off the thought, feeling a little disloyal. Jamie wouldn't show Ellie unless both he and the potential buyer's trainer thought the buyer could handle her. As long as Ellie stayed in a good program, she would be fine.

Kate wondered why she always worried about things like that more than she should, way more than other people did. Maybe she was still getting used to the way things were done on the A circuit. This wasn't that local lesson barn, where buyers almost never had trainers and sellers rarely even bothered to knock the mud off their sales horses. No, even after being with Jamie's barn for over two years, it still seemed like a whole different world to her sometimes.

"Want me to lower the fences to start?" Tommi called as Kate rode past her.

Kate glanced at the jumps. There were two lines set up, one a pair of simple verticals at about three feet and the other a pair of higher fences that Fitz had been jumping, the 3'9" vertical and an oxer at the same height.

"We should be fine," she called back to Tommi. "Thanks, though."

She aimed Ellie at the smaller line. The mare's dainty ears pricked eagerly as soon as she realized they were jumping. She took the first vertical about a foot higher than required and rushed the second, but after a couple of times through she settled down and started jumping in her usual superb form, slow off the ground, knees up and even, back rounding over the fence. That form, along with her long stride, had turned her from a jumper to a hunter and added a healthy percentage to her asking price.

"Good girl," Kate murmured, cantering the mare around to the larger jumps. "Easy . . ."

She steered toward the larger vertical, keeping her leg on. Ellie met it out of stride and cleared it smoothly. Okay, five strides to the oxer . . .

Two strides out, Kate noticed a good-sized group of people walking toward the ring. She glanced over and spotted Jamie near the front of the group. Then she recognized the tall, handsome man striding along beside him. It was world-famous rock god Zac Trask!

Kate's whole body clenched with surprise. She turned her head, wanting a better look to make sure she wasn't imagining things.

She was so distracted that she totally forgot where she was for one critical second. Ellie threw her head, annoyed by Kate's hands tightening on the reins, and her stride wobbled.

The oxer was only a stride away when Kate finally clicked back in to what she was supposed to be doing. Her eyes widened as the jump loomed ahead of her, both too close and way too far away.

She started to pull up, to yank the mare around the jump instead of trying to clear it from the scary long spot. But she instantly realized that wouldn't work. It was too late; Ellie was already locked on. So instead Kate loosened the reins, gave the mare a kick, and prayed.

For a second she thought it might actually work. Ellie pushed off hard, stretching to make it. But her front hooves clipped the back rail of the oxer, and she lurched downward; with a clatter of rails, the entire jump collapsed around them, and all Kate could see was the ground coming up fast. . . .

THREE

"Oh my God!" Tommi blurted out as she watched Kate and Ellie crash through the jump. The mare landed hard, throwing her head down to balance herself as she tripped over a falling rail. Kate was tossed forward on the mare's neck, but Ellie stayed on her feet and Kate managed to cling on and shove herself back into the saddle as the mare bolted away from the fallen jump, snorting with annoyance.

Tommi finally let out the breath she'd been holding, relieved that nobody was hurt. She couldn't remember the last time she'd seen someone miss that badly over a jump that size—especially someone like Kate.

It was only then, as she became aware of murmurs and gasps from behind her, that Tommi realized Jamie had arrived at the ring. A bunch of people were with him, including a familiar-looking girl with curly black hair, flawless dark skin, and full, pouty lips. She was around Tommi's age or a little younger, pretty in an offbeat way. Her curvy body was encased in a too-tight polo shirt and flashy custom fringed full chaps. The latest trendy helmet—the one all the big-time jumper riders were wearing these days—was tucked under one arm.

"Is that Eleganz?" the girl asked, stepping to the rail beside Tommi. "Not much of a jumper, is she?"

Before Tommi could figure out a response to that, she noticed that another member of the party was Zac Trask. As soon as she recognized the singer, she also belatedly remembered where she'd seen the girl before—she was Zac's daughter Zara, a top junior rider out on the West Coast. Tommi had never ridden against her or even met her before, but she'd seen her picture here and there.

So Zara was the potential buyer. Tommi couldn't help a flash of disappointment that Ellie might be going so far away. She wasn't the type to get overly attached to the sales horses, but this mare was something special.

"What's going on here?" Jamie asked, staring at Tommi. "I thought I asked you to ride Ellie."

"Sorry, Jamie," Tommi said. "We just thought . . ."

She didn't bother to finish. Jamie's tone was mild-mannered and his facial expression neutral, but she knew him well enough to tell that he was annoyed. And she couldn't really blame him. It was pretty obvious now why he'd asked her to ride Ellie today instead of Kate. Kate was a great rider, but a little too easily flustered. Having an international superstar watch her ride was likely to throw her off her game. Obviously.

Tommi, on the other hand, was well known for her nerves of steel. Besides, she'd met more rock stars, actors, and other celebrities than she could count, and she'd figured out when she was still pretty young that people were all about the same anyway.

"Sorry about this, folks." Jamie was instantly jovial again as he turned to face Zac, Zara, and the others, who Tommi guessed to be bodyguards and managers and such. "Let me get my rider up, and then you can see what this horse can really do."

"Sounds like a plan," Zac said with an easy smile. "Right, Little Z?"

Zara shrugged. "Whatever. But somebody should probably be taping it for the next thrills and spills video."

"This will only take a sec." Jamie gestured to Tommi, then ducked through the fence and strode out toward Kate and Ellie.

Tommi snapped her helmet's chin strap and scurried after him. By the time she caught up, Kate was on the ground staring at her feet and Jamie was holding Ellie, who was dancing nervously, her eyes rolling in her head.

"You okay?" Tommi whispered as she passed Kate.

Kate shrugged, not meeting her eye. Tommi felt bad for her, but there was no time to worry about hurt feelings right now. Jamie was already checking the girth and adjusting the stirrups.

"Ready?" he asked Tommi.

She nodded and stepped forward, already assessing the mare's mood—freaked out—and planning what she'd need to do to fix it. Time to salvage this situation if she could.

Kate watched out of the corner of her eye as Tommi mounted, gathered up the reins, and sent Ellie into a smooth trot. She'd forgotten about her jacket and was riding in just her show shirt with the collar undone, but even so she looked cool, capable, and professional. In other words, the total opposite of how Kate felt as she slunk out of the ring at Jamie's heels.

She couldn't believe she'd made such a spectacular fool of herself. But looking stupid wasn't the worst of it. After all, horses could make anyone look stupid. No, the worst part was that she knew she'd disappointed Jamie. Buying and selling horses was a huge chunk of his income, and she might have just screwed up a big sale.

Kate wanted to run straight back to the barn, hide out in a stall, and cry into a horse's mane like a little kid. But she knew she couldn't. The least she could do was stick around to help Javier take Ellie back to the stalls after this, since both Jamie and Tommi would probably have to book to make it over to the jumper ring in time. Taking a deep breath, she forced herself to step over to the group at the rail.

"H-hi." Her voice shook, but she did her best to smile. "Sorry about that. It was all my fault—I, um, really messed up the approach to that fence."

Zac shot her a smile that practically oozed with charisma. "No worries, sweetheart," he said in that raspy, distinctive voice Kate had heard on the radio and MTV a million times. "I'm impressed you stayed aboard. You could make big bucks at the rodeo."

Jamie and several members of the entourage chuckled, though Zara just rolled her eyes. She stared at Kate for a second as if she had two heads, then turned away without a word to watch the horse in the ring.

Kate turned to watch Ellie, too, relieved to see that the mare already looked calmer. Tommi was making her focus on some lateral work, helping her forget about what had happened. As they passed the group at the rail Tommi sent the mare into a canter, showing off her flawless depart. Impressed that Tommi didn't seem fazed by the identity of the prospective buyer, Kate sneaked a peek at the girl beside her.

Zara caught Kate's glance and frowned. "Can I help you?" she asked in a cool voice.

"I—I was just wondering what you thought," Kate stammered, taken aback by Zara's hostile tone. "Um, of Ellie. That's what we call her. Her barn name, you know. Eleganz, I mean?"

Zara stared at her, her moss-green eyes sizing her up. "Yeah, thanks. I never would've figured that one out."

Jamie had been chatting with Zac, but now he joined the two girls at the rail. "As you can see, Zara, the mare is a fantastic mover and a natural for the hunter ring. She went reserve in the First Year Greens at Devon last month, and I think she'll get even better as she matures."

"What do you think, Little Z?" Zac asked. "Like her?"

"She's okay. Need to see her jump," Zara said with a shrug. "Like, *over* the jump this time instead of through it."

"Of course." Jamie glanced over at Kate. "Why don't you go out and set some jumps for Tommi, okay?"

"Sure." Kate was relieved to have an excuse to escape from the group at the rail. Otherwise she had the uncomfortable feeling she might end up doing something weird out of sheer nerves, like burst out singing Zac Trask's latest hit at the top of her lungs.

Zara watched as the tall blond girl set up a line of smallish jumps. She was playing it cool as always, even though what she really wanted to do was clap her hands and squeal like a little girl. She hadn't really been expecting much out of this trip, especially after seeing that crash, but damn, this mare was gorgeous! Leggy and sleek and dainty-headed like some fantasy pony, but with a killer trot and a canter that made Zara's old junior hunter look like a lame cart horse. Plus there was something about this mare—some spark that made Zara think she wasn't just another of those boring overschooled automaton types that her trainers always wanted her to ride. She looked . . . spunky.

Zara almost smiled, but she knew better than to let her real emotions show. Ever. It was safer not to reveal too much, easier not to trust people. Trust only got her in trouble. *Real* trouble, not the fun kind.

No, the only ones she really trusted were the horses. They never lied to her. Never acted friendly to her face and bitchy behind her back. Never used her to get to her famous parents. That was a part of what had kept her riding all these years. She'd started for the thrills, always seeking out the rush of going faster and jumping higher. But she'd stuck with it for the horses themselves.

Not that she'd ever admit that to anyone. Most people thought she was just in it for laughs. And Zara was fine with that.

Skinny-Blondie finally finished setting the jumps and stepped back, and Zara leaned forward, eager to see what the mare could do. The billionaire chick—Zara forgot her name, but she'd seen her picture in the *Chronicle* enough times to recognize her face—put the horse into a smooth canter and aimed her toward the first fence.

Just then there was a commotion from somewhere behind the group. Zara glanced that way just in time to see someone burst into view from around the corner of a nearby food stand.

Great. It was Mr. Pitstains from earlier. This time he'd brought a couple of camera-toting friends. As soon as they spotted Zac, they all started snapping away.

"Get the daughter, too," one of the guys called out in a Queens accent so thick and gluey that Zara's mother would have said it was straight out of central casting.

"Oh, man," Zara murmured under her breath, shooting Zac an irritated look. The last thing she wanted was for these freakazoids to stand there snapping pictures during her test ride.

Not that she was shy. Far from it. She'd once gone skinny-dipping in the surf right next to the Santa Monica pier. In broad daylight.

But she'd only done that to piss off her parents after they'd taken away her car for partying too much. This was different. It was her own thing, not the property of the *Globe* or TMZ or whatever.

Besides, she hated looking stupid. And if there was one thing Zara had learned in her years of riding, it was that horses could be humbling. That was the flip side of them not caring who you were. They'd just as soon buck off a rock star's daughter as some anonymous suburban brat.

Zac's head bodyguard, a tractor-trailer of a man known only as Bo, was already moving in on the photographers, with a couple of the other guys backing him up. Zara turned away as they did their thing, trying to focus on the mare in the ring. Little Miss Billionaire was taking her over a vertical that couldn't be more than 2'9", and the mare was squaring her knees, pricking her ears, and looking picture-perfect.

By the time Zara checked again, the stalkarazzi dorks were nowhere in sight. Neither were the bodyguards. It gave her a moment of evil pleasure to imagine what Bo and the boys might be doing to remind those losers not to bother people. Not that it was probably really going down that way, but still. A girl could dream.

But she was irritated that the interruption had happened in the first place. Back home, everyone was used to her being around the shows. There was no fuss even when Zac turned up to watch her ride, or her mom, either. Maybe a few autographs for the tourists, but that was it.

"Frigging East Coast," she muttered.

"What was that?" the trainer, Jamie, asked politely.

She couldn't tell from his expression whether he'd heard her or not. "Nothing," she said. "Talking to myself."

Jamie nodded, glancing out at the horse. "Want to see a few more jumps, or are you ready to take Ellie for a spin?"

"I'm ready." Zara shot another quick look around for lurking camera commandos, then glanced at her father. As usual, he looked as if he didn't have a care in the world. He was testing out his pathetic pidgin Spanish on the cute young Mexican groom that had walked over with the group from Jamie's barn; the groom was grinning like a loon and looking starstruck.

Zara rolled her eyes. Totally typical. It didn't seem fair that Zac never seemed to mind being attacked by fans and the press everywhere he went. Then again, he'd signed on for this. Nobody had ever bothered to ask Zara what she thought of being stalked like a freaking eight-point buck every second of her life, even when she was supposed to be doing something fun.

But whatever. She didn't want to let those jerks—or her father—ruin this for her. She watched as Jamie waved to the girl on the horse, signaling her back to the gate.

"Ellie is willing but pretty sensitive, so you'll want to take it easy until you get to know each other a little," Jamie told Zara. "Stay soft with your hands and seat, but keep a light leg on her so she doesn't feel abandoned."

"Yeah, okay," Zara muttered, casting another glance around to make sure the photographers were really gone.

She grabbed her helmet off the fence post where she'd stuck it and jammed it on her head, not bothering to fix her hair first. If these East Coast snobs didn't like that, they could kiss her West Coast ass.

By then the other girl had ridden over and dismounted. She led the mare to the mounting block and held her while Zara checked the stirrup length. It turned out she didn't have to adjust them at all. Miss Rich Girl was a couple of inches shorter than her, but apparently had freakishly long legs for her height.

"I guess Jamie already told you that Ellie here likes a light touch, right?" the girl said.

Her tone was friendly, but Zara wasn't in the mood for small talk. "I know how to ride, okay?" she snapped. Then she swung into the saddle, grabbed the reins, and gave the mare a firm nudge with her heels to send her back out into the ring.

Ellie started jigging almost immediately, her whole body tense. "Chill out, okay, girlie?" Zara said, shortening her reins.

That only made the mare toss her head and start backing up. "Easy with your hands," Jamie called. "Why don't you just walk around on the rail for a minute, get used to how she feels?"

Zara wasn't in the mood to be told what to do, especially by some overgelled short dude she'd just met. So what if everyone around here treated him like some kind of Supreme Trainer God? She wasn't that easily impressed. Turning the mare back along the rail, she gave her another kick, planning to pick up a trot.

Ellie had other ideas. With a snort, she leaped into a canter, yanking her head forward and down.

"Keep her head up!" Jamie called, sounding a little panicky.

Zara had already figured out what the horse was up to. "Oh, no you don't," she warned through gritted teeth. The mare only managed to get in one small crow hop before Zara pulled her head up and then spun her around to the left. Ellie stopped and planted her front feet, hopping up and down a few times.

But by now, Zara's annoyance was fading away and she was actually starting to have fun. She'd been right—this mare had spunk!

"I knew it," she whispered as she sank deep into the saddle and booted Ellie forward. "Let's see what you've got, baby."

Ellie leaped into a canter again, though this time she kept her head high, evading the bit. Zara was vaguely aware that Jamie was still yelling instructions, but she wasn't paying attention. She was fully with the mare, waiting to see what she'd do next, feeling the excitement she always felt when she climbed aboard a new horse for the first time. That rush. The sensation that anything could happen.

The mare didn't try bucking again, though she remained high-headed and jiggy. Zara was tempted to spin her around a few times with her nose to her boot like the stunt rider she'd met on one of her mother's movie sets had taught her to do. But she resisted the temptation, instead just sitting chilly through it all until the mare finally started to settle down.

After that, it only took her maybe ten or fifteen minutes to get Ellie trotting and cantering around fairly quietly. Zara knew the mare probably didn't look anywhere near as relaxed and professional and huntery as she had with the previous rider. But she was able to canter the line of jumps a couple of times with little trouble.

As she was coming around for a third go and thinking about asking to have the jumps raised, she heard Zac calling her name. Glancing that way, she saw a couple of pony riders coming in through the gate. Bummer. It looked like their private ring was no more. But that was okay. Zara had gotten what she needed out of the test ride. She gave Ellie a pat and a scratch on the withers, then rode her back to the gate and hopped down.

The dark-haired billionaire girl and the skinny blonde came forward to grab the horse. "Nice seat," Billionaire Babe said. "I guess that wasn't your first bronc, huh?"

"I must admit you had me nervous for a moment there," Jamie told Zara with a wry smile. "You've got guts, that's for sure! Well done. We're here through the weekend if you want to try Ellie out in a class or two before you make a decision."

"That's okay." Zara shrugged. "A friend of my trainer's saw one of your barn rats ride her in that show last weekend. That's why I was interested in her in the first place. I know she can show."

"All right," Jamie said. "I just thought you might want to get a feel for her in the show ring before you make a—"

"No biggie," Zara cut him off as she reached up to unbuckle her helmet. "I can figure her out, don't worry." Then she glanced at her father. "I want her."

Zac raised an eyebrow. "You sure, Little Z?"

"When am I ever not sure?"

Before anyone could respond to that, she heard a shriek of excitement. This time at least it wasn't paparazzi. Just some embarrassed-looking pony rider's pudgy middle-aged mom, who'd probably made out with her first boyfriend to Zac's music back in Jurassic times. Zac was all charm as the woman searched her oversize Mom Purse for a pen so he could autograph her prize list. Zara rolled her eyes.

"That must get annoying after a while, huh?" Billionaire

Girl said quietly as the fan started gushing about what a genius Zac was, blah, blah, blah.

Zara shot her a sharp glance. "Whatever," she said. "It's life." Then she grabbed her helmet and hurried away, so totally over the whole stupid scene.

FOUR

West Maple Street was less than five miles from the lush green fields of Pelham Lane Stables, but it might as well have been in a different galaxy. The block where Kate's family lived was lined on both sides with small houses set close together, most of them tidy but all definitely looking as if their best days were behind them.

Kate was so exhausted she barely had the energy to turn the key to cut her car's engine as she pulled to the curb in front of her family's modest bungalow. Shows always wore her out—no sleep, bad food, and extra stress could do that to anyone, she figured. At least these days she could drive herself home from the barn afterward. For her sixteenth birthday last winter, her dad had bought her the cheapest halfway reliable car on the impound lot and even paid for the first six months of insurance. It was way more than Kate had been expecting, even though she knew it was mostly because of how much he'd hated the thought of her biking home from the barn in the dark. As a cop, he knew what could happen.

Grabbing her duffel, she climbed out of the car and headed up the front walk, still thinking back over the show. It was one of the smaller ones Jamie's barn attended, a low-pressure local outing meant to kick off the summer for the newer clients and ease those who didn't travel to Florida for the winter circuits back into serious showing. Kate had ended up taking a few different horses in the ring, as she usually did. One of them was an adult client's new horse, an experienced but opinionated Trakehner gelding who'd decided to buck instead of canter in the client's under-saddle class. Kate had schooled him afterward, and the nervous ammy had begged her to show him for her. They'd gone in the Large Junior Hunters and wound up as division champions. The client had been thrilled, which was nice, but it still made Kate smile to remember how grateful Jamie had been. This particular adult client was easily rattled, and after seeing how well her horse had gone with Kate, she'd had the guts to get back on and jump him around a low schooling class successfully. Disaster averted.

Kate's smile faded as she noticed that every window in her house was blazing with light. She checked her watch. It was well after eleven, and her father always worked Sunday nights. This couldn't be good.

"Mom?" she called as she let herself in.

"In here, Katie!" her mother's thin, tremulous voice drifted back from the direction of the kitchen.

Kate's heart clenched as she hurried that way. She found her mother standing in front of the small, worn butcher-block kitchen island with half the pantry's contents set out on its scarred surface. As she entered, her mother was touching each can of soup and box of noodles with the tip of one thin finger—twice, then again, then on to four, the magic number—her lips moving as she counted silently along.

"Mom?"

There was no answer. Kate gritted her teeth, knowing she might as well be patient. Otherwise her mother would only have to start the counting ritual over again.

Finally Kate's mom gave four light taps to the last of the cans in the row before her. Only then did she look up and smile uncertainly at her daughter.

"What time is it, sweetie?" she asked. "Is your horse show over?"

"Yeah, Mom. It's like quarter after eleven. Where's Andy?"

Her mother blinked and looked around, her thin, pale face uncertain. "I—I think he's in his room. Surely he's resting up. He has summer school tomorrow, after all."

Kate closed her eyes for a second, gathering strength. She had the sinking feeling that her younger brother *wasn't* in his room in the basement. He was probably still out with his rotten friends, the ones who'd distracted him enough all year to make him flunk two classes and have to attend summer school. If their dad found out he was screwing up again . . .

But that wasn't her problem to solve, and she didn't have the energy right now, anyway. Her mother was already back at it, stacking four cans neatly atop one another, then carrying the stack to the pantry, which was standing open. She set the cans down carefully, lining them up with the matching stack of four anchovy tins beside them, then touched each can four more times.

"How did your weekend go, sweetie?" she asked Kate after that. "Did you have fun?"

"Sure." Kate suspected her mother thought her shows weren't much more complicated than the pony rides she'd begged for as a child every time they went to the fair. "It was big fun. But I'm tired—I'd better hit the sack. Good night."

She scurried out of the room without waiting for a response. Watching her mother in full-blown OCD mode always made her feel uncomfortable and slightly sick to her stomach.

Her bedroom was in the gabled half-story at the top of a narrow flight of stairs, across from the spare room. In here, too, every light was on, and Kate saw right away that her mother had been there while she was gone. Four of her old stuffed animals were arranged atop the neatly made bed, which Kate had left unneatly unmade when she'd stumbled out of the room early Wednesday morning. The photos and other knickknacks she kept on her dresser were grouped into fours, and Kate knew that if she opened her underwear drawer, her bras and panties would be tidily arranged in little groups of four, too.

She reached into her pocket and pulled out her cell phone, speed-dialing her father's number. He liked her to check in so he knew she'd arrived home safely. Her car was an improvement over the bike, but he still worried about her driving home alone at night.

"I'm home," she told him when he picked up. "How's work?"

"Quiet," he said. "How'd your show go? Win any trophies?"

She smiled. He asked the same question every time she got home from a show, referring back to her very first competition, a tiny, informal student show at her old lesson barn.

She'd come in first in her walk-trot class and won a garish plastic trophy that looked as if it had come out of a gumball machine. But her father had fussed over that silly little trophy so proudly that Kate had painted it gold and given it to him for Father's Day. Ever since, the trophy thing had been their own private joke.

"A few," she responded lightly. Then she paused, wondering if she should tell him that her mother was getting bad again.

But she decided not to bother. He had to know already, right? Wasn't that why he kept taking on more overtime? Why Andy spent less and less time at home? Why she herself escaped to the barn every chance she got?

After she hung up, she flopped onto her bed, feeling guilty. She knew she should be more patient with her mother. It wasn't her fault she was this way, or so everyone always said. That didn't make it any easier to deal with—or stop Kate from wishing sometimes that she could trade lives with Tommi, or Summer, or any of the other riders at the barn, whose lives all seemed practically perfect despite their little complaints here and there.

Kate yawned so widely it felt as if her face would crack in two. But despite her weariness, she knew she was way too wired to fall asleep yet. It was always that way after a show.

She dialed Tommi's number, knowing she'd still be up— she'd left the barn only a short while before Kate did, and had a longer commute back to her family's town house in Manhattan. But the phone only rang twice before bouncing to voice mail.

"Damn," Kate muttered.

Still feeling restless, she tried another familiar number. This time, someone picked up almost immediately.

"Hey, Katie," Natalie greeted her.

Kate smiled. It helped to have a friend who was a night owl.

"Hey," she said. "What's up?"

Natalie had been her best friend since kindergarten. The two of them had started riding together at Happy Acres Riding Academy, and Kate knew that Nat still didn't quite get why she'd left the homey, relaxed barn just to ride "a bunch of inbred dumbbloods with snooty Manhattan princesses," as she often put it. Still, Kate thought of her as the closest thing to a sister she'd ever had.

"Not much," Nat said. "Where were you all weekend? I stopped by to see if you wanted to hit Frankie Pannelli's party with me."

"Had a show." Kate hesitated. Nat was one of the only people outside her immediate family who knew about her mother. Thanks to sleepovers in their younger days, she'd seen her in action more than once. "Um, didn't my mom tell you that when you stopped in?"

"Didn't see her. Andy said you'd killed yourself by jumping off the Brooklyn Bridge."

Kate rolled her eyes. Yeah, that sounded like Andy, at least lately.

"Probably just as well," she said with a sigh. "Mom's cheese is sliding off her cracker again these days."

"Really? She ever go see that shrink your dad found?"

"I dunno." Kate didn't really feel like talking about it right now. Actually, she didn't really feel like talking about it *ever*. She decided to change the subject. "You ride this weekend?"

"Just when Roscoe decided to be a brat for one of the kiddies I was teaching. Had to hop on and remind him how to behave himself."

Kate couldn't help wincing. Ever since Nat had started teaching up-down lessons at Happy Acres last summer, she'd gotten a little too big for her breeches, to the point where she could be kind of rough on the school ponies, who were mostly of saintly temperament but often half lame and usually less than half trained.

"Sounds like an adventure," she said lightly, knowing her friend would take offense if she asked too many questions or sounded the least bit disapproving. "Speaking of good old Roscoe, I saw a pony at the show that reminded me of him. Same type of markings."

"Hmm." Nat didn't sound too interested. She never seemed interested in hearing about anything that happened at Jamie's barn or the A shows Kate attended. It seemed strange to think that the two of them didn't have much in common anymore when it came to horses. Especially considering that horses were what they'd bonded over in the first place, playing together for hours with their Breyer models long before either of them ever got the chance to touch a real live horse.

Still, Kate knew better than to force things with Nat. She didn't deal well with that sort of thing. Time for another change of subject.

"So you said Frankie had a party," she said. "Fun?"

"Totally!" Nat's voice brightened immediately. "Justin

swiped some vodka from his drunken mom's stash, and snooty Stacey Wilcox got plastered and ended up making out with that loser Dave Duffy and then posting all over Facebook today how much she hates him."

They chatted about the latest high school scandals for a few more minutes. By the time she hung up, Kate felt better, or at least more normal. She peeled off her filthy barn clothes and wrapped herself in a clean towel—one of exactly four stacked neatly on the chair near her closet—and headed downstairs to the bathroom for a much-needed shower. A few minutes after that, clean again, she climbed into bed and fell asleep the moment her head hit the pillow.

Tommi opened her eyes on Tuesday morning to a beam of bright sunlight slashing across her room. Instantly wide awake, she glanced at the clock beside her four-poster and groaned. Six thirty. Her body was still on school time, even though summer vacation had started over a week ago.

Summer vacation. Tommi stretched and smiled, relishing the thought of long summer days at the barn and nights out on the town with her friends. What could be better?

A few minutes later, showered and dressed, she headed downstairs. Mrs. Grigoryan was in the kitchen bustling around with the dishes, and Tommi's father was in the dining alcove with a cup of coffee at his elbow and that morning's *Times* spread all over the table. He glanced up as she came in.

"Morning, sunshine," he greeted her.

"Morning. What are you still doing here?"

Her father raised one bushy eyebrow. "Aren't you happy to see your old father, Thomasina?" he asked in a mock-insulted tone.

Tommi rolled her eyes. Her father only used her full name when he was angry with her—which he clearly wasn't at the moment—or when he was feeling extra jovial.

"Usually you're at the office by now," she said, dropping into a chair.

"Got a tennis date with the mayor at eight." Mr. Aaronson folded back another page in the business section. "Figured there's no point in heading downtown until afterward."

That explained his good mood. Tommi's father and the mayor had a standing tennis date, and her father almost always won. Winning made him happy.

"By the way," he added, "I have some exciting news."

"Oh?" Tommi was already back on her feet, heading toward the fridge for some OJ.

"Your sister's coming home next weekend."

"Isn't that nice, dear?" Mrs. Grigoryan cooed in her thick Armenian accent. "It will be so lovely to have Miss Callie around the place again, if only for a short while."

"Callie's coming home?" Tommi stopped for a moment, staring into the open refrigerator with surprise. Then she grabbed the orange juice carton and a glass and headed back out to rejoin her father. "What's the occasion?"

"No occasion. She just misses her family, I suppose," her father said.

Tommi wasn't sure how to feel about the news. This would be her older sister's first trip back to New York since graduating from Yale in May and moving to DC to take a job on Capitol Hill. It would be nice to see her, of course.

On the other hand, she hadn't really been gone that long. Definitely not long enough for Tommi to get used to the way everyone in her parents' social circle had started talking about how Callie would probably be the first female president someday. Tommi didn't doubt that at all, of course—what Callie wanted, Callie went out and got. But it always made her feel a little uncomfortable when people would finish the thought by glancing at *her*, as if wondering how little sister could possibly measure up.

Realizing her father was staring at her, waiting for a response, Tommi pasted on a smile. "That's cool. When's she coming? I've got a show next weekend, so I hope I get to see her."

"Another show?" Her father's smile faded. "How about you give this one a pass? It's not every day your sister comes home."

"I can't skip the show." Tommi felt her temper bubbling up, as it always did when her father refused to understand how important showing was to her. "Jamie's counting on me, and everything's already set."

Her father was frowning now. "Well, I expect you to be here for Callie's welcome-home dinner on Friday night. Your stepmother and Mrs. Grigoryan have a nice meal planned."

Tommi opened her mouth to protest—she wasn't afraid to say no to her father, even if half of Wall Street was—but then realized she didn't have any classes scheduled until Saturday anyway. "Fine," she said. "I'll be here Friday for dinner. But I'm showing the rest of the weekend."

Tommi was still stewing over her father's news when she

arrived at the barn later that morning. She stopped by Toccata's stall to feed him a peppermint, then spotted Kate grooming a horse in the cross-ties nearby. Chaucer was dozing near the horse's front end, while one of the other farm dogs, a young Lab mix named Hugo, sniffed around hopefully for interesting things to eat.

"Hey," Kate greeted Tommi as Hugo bounded over to say hi. "How was your day off?"

Like many top stables, Pelham Lane was closed to clients on Mondays. It was Jamie's day off, and a day for the staff to relax a bit and take care of things they didn't have time to do the rest of the week—fixing or painting fences, doing maintenance work on the trailers and other vehicles, catching up on barn laundry. The farrier had a standing appointment, and if any horses needed shots or teeth floating or any other routine work, Monday was the day the vet came out as well.

Tommi knew that Jamie didn't really mind if the more serious juniors wanted to come ride on Mondays, as long as they didn't mind grooming and tacking up for themselves. And occasionally Tommi would take advantage of the quiet to come and school before a big show. But most of the time she tried to respect the rules and stay away.

"Boring," she told Kate, rubbing Hugo's floppy ears. "Did some shopping in the morning, then drove up to a friend's place in Greenwich for a swim. Need some help?"

"Wouldn't mind." Kate tossed her a brush, and the two of them set to work on the horse's already gleaming coat. "Ms. Hamilton is supposed to have a lesson at ten, and I'm running late getting Reno ready for her."

Tommi nodded. "So here's some news," she said as she

flicked dust off the horse's hindquarters. "My dad just told me Callie's coming home this weekend."

Kate glanced at her over the horse's back. "She tired of DC already?"

"Doubtful," Tommi said with a snort. "Probably just wants a fresh audience for her stories about how important her job is and how much everyone loves her."

Kate laughed. "You're bad!"

"I know." Tommi sighed, switching hands to reach under the horse's belly with the brush. "I'm totally going to hell. But I can't help it."

Kate shot her a sympathetic look. Before she could say anything, Fitz sauntered into view around the corner, both hands shoved in the pockets of his jeans. Hugo let out a bark and rushed to welcome him, his tail wagging a mile a minute.

"What's up, ladies?" Fitz asked as he reached them.

"Hi, Fitz," Tommi said. "You look bored. If you don't have anything better to do, why don't you grab Ms. Hamilton's stuff from the tack room for us?"

"I'm not quite *that* bored." Fitz leaned against the wall, ruffling Hugo's ears and grinning that lazy, slightly crooked grin that had charmed half the girls in the New York metro area. If you believed even a fraction of his stories, anyway. "So Kate, I heard you totally rescued Greta Phillips from her horse's rodeo show."

"Something like that, I guess," Kate said softly. "It wasn't a big deal. You know how nervous she gets sometimes."

"Don't sell yourself short," Tommi told her. She glanced at Fitz. "She laid down the law with that horse and turned in a great trip each time."

"I'm not surprised." Fitz bent down to give Chaucer a scratch on his big round head. "Our Kate's an awesome rider. Not a bad-looking one, either."

Kate blushed, and Tommi rolled her eyes. Shameless flirting was Fitz's default mode. Tommi was one of the few who seemed immune to his charms, preferring a guy who required something more than two X chromosomes to turn him on. She'd shut him down on his first attempt to hit on her, though they'd ended up pretty good friends.

"Too bad you couldn't beat me in the High Juniors this time." Tommi shot Fitz a smirk.

"Yeah, the Chipster did his best, but I kept screwing him up by leaning at all the fences. Maybe I need some extra private lessons. What do you say, Kate? Think you could whip me into shape?"

Kate shot him a half smile, clearly not sure whether he was joking or not. Tommi wasn't surprised. Fitz usually went for the more obvious targets, like Summer or some of the others—confident girls who gave as good as they got from him. He'd never paid any particular attention to Kate, who was usually too busy for much socializing.

"You're a really good rider," Kate told Fitz softly. "I'm sure you were just having a bad day. It happens, right?"

"Sure." Fitz shrugged. "But you can't blame a guy for trying to get some one-on-one time with the barn superstar, right?"

Now that Tommi thought about it, maybe she shouldn't be surprised that Fitz was hitting on Kate. In fact, it was about time, given that he'd worked his way through most of the barn's young female population already. Even if Kate wasn't putting herself out there the way some girls did, why *wouldn't* he notice her? She was gorgeous, talented, and sweet—probably way too sweet for the likes of Fitz. Tommi made a mental note to mention something to Kate as soon as he left. Call it a friendly warning.

At that moment the horse they were grooming pricked its ears toward the far end of the aisle. A split second later they all heard the clatter of hooves from that direction. A tall, attractive chestnut gelding walked in, dressed in shipping boots and a fleece-padded halter. Javier was at the horse's head, cooing to it in Spanish as he coaxed it along.

"Who's that?" Fitz asked.

Tommi shrugged. "Nice-looking horse, but I don't recognize it," she said. "Maybe a new sales horse?"

"Jamie didn't mention buying anything new lately," Kate said. "I wonder if—"

She stopped mid-sentence as someone else hurried into the barn right behind the horse. Tommi's eyes widened as she recognized her. It was Zara Trask, the rock star's daughter who'd bought Ellie! She was casually dressed in shorts, flip-flops, and a spaghetti-strap tank that left little to the imagination.

"Who's *that*?" Fitz sounded much more interested in the girl than he had in the horse.

"What's she doing here?" Tommi murmured at the same time, shooting Kate a glance. Kate shrugged.

Zara spotted them and hurried forward. "Hey, where's Jamie?" she demanded. "He was supposed to have a stall waiting for Keeper."

"Keeper?" Kate echoed uncertainly, glancing at the horse.

"Keeper. Keeping Time." Zara sounded impatient. "My horse!" She waved a hand at the big chestnut, who was staring around with interest at his new surroundings, ears pricked.

Just then Elliot hurried in from the opposite direction. "Is this the new jumper horse?" he asked Zara politely. "Please come with me—I have his stall ready."

"What's going on?" Tommi asked.

If Zara heard her, she didn't show it. She hurried out after the horse.

A second later, Summer rushed into view from the other direction. "Is she here yet?" she demanded breathlessly.

"Who?" Kate asked.

Summer rolled her eyes. "Duh! Zara Trask!"

"How did you know Zara Trask was here?" Tommi was feeling more confused by the second.

"Are you kidding me? Everyone knows!" Summer exclaimed. "I mean, how huge is it that she's moving to our barn?"

"She's what?" Tommi said. "What are you talking about? I thought she lived in LA."

"Don't you ever, like, watch the news or check TMZ or anything?" Summer rolled her eyes dramatically. "Her family just moved to New York City so her dad could open some new studio or something. She and her horses are going to be right here at our barn!"

FIVE

━ ━ ━ ━ ━

"Got everything you need, sweetheart?"

"Yeah." Zara climbed out of the Mercedes convertible, then leaned back in to grab her bag out of the backseat. "Thanks, Mickey. Pick me up at like five thirty, okay?"

Mickey nodded, flicking his cigarette out over the side of the car and then gunning the engine. He was probably Zara's favorite member of her father's entourage, partly because his shaggy black hair and pale, gaunt face made him look like an extra from a zombie movie, but mostly because he was totally chill and never freaked out about any of the stuff she did. And he'd drive her anywhere, anytime, no questions asked.

As the car peeled off down the winding drive, its tires kicking up gravel, Zara headed for the main barn. She'd only been there twice, but she could already tell that Pelham Lane was going to be a major change of pace from LA. It was like some fantasy from one of her mom's movies. Gorgeous barns, acres of lush grass, miles of perfect whitewashed board fencing, the whole deal. Nothing like the cramped equestrian center back in LA, where horses were lucky to get twenty minutes of turnout a day in one of the riding rings.

Nobody was around when she entered, though she could hear voices from somewhere else in the barn. Turning the opposite direction, she found her way to her stalls. Ellie's was empty, and Zara guessed someone was getting her ready for their first lesson together.

She checked her watch. The lesson was supposed to start in five minutes. Jamie wanted her to do a private first, which he said was so she and Ellie could get to know each other before they joined group lessons. But this wasn't Zara's first barn. She knew he wanted to check her out, make sure she could ride before he threw her in with all his high-powered juniors.

No biggie. Zara didn't mind proving herself. If there was one thing she could do, it was ride. If Jamie hadn't figured that out after seeing that test ride, she'd make sure he knew it today.

Figuring she still had plenty of time, she walked down the aisle to say hi to Keeper. The tall chestnut looked up from his hay pile at the sound of her voice, then stepped over to greet her.

"Hey, buddy," she said, digging a carrot out of her pocket. "How's the new crib?"

Keeper crunched the treat and then lipped Zara's palm, looking for more. She laughed and rubbed his long nose.

"Nice horse," a voice spoke behind her.

Zara glanced back. It was that guy—the sexy-skinny-sarcastic one she'd met earlier in the week when Keeper had arrived. Tall and lanky and oozing wicked charm. What was his name again? She knew it was something kind of different and preppy.

"Fitz Hall," he said, as if reading her mind. "We met the other day."

"I remember." Zara leaned against the stall door behind her, making sure he had a good view of her assets. "I never forget a pretty face."

Fitz grinned, leaning a little closer and resting one hand on the doorframe beside her. "Me neither. By the way, did I mention I'm the official barn welcome committee?"

"Oh yeah? So what does that mean?"

"What do you want it to mean?" he countered.

She smirked. "We'll see." Just then Keeper thrust his muzzle past her, still hoping for another carrot. She caught him around the nose and gave him a quick face hug.

Fitz reached out to give the chestnut a pat on the neck. "So you shipped this guy out from LA, huh?"

"Yeah. We sold my hunter and my large pony, but I told my parents I wasn't moving without Keeper." Zara shot Fitz a sidelong look. "And once you get to know me better, you'll find out I almost always get my way."

"Really?" Once again, Fitz leaned closer. "I hope I get to know you better real soon."

Zara almost laughed. She could already tell that Fitz was used to getting what he wanted, too. And that he wasn't afraid to go after it, corny lines and all, whatever it took. Definitely her type. But she wasn't going to make it *too* easy for him. Where was the fun in that?

"Gotta go," she said, casually glancing at her watch. "I'm late for my lesson."

"Want me to show you to the indoor?" Fitz offered.

"No thanks. I remember how to get there."

That was a lie. Zara hadn't paid much attention when Jamie gave her the grand tour. But she hurried off around the corner, figuring she'd find it sooner or later.

The barn was laid out in a big rectangle, with two long aisles on either side and shorter ones on the ends. Stalls lined both side aisles, with space in the middle for a huge tack room, bathrooms, and other storage areas.

Okay, so where was the indoor? Zara wandered down the aisle, glancing into the stalls as she passed. She stopped short when she saw a guy cleaning one of them. His back was to her, and he was grooving to his iPod as he scooped up manure and shavings. She just stood there and enjoyed the show for a minute, smiling as he wriggled his tight little ass to the rhythm. Sweet.

"Hi there, sexy," she said loudly. "Mind helping me out?"

The guy spun around, clearly taken by surprise. Yanking the iPod earbuds out of both ears, he looked her up and down.

Zara returned the favor. He looked just as good from the front as he had from the back. Maybe late teens, early twenties, dark hair, ripped arms, a little rough around the edges.

"I'm Zara," she told him. "What's your name?"

"Sean," he said, taking in her boots and breeches. "You're new here, right? You the one who's supposed to be some kind of celebrity or something?"

"My parents are the celebrities, not me. My dad's Zac

Trask, and my mom's Gina Girard." Zara shrugged. "Rock star marries movie star. Total cliché, right?"

Sean took a step closer. "I wouldn't know. But, you know, welcome to New York."

Zara smiled. She could tell the guy was pretending not to be impressed by who she was. But so what? At least he was trying. And he was totally adorable in a raw, blue-collar kind of way. Nice change of pace from all those overprocessed California boys. Maybe switching coasts—and barns—wouldn't be so bad after all.

Not that she'd had a choice. She hadn't even found out about the move until everything was settled. Both of her parents had thought the other had told her, and she'd ended up finding out from the housekeeper who was supposed to start packing up her room. Classic.

But she shoved those thoughts aside, focusing on Sean and the way his eyes were eating her up. On the rush she always got from making a new guy want her. "So you work here or what?" she asked. "What's your story?"

"Nothing much." Sean leaned on his manure fork. "Graduated from high school earlier this month. Work here part-time for some extra cash. My real thing's BMX."

"Cool. Maybe you can take me for a ride sometime."

Sean smirked. "Anytime. I'm sure I could teach you a few things."

Oops. That reminded Zara that she was getting really late for her lesson now. "Hey, where's the indoor?" she asked, glancing at her watch again. "I'm supposed to be in a private lesson like ten minutes ago."

"Out the far end and across the courtyard," Sean said. "But hey, I'll give you a private lesson right here and now if you want."

"What would Mr. Vos say if he heard you proposition a paying client that way, young man?" At Sean's sudden shocked expression, she burst out laughing. "Just shitting you," she said. "But just so you know, I doubt there's anything *you* could teach *me*."

"Is that so?" Sean countered. "I guess we'll have to see."

"If you're lucky." She ducked out of the stall and hurried down the aisle before he could answer.

Moments later she was slipping in through the big sliding door, which was open to catch the summer breeze. Ellie was already in the ring, fully tacked up. A groom was holding on to her reins as she danced around impatiently. Jamie was perched on the fence nearby. He looked a little impatient, too.

"Sorry I'm late," Zara sang out.

Jamie glanced back at her and hopped down from the fence. "Okay, at least you're here now," he said calmly. "But listen, before we get started I should probably fill you in on how this place works. We run a full-service program here, and everything goes pretty smoothly thanks to great help." He nodded toward the groom, who was jiggling the reins lightly to distract Ellie from pawing at the footing.

"Yeah, I know the drill. It's like my old barn in LA."

"Right. But the thing is, the program only works if everyone here is responsible for themselves. Including getting themselves where they need to be on time. I realize some barns are more casual about start times, but here when I say a lesson begins at a certain time, that means I expect everyone in the ring, ready to get started, and . . ."

Zara tuned out after that, her mind wandering back to Fitz and Sean while she waited for the lecture to end. She didn't take Jamie's huffing and puffing too seriously. So she'd been a few minutes late; so what? Most people cut her plenty of slack.

"Again!" Jamie called out from the center of the ring. "Don't let her put in any trot steps this time. She knows how to canter from a walk."

"She's not acting like it," Zara complained. When Jamie didn't respond, she gave Ellie a squeeze to send her back to the rail. "You're making me look bad, mare," she muttered under her breath.

Ellie tossed her head, jigging a few steps. She'd been giving Zara trouble throughout the lesson, spurting through her aids, spooking at nothing, and generally being a pistol. Spunky was one thing, but this was getting annoying.

"Easy," Jamie called. "Let her settle for a sec, then pick up your left lead when you feel ready."

Zara sank deeper into the saddle, doing her best to "sit heavy," as her old trainer had put it, hoping that would settle the mare. It seemed to work for a moment. Ellie took several flat-footed walk steps. But as they neared the spot where Zara had decided to pick up the canter, Ellie tensed and broke into a trot.

"Aargh!" Zara exclaimed, half-halting sharply to bring her back.

"What was the problem there?" Jamie asked calmly.

Zara shot him an irritated look. "You're the trainer. Aren't *you* supposed to tell *me*?"

"It looked to me like you tensed up in anticipation of the depart, and she felt that and took advantage."

"I can't help it. She keeps looking at stuff!" Glancing around, Zara saw a big, lazy-looking bulldog lying just outside the arena fence. "I think she's scared of the dog."

"She's not scared of the dog," Jamie replied. "She's just not listening to you. You have to convince her to listen. Take her around and try again."

Grumbling under her breath, Zara did as he said. So far, this lesson wasn't much fun. She'd expected Jamie to warm her up on the flat for a few minutes, then set up some jumps to see what she could do. She'd been looking forward to trying her new horse over something a little higher. But they hadn't gone near the jumps yet, focusing instead on boring flatwork.

The next time around, they got the canter depart. "Nice!" Jamie called. "See, I knew you could do it."

Zara rolled her eyes, not sure whether to be pleased or insulted that he was praising her like an up-downer nailing her very first canter. Before they'd gone more than a few strides Ellie spooked, surging in off the rail, popping her shoulder, and totally cutting the corner. This time Zara tried to blame it on the birds flying around up in the beams, but Jamie didn't seem impressed by that explanation, either.

"Let's change directions and try it on the other lead," he said.

"But she keeps spooking and being goofy!" Zara exclaimed. "I thought this horse was supposed to be trained. She certainly cost as much as a trained horse."

"She's well trained for her age, but she's not a machine, Zara." Jamie's voice didn't get any louder, though it took on a steelier edge. "You need to ride her so she knows what you expect of her."

Zara dropped her reins on the mare's neck, pushing her full lips out in a pout, and kicking her feet out of the stirrups. "Maybe you need to get on and school her for me."

"You'll be fine." Jamie pointed to the rail behind her. "Reverse, please. Make sure she's pushing from behind at the walk, then ask for the right lead when you pass me."

Zara debated throwing a tantrum, but decided it wasn't worth the effort. Not yet. It was already looking as if Jamie was going to be tougher to handle than her old trainer, who had pretty much let her do whatever she wanted. What was the point of taking a lesson—or riding at all, for that matter—if it wasn't fun? Pelham Lane might be the best, most prestigious, and winningest show barn in the area. But that didn't mean it was going to work for her. Jamie did seem to know his stuff, so she figured she'd give him a little longer, see if he chilled out once he got to know her. If not, she'd just have to find a barn with a more relaxed trainer.

Zara jammed her feet back in her stirrups, gathered up her reins, and nudged Ellie into a walk. For now, she'd go along for the ride and see what happened.

"Hi, Javier," Tommi said, poking her head into the feed room. "You seen Jamie?"

The young groom looked up from mixing feed and smiled. "Si, he's in the indoor, Miss Aaronson," he said.

"Thanks." Tommi returned his smile, then headed for the indoor. When she entered, she saw that Jamie was teaching a private lesson. It was the new girl, Zara, riding Ellie through a simple gymnastic exercise. Not wanting to interrupt—and a little curious about the newbie—she leaned against the bleachers and watched the last few minutes of the lesson. Finally Jamie called for a halt.

"Well done, Zara," he said. "I think you and Ellie will make a good team with a little work. Let's quit there for now, okay?"

As he left the ring, Tommi stepped forward. "Want me to ride Legs today?" she asked him.

"Hi, Tommi." Jamie sounded distracted as he checked his watch. "Yeah, that would be great. You didn't see Mrs. Walsh on your way over here, did you? I'm late for her lesson in the jumping ring."

He rushed out without waiting for an answer. "Hey," Zara complained. She'd just dismounted and run up her stirrups. "I thought this was a full-service barn. Where's the groom?"

"Jamie usually expects us juniors to cool out our own horses and bring them back over to the barn when we're at home," Tommi explained. "Then if you don't have time to untack, you can ask a groom to do it." She reached over the fence to give Ellie a rub on the nose. "You two looked pretty good out there," she added. "I'm always tempted to float the reins through a gymnastic with a forward horse like Ellie, but I've found she actually goes better with a little more support."

"What are you, the junior trainer or something?" Zara rolled her eyes. "I know how to ride a gymnastic, okay?"

Tommi frowned. So much for being friendly. With that attitude, Zara wasn't going to fit in too well at Pelham Lane. Sure, the juniors who rode there were competitive, but that wasn't synonymous with bitchy or cutthroat. Not here. Jamie liked to foster an atmosphere of teamwork, expecting them all to challenge, push, and support one another. Zara had better figure that out fast, or she wasn't going to find too many friends here. For a second Tommi was tempted to tell her exactly that.

But she bit her tongue. Why stress about it? Jamie would whip Little Miss Rock & Roll into shape soon enough.

"Oh wow, there you are, Zara!" Summer rushed into the indoor, pushing past Tommi as she headed straight into the ring, finally skidding to a stop in front of Zara. "I heard it was your first day actually riding here and stuff, and I totally wanted to, like, officially welcome you to the barn!"

"It's about time. Here." Zara tossed Ellie's reins in Summer's direction.

Summer caught the reins, looking startled. She stared down at them, then at the horse attached to them, as if she wasn't quite sure what to do with either.

"Make sure my tack gets put away in the right spot," Zara ordered. "That's an expensive saddle." She gave Ellie a quick pat, then spun on her heel and marched out of the ring.

Tommi smirked at the look of astounded confusion on Summer's face. "Wow," she said with barely contained amusement.

"Bet it's not every day you get mistaken for a groom, huh, Summer?"

"That's not what happened." Summer recovered quickly. "Um, I'm sure she just realized I wanted to help her out. You know, as like a friend." She shot Ellie a slightly nervous look as the mare jerked her head, nearly yanking the reins away. "Come on, sweetie pie!" Summer cooed. "Come with Mummy and we'll find Miguel so he can hose you off."

She gave a tentative tug at the reins, causing Ellie to toss her head again. Tommi was tempted to step in before someone got hurt. But at that moment Kate came rushing in, pink-cheeked and breathless.

"Here I am!" she exclaimed. "Sorry I'm late, I was getting the ponies ready for my next lesson, and . . ." Her voice trailed off as she stared at Summer holding Ellie.

"Here." Summer thrust the reins at her, looking relieved. "Zara says make sure Ellie gets taken care of really well. Now I'd better go see if she needs me to show her around or anything."

She rushed out of the ring. Kate glanced at Tommi. "Okay, what'd I miss?"

"Tell you later." Tommi grinned. "I don't want to keep you from your orders."

"Good boy!" Tommi exclaimed as the horse she was riding arced over a fair-sized jump. As he landed, the lanky bay gelding sped up, flagging his tail and tossing his head joyfully.

Tommi laughed as she pulled him up and gave him a pat.

Legitieme, barn name Legs, was a young Dutch Warmblood that Jamie had imported recently from Europe. He was super talented and scopey, but also green and quirky. Most of the other juniors didn't like riding him much, but Tommi found him a fun and interesting challenge. She enjoyed trying to figure him out, working with him to bring out his best. Jamie had noticed how well they got along and made the gelding her personal project.

"If you keep jumping like that, we're going to tear up the Training Jumpers at the show this weekend," she murmured, sending the horse around the outdoor ring at a walk on a loose rein to cool out. It was a hot afternoon, and they'd worked hard. Both horse and rider were sweaty and a little tired, but content. Legs ambled around for a moment, then suddenly leaped into a trot, pricking his ears at the nearest jump.

Tommi laughed again, pulling him away from the jump and making him slow down. It was fun to ride a horse that loved to jump as much as she did. And Legs definitely loved it. He was no hunter, that was for sure—too hot, too fast, too high-headed. But he was perfect for jumping the big sticks, if his rider could channel his energy and keep him under control.

As they made their third circuit of the ring, Tommi saw Kate walking toward the gate at the head of a little parade of ponies. Kate was helping a tiny eight-year-old girl lead the first pony, a fancy dapple-gray medium that kept tossing its head. Three more ponies were behind them, led by their small owners, who ranged in age from six to eight.

"Hi," Tommi called, steering Legs toward the gate and then dismounting. "Don't worry, we're finished. The ring's all yours."

"Thanks." Kate looked harried. "Okay, girls. Stand back until Tommi's out of the ring, okay?"

Tommi shot her a sympathetic smile as she led Legs out. She was sure this was going to be an interesting lesson. The pony Kate was leading was young, green, and opinionated. His owner was a tough little rider who'd cleaned up in the Smalls for the past couple of years, but she definitely had her hands full with her new mount.

Stopping just outside the ring, Tommi loosened Legs's girth. When she turned around, she almost jumped out of her skin. Zara was standing about six feet away, watching her. How long had she been there?

"Nice horse." Zara flicked her moss-green eyes at Legs. "Yours?"

"No, he's Jamie's." Tommi felt cautious, considering their previous exchange. "But thanks, he's a good boy."

Zara nodded. "He looks like fun. I liked how you handled him over that tricky combination."

"Thanks," Tommi said again, trying not to sound surprised. She wondered if she'd misjudged Zara earlier. Maybe the tough exterior was just that, a way to protect herself. Tommi knew as well as anyone that it wasn't easy coming from a well-known family.

Before she could think about it much, she heard a shout from nearby. Zara heard it, too, and spun around.

"Shit," she spat out.

"What?" Tommi turned, too—just in time to see a pair of paparazzi types rush toward them, cameras raised.

SIX

— — — — —

"Don't forget to tighten your girth," Kate told little Gigi Jones, who would probably forget her own head if someone didn't keep after her. "I'll check it in a second."

As she turned to help Mackenzie with her green pony, she heard someone let out a yell from the direction of the nearest building. Glancing that way, she saw two strange men running at full speed toward the ring.

"There she is!" one of them hollered. "Zara, wait! We just want to talk to you!"

Confused, Kate glanced at Zara. The girl's face had gone hard. Without a word, she turned and dashed away, disappearing into the quarantine barn.

"Get out of here!" Tommi yelled at the men. "You're going to spook the horses!"

The first man ignored her. "Go after her!" he shrieked, waving his arms in the air. The other man obeyed, vaulting over the ring's post-and-board fence, clearly seeing that as a shortcut to catch up to Zara.

"Stop!" Kate cried in alarm. She'd let go of Mackenzie's pony, Dazzle, once they were all safely inside the ring. Now she lunged toward him, trying to grab his bridle before he spooked.

Too late. Seeing the large man come hurtling over the fence had blown the sensitive pony's mind. He yanked loose from Mackenzie and reared, snorting with panic. When he landed he spooked violently to one side, almost knocking Mackenzie down before crashing into Gigi's pony.

That pony, a cute little flaxen chestnut, was a pretty quiet type, but it had to lurch and fling its head up to keep from being knocked over, which startled the other two ponies. One of them, a fancy but rather ornery Welsh cross, let a kick fly at the chestnut, missing its hock by a hairsbreadth. The other pony, a stout pinto, threw its head in the air and started backing up.

"Get out of there!" Tommi screamed at the man, who'd stopped to stare at the upset ponies.

He shot her a look, then shrugged and sprinted across the ring, dodging around the pinto, which stopped backing up and started prancing in place instead. The little girl holding it shrieked with fear, dropped the reins, and ran away.

"Hey!" the other man said loudly. "Aren't you Rick Aaronson's daughter?"

If Tommi answered, Kate didn't hear her. She had her hands full. Dazzle was rearing again, his hooves waving dangerously close to Mackenzie's face.

"Get back, sweetie," Kate ordered tersely. "I'll catch him."

Mackenzie backed away. Kate eased past her, waiting until the pony's front end landed and then grabbing his dangling reins before he could go up again. "Easy, boy," she said. "Chill out, little man."

Out of the corner of her eye, she could see Tommi hanging on to Legs with one hand as he spun around her in circles. With her other hand, Tommi was texting madly.

Good. That meant help would be here soon. But would it be soon enough? The first photographer had disappeared into the quarantine barn after Zara, but the other guy was snapping pictures of Tommi as she attempted to hold on to her horse, who was becoming increasingly agitated.

Keeping a tight hold on Dazzle, who was still threatening to rear, Kate glanced around the ring. The girl with the pinto was clinging to the rail, crying as she watched her pony trot around with its reins dangling. Gigi was still holding on to her pony, though his head was up and his ears on alert as he clearly weighed whether it was worth the effort to act up. The last little girl was trying to grab the Welsh cross as it lunged at the pinto with teeth bared.

Worst-case scenarios flashed through Kate's mind before she could stop them. Dazzle pulling away from her and bucking around the ring. The other ponies getting away from their owners, trampling them, and then running around wildly until they all ended up with suspensory injuries or worse. Tommi getting knocked over by Legs, who could easily clear the perimeter fence and end up on the highway . . .

Stop it, Kate ordered herself. If you freak out, it's only going to make matters worse.

"Hey! What's going on here?" a familiar voice broke through the hubbub.

"Fitz!" Kate blurted out.

Fitz had just ridden into view aboard his semiretired children's hunter, a placid older Appendix quarter horse named Beacon. He liked to ride the chestnut gelding around the farm under Western tack for fun. Kate suspected most of that fun came from Fitz teasing Jamie by saying he was going to give up showing and become a cowboy.

Taking in the scene, Fitz vaulted off his horse, leaving him ground-tied. Then he ducked into the ring.

"Go help the littles," he told Kate. "Let me deal with Dazzle."

"Thanks." Kate had never been so grateful to someone in her life. Hurrying over to grab the Welsh cross before it could rile up the other two ponies any further, she quickly got the situation back under control.

By the time she glanced back at Fitz, he'd taken Dazzle out of the ring. "Hey, you," Fitz said to the photographer, who was still hassling Tommi. "What do you think you're doing?"

"Trying to earn a living, kid." The photographer smirked. "Guess none of you trust-fund brats would know about that."

"Okay, you've had your fun. Time to get lost before someone gets killed." Fitz maneuvered Dazzle around, forcing the agitated pony to sidepass toward the man.

"Hey, keep that thing away from me," the man complained, suddenly looking a lot less cocky.

At that moment Dazzle tossed his head, almost breaking loose from Fitz's grip. "Uh-oh!" Fitz shouted. "Dangerous horse! Clear the decks!"

Mackenzie's eyes widened in alarm. "Don't worry, sweetie,"

Kate whispered, sidling closer. "Fitz is just kidding around. Dazzle will be fine."

She watched as Fitz continued to angle the pony toward the man. Finally Dazzle reared in annoyance, letting out several loud snorts. Fitz let the reins slip through his hands, then reeled the pony back in. The photographer was frozen in place, looking terrified.

Kate noticed that Tommi had taken advantage of the distraction to slip off toward the barn with Legs, who was jigging a bit but behaving well otherwise. Unfortunately the photographer noticed, too.

"Hey! Miss Aaronson!" he called, darting around Fitz and the pony.

Great. So the pony's antics hadn't totally distracted him. Still, Kate wasn't too worried. Tommi could handle herself. At least now that both intruders were gone, she should be able to get things back under control.

"Everything all right in here?" Fitz asked, leading Dazzle back into the ring and kicking the gate shut behind him.

Kate shot a look around. Dazzle had settled as soon as he was back in with the other ponies. Mackenzie had already caught the pinto and returned it to its owner.

"Yeah, I think so," Kate said. "Thanks to you. I don't know what would have happened if you hadn't shown up when you did."

"I aim to please." Fitz handed Dazzle's reins to Mackenzie as she hurried over. "But if you really want to thank me, I can think of a good way."

"Really? What?" Kate was a little distracted as she watched Mackenzie croon to her pony.

"With a kiss."

"Huh?" That got Kate's attention—and the attention of all four pony girls, who immediately started giggling.

"Kiss him, Kate!" Gigi cried.

"Yeah!" another girl added. "Give him a big smooch!"

Kate felt her cheeks go hot. "Girls, he's just kidding around," she said quickly.

"No, I'm not." Fitz grinned at her, looking as completely comfortable as she was embarrassed. "Come on, Kate. I thought I was your hero. Doesn't that deserve a measly little kiss? You know, like in all the Disney movies?"

"Kiss him! Kiss him!" Mackenzie chanted.

Glancing around at the giggling girls, Kate felt trapped as she realized Fitz had done it again. After what had just happened, she'd expected to spend at least three-quarters of the lesson coaxing the riled-up, nervous little riders onto their mounts. But now, with his simple request, Fitz had them all laughing. That would make her job a lot easier.

So what choice did she have? It was the least she could do to thank him.

"Fine, if you insist." Kate did her best to sound casual and amused, though she had a feeling she hadn't really pulled it off. Her face was still flaming, and her heart was thumping so hard and fast that it sounded like a herd of galloping horses. She could only hope the girls' giggles covered it so Fitz couldn't hear.

She stepped toward him, feeling awkward. He leaned a little closer, still grinning. Taking a deep breath, Kate stood on tiptoes just long enough to give him a quick peck on the cheek. Up close, his skin smelled surprisingly sweet, like fresh hay and citrus.

"Very nice, but you missed," Fitz exclaimed. He tapped himself on the lips. "A little to the left . . ."

"Hey, Fitz." Mackenzie pointed outside the ring, where Fitz's horse was wandering off toward the nearest patch of grass. "You'd better get out there. Beacon is leaving without you!"

"Almost there, buddy," Tommi whispered to Legs, keeping a tight hold on his reins as she led him down the barn aisle.

She was all too painfully aware of that photographer still following them. He was just a few steps behind—well within range if Legs happened to feel like kicking, she couldn't help noting.

But alas, the horse behaved himself, and the man was still with them as they reached the gelding's stall. Tommi led Legs inside and stopped, not sure what to do now. She'd already texted Jamie and Miguel, so help would be there soon. In the meantime, the last thing she wanted to do was stand in the cross-ties untacking and grooming the horse while this loser snapped pictures. Instead she slipped off the gelding's bridle, slinging it over the stall's Dutch door. The saddle could wait.

"Hey, Tommi!" the photographer called, leaning in over the door. "What was it like growing up the daughter of the richest guy in New York?"

Tommi turned away, patting Legs and keeping her eyes trained on the back wall of the stall.

"Come on, Tommi. It's a simple question. Don't you owe your fans an answer?"

Legs nuzzled at Tommi, looking for treats. She dug into the front pocket of her Tailored Sportsmans, finding a chunk of an apple-flavored treat, which she fed to him. But she didn't change positions as the man kept shooting questions at her despite the lack of response.

After what felt like a million years but was probably less than five minutes, she heard stern voices moving rapidly toward them. Thank god. Miguel and Elliot to the rescue.

After a few polite but serious words from Elliot, the biggest and most muscular groom in the barn, and a whole lot of swearing and complaining from the paparazzi guy, all was quiet again. Miguel had taken Legs off for a bath and grooming, and Tommi was free. She headed straight back outside, wanting to make sure none of the ponies or their riders had been hurt. When she thought about what could have happened, it made her angry all over again.

Halfway to the door, she ran into Zara. "The ugly one gone?" Zara asked, shooting a look around.

"Yeah. The guys just tossed him off the property," Tommi said. "What about the other one?"

"Ditto. Couple of grooms turned up and booted the jerk." Zara shook her head. "Man, took them long enough, though." She shot Tommi a rueful look. "Sucks dealing with that kind of shit, doesn't it?"

"Yeah, well, we've never had much trouble with it here," Tommi said. "You know—until now."

Zara's expression darkened. "What, you blaming me for those assholes?"

"Who else would I blame?" Tommi realized she was being

kind of harsh, but she couldn't stop herself. Zara had to know that this wasn't cool. "I've seen the tabloids and the TV stuff. You've never exactly gone out of your way to avoid the press, have you?"

"You don't know anything about me!" Zara retorted hotly.

"I know this," Tommi said. "You'd better figure out how to keep it away from the barn. Because the rest of us don't want it here."

Zara glared at her. "I thought of all people, *you* might actually understand. Shows what I know!"

She spun on her heel and stomped away. "Hey!" Tommi called after her, already feeling bad. Those loser paparazzi deserved her temper; Zara didn't. Not really. Not for this.

But she did her best to shrug off the guilt. It was too late to take it back now. Zara was already gone.

Tommi stayed busy for the rest of the morning, taking Toccata for an easy hack in the fields, giving her junior jumper a quick lunge, and then schooling one of Jamie's greenies on the flat. By the time she'd finished, her stomach was grumbling.

"Hey," she said, sticking her head into the utility room. "You eat yet?"

Kate looked up from pulling a load of damp barn laundry out of the washing machine. "What time is it?"

"Almost one. Want to take a break and hit the diner with me? My treat."

"One o'clock?" Kate sounded panicked. "Oh, man, I'll have to pass. I've got to finish two more loads, and I'm supposed to teach a lesson at two thirty."

Tommi stepped into the room. "No biggie. I'll help you finish up here, then we can do a quick lunch run and be back in plenty of time."

"Thanks, Tommi, but that's okay." Kate's hands flew as she separated the next load of dirty laundry—polo wraps in one pile, baby pads in another, grooming towels separate. "I'd better not. I still need to dump and scrub the outdoor water tubs, too—oh! And speaking of water, I told Jamie I'd keep up with the hanging baskets outside the office, and I noticed the flowers in them are starting to wilt already . . ."

Tommi sighed. She knew better than to press Kate when she got like this. Total perfectionist mode.

"Okay," she said. "But you've got to eat, right? I'll bring you back a sandwich or something."

"You don't have to do that," Kate said.

"I know. See you in a while." Back in the aisle, Tommi wondered who else was around. She hated eating alone, especially at the crowded local diner where party-of-one customers always got stuck at the counter, with its rock-hard vinyl seats.

She noticed Javier leading Ellie down the aisle in the direction of the turnouts. What about Zara? Maybe she should invite her to lunch as an apology for snapping at her earlier.

As quickly as the idea entered her head, Tommi shrugged it off. It had been a couple of hours since she'd seen Zara; who knew if she was even still at the barn? She didn't really seem like the type to hang around looking for ways to help out. Besides, when Tommi thought back to the paparazzi incident, she felt herself tense up all over again. Whether she'd meant to or not, it seemed Zara had brought the trashier element of the press to the barn. No, maybe she wasn't ready to make nice quite yet.

Just then she spotted two of the barn's other junior riders, Marissa and Dani, wandering out of the tack room. Bubbly, always-smiling Marissa was the type of person who got along with everybody; she wasn't the bravest or most naturally gifted rider in the world but made up for that with hard work. Dani was athletic and fun-loving, though way too ADHD to have much success in the hunter or equitation rings. Jumpers was her thing—she'd never seen a big fence she didn't have the guts to try. Like Kate's, her family didn't have tons of money to throw at the horses, but Jamie had found her an inexpensive but talented off-the-track Thoroughbred, and the pair had been cleaning up in the Low Juniors all year with plans to move up soon.

"Hi," Tommi said, hurrying over. "I was just heading out to the diner. Want to come?"

"God, yes!" Dani exclaimed. "I was just telling Marissa I had to eat something soon or I'd pass out."

Marissa giggled. "Yeah, well, it's her own fault," she said. "If we hadn't had to stop halfway through to look for your cell phone after you dropped it, our ride wouldn't have taken so long."

"Whatever," Tommi said with a smile. "Come on, I'll drive."

Soon all three of them were climbing into Tommi's BMW Roadster, a birthday gift when she'd turned sixteen. Fifteen minutes later, they were seated in a window booth at the diner.

"I'll take one of everything," Dani joked as she grabbed a menu.

Marissa was staring at something over Tommi's right shoulder. "Me too," she said. "Especially one of *him!*"

Tommi turned and saw a good-looking young construction worker wolfing down a piece of pie at the counter, totally oblivious to their stares. "Nice," she said with a grin. "Why don't you go over and say hi?"

"Are you kidding?" Marissa grinned back. "My parents would have a heart attack. I mean, he's probably not even Jewish."

Tommi laughed, then turned her attention to the menu, even though she practically had it memorized. "Remind me to grab something for Kate on our way out, okay?" she told the others.

"Let me guess," Marissa said. "She's too busy to stop for lunch, right?"

Her tone was light and friendly, but Tommi couldn't help feeling a little defensive on her friend's behalf. Still, what could she say? Marissa wasn't wrong.

"What's up with her, anyway?" Dani asked. "Kate's been even more spastic than usual lately. Is she trying to put Jamie and the grooms out of a job and run the whole place on her own?"

Marissa took a sip of her water. "She really pushes herself. I hope she doesn't burn out."

Tommi bit her lip, feeling a flash of worry. Were the other girls right? Was Kate working too hard? Tommi made a mental note to check on her, then decided to change the subject.

"Hey, listen," she said. "I was just realizing the big Hounds Hollow show is really coming up fast! Can you believe it's only a few weeks away?"

Marissa shrugged. "I guess. I'm not going to worry about it until after I survive the next one. But listen, Tommi, you're probably Kate's best friend in the barn, right? Do you think she's working too hard?"

Okay, so that attempt at changing the subject hadn't worked. "I'm sure Kate's fine," Tommi said. "But listen, I meant to ask, have you guys met the new girl yet? You know—Zara Trask."

"Oh my God, yes!" Dani's eyes lit up. "Is she a piece of work or what? I heard she totally bitched out Miguel because there was poop in Ellie's stall when she stopped by to see her."

"Are you sure that's true?" Marissa looked dubious. "Summer says she's really nice."

"Summer likes anyone who's richer than she is," Dani retorted. "Anyway, I saw this story about Zac Trask on TV last year, and it said . . ."

Tommi sat back as the gossip continued to flow, keeping them all busy until the waitress arrived to take their order.

SEVEN

Tommi sat in the brownstone's classically elegant dining room staring into her soup, trying to zone out her sister's prattling about her latest *fabulous* luncheon with some bigwig senator. They were only twenty minutes into dinner, and Tommi was already bored. Definitely not her favorite way to spend Friday night.

She glanced around the table. Her father was leaning forward, hanging on Callie's every word. Her stepmother was smiling vaguely as she sipped her wine. Tommi's aunt and uncle, who lived in Connecticut but had made a trip into the city for this family dinner, were their usual mellow selves.

Then there was Grant. Tommi still couldn't quite believe he was there, sitting right next to her. She hadn't seen him in two years and hadn't even realized he was back in the country until he'd turned up at the door, looking taller, broader, tanner, and handsomer than she remembered in a linen sport coat. Surprise!

"In any case," Callie said, reaching for her wineglass, "I have no interest in switching jobs right now, but it's nice to know I have options."

Her father chuckled. "Of course you do, sweetheart," he said. "With your education and brains and hardworking attitude, it's no wonder you're in demand!"

Callie smiled, leaning back in her chair. She was slightly taller than Tommi, her face a little narrower, her brown hair cropped into a conservative hairdo that practically screamed Washington DC. But there was no mistaking that she and Tommi were sisters. Maybe that was why everyone always seemed to be comparing them.

Tommi grimaced, trying not to think about that. She was only seventeen. Her senior year still months away. That hadn't stopped her family from starting to make noises about college, career . . . basically, Life After Horses. So far she'd managed to ignore all that. But Callie's visit was making it harder.

Stirring her soup, Tommi let her mind wander to the horse show that weekend. She wondered if all the horses had settled in over the past couple of days. How Kate and her other friends had done in their classes that afternoon. What else was going on. Whatever it was, it had to be more interesting than sitting here listening to Perfect Callie talk about her Perfect Life.

"So what are you up to these days, Tommi? Still doing the horse thing?"

Tommi glanced up, snapping back to the here and now. Grant was smiling at her. Callie had apparently paused for breath, because everyone else was looking at Tommi now, too.

"Um, yeah," Tommi told Grant. "I'm showing tomorrow, actually."

"You are?" Callie glanced over at their father. "Maybe we should go. I kind of miss being around horses." She grinned. "There aren't many on Capitol Hill. Just horses' asses."

Her father roared with laughter, and everyone else joined in as if the lame joke was the funniest ever. Tommi sipped a spoonful of soup to stop herself from rolling her eyes.

"Seriously." Callie turned to stare at her. "Where's the show?"

Tommi shrugged and told her. She doubted Callie would actually decide to go—she'd ridden as a junior herself, but had never been that into it.

"So do you show a lot?" Grant asked. "I mean, I remember you going to a lot of horse shows when we were kids, but . . ."

"I show as much as I can," Tommi told him. "I love it."

"Really? Maybe I should tag along to this show tomorrow, if Callie and your dad don't mind," Grant said. "See what it's all about."

"The more the merrier," Tommi's father said jovially. "We can all make a day of it."

Tommi did her best to ignore the smug look her father shot her stepmother. That confirmed it—this was supposed to be a setup. Grant was exactly the kind of guy her father adored. Tall, square-jawed, smart, polite, ambitious, from a good family, the whole deal.

Not that Tommi minded seeing him, of course. Grant was one of her oldest friends—they'd taken tennis lessons together when she was six and he was seven, and had been pretty tight for a while. But he'd spent his last two years of high school in Europe, and aside from an occasional e-mail or Facebook posting, they'd pretty much drifted apart.

"So what are your plans for the summer?" she asked him, hoping to focus the dinner conversation on someone other than her sister. "Dad said you're starting at Columbia in the fall?"

"That's right," Grant said. "Everyone says I won't believe how much work it is, so I'm just planning to chill this summer to rest and prepare myself."

Tommi's father chuckled. "Good. That gives me the whole summer to convince you to transfer to Georgetown." He shot a broad wink at the other adults, who all smiled.

"You can try, Mr. Aaronson," Grant joked in return. "But you know my dad's a Columbia man, so I think he'll have something to say about it." He turned to Tommi. "And what about you? Got big plans for the summer?"

"Just the usual," Tommi said. "You know—ride, show, hang out, whatever."

"And start thinking about colleges, right?" Her father shot her a look.

Tommi shrugged. "I guess."

"You need to start narrowing down your choices, Tommi," her uncle spoke up. "The right school can open a lot of doors, depending on what you want to do with your life."

"That's true," Grant agreed. "Do you know what you want to do, Tommi? I know you always talked about moving to Antarctica to study penguins when we were kids, but I'm assuming you're over that."

Once again, all the adults chuckled. Tommi smiled tightly. "Yeah, I'm thinking ice floes and riding don't mix too well."

"So you still think you're going to keep riding in college?" Callie raised one tweezed eyebrow.

"Of course," Tommi told her evenly. "Not everybody quits the second they get accepted to the university of their choice like you did."

Their father set down his spoon and dabbed at his mouth with his napkin. "Nobody says you have to quit entirely, Tommi," he said in his Father Knows Best voice. "But you'll have to scale back a bit, of course. As Grant says, your studies will be much more challenging than high school."

"Yeah. It's not like showing would be as much fun anyway once you age out of the juniors," Callie put in.

Tommi frowned. She'd planned to just drift along, try to get through this dinner without making waves. But now Callie was pissing her off.

"Who says it's no fun?" she retorted. "For your information, I'm not planning to quit. Or scale back, either." She turned toward Grant. "In fact, I'm seriously thinking about turning pro as soon as I age out of the juniors and making a career out of riding."

She hadn't known what she was going to say until it was out of her mouth. But now there it was, hanging in the air over the Tiffany china and Tuttle flatware like a horse's fart. But despite her family's surprised looks, Tommi felt pleased with the whole idea. Her, going pro? It sounded right somehow.

"Oh, please." Callie rolled her eyes.

Meanwhile their father was scowling. "Grow up, Tommi," he snapped. "Nobody does that."

"Oh, right. All those pro riders are just figments of my imagination, right?" If her family was going to turn on the sarcasm, Tommi could match them snide remark for snide remark.

"Well, she still has plenty of time to decide," Tommi's aunt spoke up, clearly trying to defuse the tension. "No need to worry about it now, when she still has her whole senior year to enjoy."

Mr. Aaronson was still glaring at Tommi. She met his eye, not backing down. Not this time.

"So can you really make a living riding horses?" her uncle asked.

Her stepmother sipped her wine. "A girlfriend of mine once dated a jockey," she said. "He did fairly well for himself, I think. Had a lovely place in the Berkshires."

"That's different," Callie said. "Tommi doesn't ride racehorses."

"Right, right," her uncle said. "Hey, what's that old joke? You know—how do you make a million in the horse business?"

"Start with two million." Grant chuckled. "Yeah, I've heard that one."

Tommi finally tore her gaze away from her father's. "Whatever," she muttered. "I guess my trainer's nice car and huge farm are just figments of my imagination, too. Because clearly there's no money in show horses."

"Speaking of racehorses," Callie said, as Mrs. Grigoryan bustled in to clear the plates for the next course, "the senator got invited to speak to some constituents' group next month, and the only place big enough is the local racetrack, so . . ."

She was off and running again. Tommi sneaked a look at Grant, who was listening with apparent fascination just like everyone else.

☙

"Another weekend, another show," Zara said as Mickey pulled the car up to an elegant stone barn on Saturday morning. The fields off to the right were packed with horse trailers of all shapes and sizes, from two-horse bumper pulls behind SUVs to huge custom rigs.

"Have fun, Z-girl." Mickey glanced at her over the top of his sunglasses. "Text me when you're ready to cut out, and I'll come get you."

"Sure you can't stay to watch?"

"Sorry." Mickey shrugged his skinny shoulders. "Got to get back to the city. Your dad's got a lot going on today."

"So I heard." Zara frowned. This would be her first time showing with her new barn. Was it really too much to ask for someone to come watch her ride?

Yeah. Apparently it was. Back home, she'd never lacked for a cheering section. Even when her parents couldn't make it— which was more often than not—there were always plenty of friends, admirers, and assorted groupies who were more than thrilled to come cheer her on. But those people were all back on the West Coast. Her dad had some kind of publicity deal going on this week, her mom was still off in Vancouver shooting some lame-ass old-farts-in-love movie, and so Zara was on her own.

Whatever. It beat sitting around the new apartment, so she might as well make the best of it.

She found her way to Pelham Lane's show stalls. When she got there, one of the grooms was just leading Ellie into a stall. It was that quiet, shy young one who always seemed to be scuttling around like a mouse—what was his name? José or something?

"How is she?" Zara asked, stepping over to give the mare a pat.

The groom unclipped the lead rope and shot Zara a tentative smile. "She's fine," the groom said in his soft, accented voice. "I just groomed her so she'd be ready for you later."

"Cool, thanks," Zara said. "She looks great. You been grooming for long?"

The groom looked a little surprised by her friendly question, which amused Zara. Did she have that much of a rep already? Whatever—she liked keeping people on their toes.

"Yes," the groom blurted out. "I mean no. That is, I've worked with horses for many years, but only a few months here. I mean, for Mr. Vos."

"Javier!" A girl with bulging brown eyes and wavy dark hair rushed in with her show collar flapping. "Is Miles tacked up yet? Jamie wants me to start warming up for my eq course, even though I thought I still had like half an hour."

"I think Max is doing it, Miss Marissa, but I'll find out." Javier—oh right, *that* was his name—rushed off down the aisle.

The girl shot Zara a look. "Oh, hi," she said, sounding distracted as she fiddled with her collar. "Are you showing today?"

"Yeah, supposedly." Zara was about to elaborate, but the other girl was already hurrying off.

"Good luck!" she called back over her shoulder.

"Yeah, thanks," Zara muttered, though the girl was already out of sight around the corner.

She wandered down the aisle, feeling out of place and unwanted. And those sorts of feelings always pissed her off, made her want to do something crazy just to get people to look up out of their own stupid little worlds and notice her.

Then she spotted someone pushing a wheelbarrow into an empty stall nearby. It was that cute part-time mucker, Sean. She hadn't really talked to him since their first meeting, but he always shot her a little smirk or wink when they passed each other at the barn.

"Hey, gorgeous," she said, leaning against the stall door. "How's the shit business going?"

"Shitty." Sean shot her a lazy grin. "But why don't you come in here and find out for yourself? Or are you the kind of girl who's afraid of getting her hands dirty?"

"Do you really want to know what kind of girl I am?" Zara stepped into the stall, easing around the wheelbarrow until she was beside him. "Because I'm thinking I already know what kind of guy you are."

"Oh, yeah?" Sean lowered his pitchfork, wiping his free hand on his jeans. "How would you know that?"

"I have my ways." Zara leaned closer, already feeling the rush. Seeing the way he was looking at her. Knowing he wanted her. It was the most powerful feeling she knew, even better than nailing a big jumper course.

"I'm starting to figure out what kind of girl you are," Sean said, his voice a sexy growl. "And I think it's the kind I like."

He dropped the pitchfork and reached for her, pulling

her to him. She relaxed into him, pressing her body against his. His hands were already wandering by the time their lips met. Cool. Zara liked a guy who got right to the point; she wasn't the type to waste time either.

"Excuse me! Am I interrupting something?"

The disapproving voice snapped Zara out of the moment. She pulled her mouth away from Sean's and glanced back to see Jamie standing in the stall doorway looking annoyed.

Oops. She felt Sean jump away quickly.

"Sorry, boss," the mucker muttered. "We were just, uh, talking."

"Right. Maybe it's time to stop, uh, *talking* and get back to work." Jamie glared at him for a second, then turned to Zara. "I was looking for you. Marissa said you were here, and I wanted to talk to you about the show, since it's your first with us."

"Okay, whatever." Zara quickly tucked her shirt back into the waistband of her breeches, then shot Sean a look. "Later."

Sean didn't answer, already digging his fork into the soiled shavings. Zara shrugged and wandered out of the stall. Jamie was waiting in the aisle.

She expected him to say something about what had just happened, but he didn't. "I showed Ellie in the First Years yesterday to prep for your division today," he told her instead. "I thought you could start off in the Children's Hunters later this afternoon."

"The Children's?" Zara echoed. "I haven't done that in like two years. Low jumps annoy me."

"I realize you're experienced at 3'6". But you and Ellie are still getting to know each other, so I'd like to see you ease into things. If all goes well you can move up to the Juniors next time."

Was that a whiff of disapproval in his eyes? Zara knew Jamie had wanted her to do a couple of lessons last week before the barn had packed up for this show. But she'd been busy, what with moving to a whole new city, unpacking, getting familiar with NYC, and reconnecting with some people she knew there. She hadn't had any spare time to ride.

That didn't mean she needed to go back to Children's. But it didn't seem worth arguing about.

"Okay, fine," she said. "Children's it is. *This* time."

Jamie nodded and checked his watch. "There's a major holdup at the hunter ring, so I have a little time right now," he said. "Why don't we do a quick lesson? Your division isn't going until later, and Ellie could stand to stretch her legs."

Zara almost said yes. Riding would help her feel less out of place, and it would be fun to give her new mare a whirl before showtime.

Then again, she wasn't sure she should let Jamie win so easily. Yeah, he was a hardass. But she was no pushover, and maybe it was better to start letting him know that. He needed to understand exactly who worked for whom in this relationship.

"No thanks," she said with a casual shrug. "I don't need a lesson to ride some dinky Children's course. It's not like this is my first show."

"But—" he began.

"If Ellie needs exercise, you can deal with it," Zara cut him off. "If you've prepped her right, we'll be fine this afternoon. Right?"

Jamie hesitated, the shadow of a frown crossing his face. He opened his mouth to respond, but before he could say a word, a frantic-looking pony rider rushed in with her red-faced mother at her heels.

"Jamie, OMG!" the small rider exclaimed. "I think Goldie just threw a shoe! And Kate said I'm supposed to start warming up soon, but I can't find her anywhere, and what if Goldie is, like, lame or something?"

Jamie turned to face them. "It's okay, Gigi," he said soothingly. "I'm sure Goldie is fine, and you won't miss your class. Just ask Miguel to call the show farrier, and . . ."

Zara didn't hear any more. Taking advantage of the distraction, she made her escape.

🐎

"Oh, man," Kate muttered, unwrapping the big bay horse's right front leg for the third time. She'd already done the other three legs, but for some reason she just couldn't get this one to lie right.

The horse shifted its weight, letting out a long sigh. He was an older jumper who tended to stock up after jumping if he didn't get either wrapped or turned out.

"Sorry, buddy," Kate said, glancing up. "I'm a fumble-fingers today."

She shook out the wrap and started again, feeling frustrated with herself. Shows always made her a little tense—there was so much to do, and even less time than usual to do it—but normally she thrived on the pressure, embracing it to help herself keep moving and get things done. But today she'd stalled out on what should be a quick, mindless task. What was wrong with her?

She started yet again. This time she was almost finished when she noticed a bulge halfway down.

"Aargh!" she cried, yanking the wrap loose yet again.

"Kate? Is that you?" Summer hurried around the corner. "Thank God! I need someone to come clean the schooling-ring gunk off my girth."

"I can't, Summer." Kate was too annoyed with herself to be patient. Besides, even Summer should be able to manage to wipe down her girth herself. "I need to finish this first."

"So finish already." Summer shot a dismissive look at the wrap. "How long does it take to wrap a leg?"

Kate didn't bother to point out that Summer probably wouldn't be able to properly wrap a leg if she had all the time in the world. Instead she just gritted her teeth and started again. This time she was hardly halfway done before she had to give up.

"What are you doing?" Summer complained.

"It's not laying right," Kate said. "It needs to be even."

Summer rolled her eyes. "Are you kidding me? You're getting just as OCD as Jamie about that stuff."

Kate froze, stung by the comment. Was that really how she came across to other people when she did stuff like rewrap a leg ten times until she was sure it was right? Kate had always thought of herself as a perfectionist. But now, for the first time, she wondered if maybe that was how her mother thought of herself, too. . . .

She squeezed her eyes shut, not liking where those

thoughts were taking her. Pushing them aside, she quickly did the wrap again, this time trying to ignore the tiny imperfection in the edge, which even Jamie would never notice.

"I'm done," she told Summer. "Just let me put this horse away, and I'll come deal with your girth."

EIGHT

▬   ▬   ▬   ▬   ▬

Summer's girth was sparkling clean, and Kate had moved on to picking out stalls when Jamie found her. "Got a minute?" he asked. "I'd like to talk to you about something."

"Sure." Kate's mind immediately flashed back over the past hour or so, wondering if she'd done something wrong—missed a tack change, screwed up a medication.

"I didn't get a chance to tell you earlier, but you did a great job with the new Irish gelding in the schooling classes yesterday," Jamie said.

Kate couldn't help feeling flattered. Jamie was pretty stingy with the compliments, at least with his ambitious juniors. The nervous adult amateurs got plenty of praise whether they found eight perfect spots or accidentally rode the course backward. But Jamie expected Kate, Tommi, and the rest to perform at a certain level, and usually only mentioned it if they went above and beyond.

"Thanks," she said, thinking back to her rides on one of Jamie's sales horses. "But it was mostly him. I could've done a lot better. I totally biffed the approach to the second line, and reacted too slowly when he cut in on the turn—"

Jamie waved a hand to silence her. "Listen, I don't have much time before I have to book it to the pony ring," he said. "But I'm impressed by how hard you've been working on your riding. I think you could do really well in the Big Eq."

For a second Kate wasn't sure what to say. The Big Eq? Sure, she'd done an equitation class here and there, but she'd never even dreamed about competing seriously in the highly competitive 3'6" junior equitation classes commonly known as the Big Eq. Did Jamie really think she was that good? Good enough to put her riding up against people like Tommi, Summer, Fitz—people who'd been showing with top trainers on top horses for their entire riding careers?

Even if he did, it didn't matter. Eq horses were like a species unto themselves, quieter than jumpers, more adjustable than hunters. The price even to lease a good one was stratospheric. There weren't enough hours in Kate's entire life to work off that kind of money.

"I—um, thanks," she said. "But I'm not sure—"

"I'm serious about this, Kate," Jamie said before she could go any further. "And I think I have the right horse for you. Fabelhaften."

"Fable?" Kate had ridden the big, flashy gray in five or six lessons so far. He was a well-trained Hanoverian who'd already had a successful career as a third-level dressage horse and a somewhat less illustrious one as a hunter. He'd come to Jamie's barn to be sold when his current owner moved overseas. Fable was a dream to ride, though Kate had already discovered that he had a few quirks, like a strong sense of justice and an unpredictable and athletic buck.

"You handle him well and seem to bring out the best in him," Jamie said. "I think you could be just the rider to help me turn him into an eq specialist." He smiled. "And he's just the horse to take your riding to a new level. Maybe even help you qualify for a finals or two."

"Wow," Kate said, still having a little trouble taking this in. "I don't know what to say."

"Say you'll give it a try," Jamie said. "That's all I ask."

"Okay. I'll give it a try."

"Good girl." Jamie checked his watch. "Gotta go. We'll talk details later."

He raced off toward the rings, and Kate wandered in the other direction, her mind spinning. Big Eq. Her. Could it really happen? It sounded as if Jamie was saying Fable would be *her* eq horse—her way to compete regularly and really learn the ropes. And with the owner who was trying to sell footing all the bills, she wouldn't even have to figure out how to swing entry fees.

She turned the corner and almost bumped into Fitz. He was standing in the aisle giving Marissa a back rub while an Asian girl Kate didn't know leaned against the wall nearby.

"Hey, Kate," Marissa said. "What's up? This is my friend Susan."

"Hi." Kate flashed the other girl a smile, noting her expensive-looking beaded cami top, short shorts, and strappy sandals. Not exactly riding attire. "Are you here to watch Marissa ride?"

"Yup. Here to watch. And I'm definitely enjoying the view." Susan shot a look at Fitz.

Fitz didn't seem to notice. He dropped his hands from Marissa's shoulders and cracked his knuckles.

"Dr. Feelgood is closed for business," he announced with his usual rakish grin. "I've got to jet. Later, ladies."

"Bye, Fitz!" Marissa and her friend singsonged.

Kate recognized the look in Susan's eyes. She'd already fallen for Fitz's charm. Chances were pretty good she'd be a notch on his Gucci belt before the end of the show.

But that wasn't any of Kate's business. She hurried past, wanting to steal a few minutes of alone time to think about Jamie's offer. She'd just rounded the corner at the end of the aisle when Fitz caught up with her.

"Yo," he said. "You okay? You look kind of—I don't know, like worried or something."

"I do?" She forced a smile. "Probably just lack of sleep."

He trailed along behind her as she headed into the equipment stall to grab a bucket. "Nope, not that," he said. "Seriously, is anything wrong?"

She shot him a look, surprised by the sincerity in his voice. Since when was he Mr. Sensitive?

"It's nothing," she said. "I was just talking to Jamie about maybe riding Fable more from now on."

"That's cool," Fitz said. "I watched you ride him in lessons last week. You looked good on him. Really fit him well. And you handled it great when he tried to balk at that one jump."

Kate was a little surprised. So apparently he'd been watching her closely enough to remember that sticky jump. What did that mean?

"Anyway," she said, "Jamie wants me to do him in the Big Eq."

"Really? That's awesome! You'll totally kick butt!" Fitz exclaimed.

"You really think so?" Kate smiled uncertainly.

"Absolutely." His eyes slid up and down her body. "Not only are you a badass rider, but you're totally built for eq, too. Judges love that long, lean, leggy look."

Kate tried not to notice how long his eyes lingered on various portions of her anatomy. Okay, so he was still a hound dog. She knew that. But it was nice having someone be so supportive. It made this whole crazy eq idea of Jamie's seem like it could actually happen.

Besides, she couldn't forget how Fitz had ridden in like Prince Charming to save her pony riders last week. He could've just ridden on by, let Jamie or the grooms handle the problem, but instead he'd waded right in to help. And now here he was being super nice about her big news.

Was she being unfair, judging him by barn gossip all this time and keeping her distance? Maybe there was more to him than his rep let on. If she wasn't careful, she might just start thinking of him as a friend.

Tommi was still brooding over what had gone down at last night's dinner as she steered Legs through the chaos of the warm-up ring. She was used to having to prove herself to most of the world—of having to show everyone that her success in the show ring was due to hard work and dedication, not an easy result of her family's money.

But now she felt as if she had to prove herself to her family, too. Especially her father. She had to show him she was serious about making riding her life. That meant getting serious herself. Thinking about the future. Something she generally tried to avoid.

"It's okay," she murmured automatically as Legs spooked at an out-of-control pony coming straight at him. Kicking him forward, she sought out Jamie's familiar face in the crowded ring. He was standing beside one of the schooling jumps, which he'd just raised a notch.

She rode toward it, purposely taking Legs a little close so he'd rub the rail. That would make him more careful when they went in the ring.

"Perfect," Jamie called as they landed. "Come on, you're on deck."

Minutes later Tommi was riding Legs in their opening circle, all thoughts of her problems gone as she focused on what she had to do. This was supposed to be a schooling ride, an easy class to start getting the horse used to showing. The jumps were a good six inches lower than they'd been schooling at home. But that didn't mean Tommi was going to take it any less seriously.

She was checking out one of the jumps when she heard a burst of laughter from the rail. Glancing over, she saw Callie standing there with her father and Grant, all laughing over something. Probably some supremely witty comment made by Tommi's brilliant sister, as usual.

Just then Grant glanced into the ring and spotted her. He lifted his hand to wave, then seemed to realize that Tommi couldn't exactly wave back at the moment. Lowering his hand, he shrugged and smiled sheepishly. Tommi almost laughed, but swallowed it back as her horse neared the timers. She was ready to go to work.

"Let's go, bud," she whispered, aiming Legs toward the first fence.

"Nice horse," Callie said, stroking Legs on the nose as he stood in the cross-ties. Tommi was grooming the horse while Miguel expertly rubbed down his legs. Tommi's father and sister had come back to the show stalls to see her while Grant was off buying them all sodas.

"He's a good boy," Tommi said, pleased by the admiration in her sister's eye as she looked Legs over. Callie hadn't taken showing that seriously even while she was doing it. But Tommi had to admit that she'd always had a pretty good eye for a horse.

"He must be good if he came in third in his very first class!" Tommi's father said.

This time Tommi just nodded. It was still a little weird to have him there in the barn. He hardly ever came to shows anymore unless he was presenting a trophy or something.

"He's not the easiest ride, but when he's on, he's on," Tommi told Callie.

Their father stepped forward to give the gelding a pat. "Who says it had to be easy? Isn't that why you take all those lessons? Anyway, there's nothing wrong with a little spirit. That's what makes a winner. Fire in the belly."

"Oh, Dad!" Callie rolled her eyes.

But Tommi barely noticed. Her father's words had just given her an idea. It was kind of crazy, maybe a little scary. But it just might be the perfect way to grab hold of her own future.

NINE

— — — — —

"She almost ready?" Zara hurried toward Ellie, who was pawing impatiently in the cross-ties. Javier and Kate were tacking her up and getting her ready for the ring.

Kate glanced up from rubbing chalk into the mare's white sock. "Getting there," she said. "Don't worry; Jamie just called to say you've got plenty of time. The barn ahead of us in the order of go just added like five more riders."

Zara nodded, taking a sip of her soda and watching as Javier tightened the mare's girth another notch. Then she heard someone call her name.

It was Summer. "OMG, Zara, I'm totally in love with your show shirt!" she gushed as she hurried over. "That color is so cool! Is it what everyone's wearing in California?"

"I dunno. I don't pay attention to what everyone's wearing." Zara chugged more of her soda, wishing it was something stronger. She had the worst case of show nerves she'd had since she was in little-kid jods and garters. What was up with that?

Summer glanced at Ellie. "So you're riding in the Children's today, huh?" she asked. "That's cool."

"Not really." Zara shot her an irritated look. "I should be riding in the Juniors, like I usually do. Hardly seems worth doing my hair just to pop over those tiny jumps."

Kate looked up at her again. "Jamie's like Mr. Conservative about stuff like that," she said. "He always wants to start slow. He'll probably let you move up soon."

Zara just shrugged, not bothering to answer. She wasn't interested in psychoanalyzing her stupid new trainer. She just wanted to get through her first round and hope her nerves went away after that.

She couldn't figure out why she was so nervous. Yeah, she was in a new place, showing in front of a whole new group of people. So freaking what? She was an adrenaline junkie, right? She should love this! But she didn't, which freaked her out even more.

Zara clenched her fists in her calfskin gloves, feeling as if she'd just been dropped at the start of a tricky jumper round without knowing the course. Too bad there wasn't a course diagram for life. Zara's mouth twisted into a grimace at the thought. Yeah. A Course Diagram for Life. Sounded like the title of one of those cheesy made-for-TV movies her mom had done early in her career.

"Hey Kate, don't forget the hoof oil," Summer said as she watched Kate and Javier fuss over the horse. Then she turned and smiled at Zara. "I'm sure you'll do great," she added. "Everyone says you're a fabulous rider, and Ellie's such a cool horse. You'll probably get champion today."

Zara had gotten so lost in her own stress that she'd almost forgotten Summer was still there. The girl was irritating at best—reminded Zara of some of the groupie losers who'd called themselves her friends back in LA. The ones who were always up for a night at the clubs or walking the red carpet at a movie premiere, but seemed to be busy anytime Zara invited them somewhere a little less flashy.

"Yeah, we'll see." Zara shot Summer a look. "But who knows. If I have to ride some boring dinky Children's course, maybe I'll do something to make it more interesting. Like ride the course backward."

"Huh?" Summer looked confused. "You mean, like, go off course on purpose?"

Zara smirked. "Nope. I mean spin around in the saddle so I'm facing the horse's tail. I've jumped that way a bunch of times. It's kind of a rush, especially if you're riding a bucker."

Summer's eyes widened. "Seriously?" she exclaimed. "No way—you're joking, right? Jamie would freak out! He's all about being professional and stuff."

"Whatever. *I'm* all about having fun, so we'll just have to play it by ear."

Summer's pale eyes darted around, as if she wasn't sure how to react. "I just remembered I haven't seen my dog for a while," she said. "I'd better go check on him. Good luck, Zara." She hurried off.

Zara leaned back against the wall, watching Kate and Javier put the finishing touches on Ellie's turnout. Messing with Summer had been fun, had even taken her mind off her nerves for a while. But now they were back, big-time.

"Oops, I think I forgot to grab Ellie's martingale," Kate said as she reached for the bridle.

"Don't worry, I'll get it," Javier offered, hurrying toward the tack stall before Kate could respond.

When he was gone, Kate glanced at Zara. "You okay?" she asked softly. "I know the feeling. I'm always super nervous before I show, no matter how many times I do it or how pre-pared I am."

Zara wasn't sure how to answer for a second. Was Kate for real, or was she just another suck-up? It wasn't like they were friends—Zara had barely said two words to the girl unless it was to order her to do something.

Deciding that figuring it out was too much trouble, she turned away without a word. "Tell the groom to bring the horse to the warm-up ring," she said as she headed for the exit. "I'll meet them there."

"Learn to steer, moron!" Zara yelled as some kid on a pig-eyed bay gelding nearly sideswiped her.

The warm-up ring was a zoo. *Quelle surprise.* Normally Zara kind of enjoyed the chaos. In her wickeder moods, she'd even add to it, looking for any chance for a game of chicken over a schooling jump. But that was with her old trainer, who mostly stood there meekly and let her do whatever.

Jamie was different. He was warming up three or four riders at the same time, but somehow seemed to have no trou-ble keeping track of all of them. Zara saw him watching her as she guided Ellie to the rail for a breather at the walk.

Ellie was prancing a little after the close call with the other horse, but otherwise she was handling the warm-up pretty well. She felt fit, alert, and focused. In other words, definitely well prepped. Plus one for Jamie.

Zara glanced at the trainer. He'd turned away from her to watch one of his other students, a nervous-looking ten-year-old on a calm-looking bay large pony, clear the jump he'd claimed for his people.

"Very good," he called to the younger girl, his voice cutting through the noise of the dozens of other people in the ring. Then he turned and waved to someone else. "Tommi, you're up. Nice and easy."

Zara searched the crowds, finally finding Tommi aboard her junior hunter, Toccata. They made a pretty impressive pair. No wonder they'd won so much.

"Don't worry, girlie," Zara whispered to Ellie, patting the mare on the neck. "Once we're in the Juniors where we belong, we'll start kicking their butts."

Ellie tossed her head and skipped sideways as a pair of glossy bay hunters trotted straight at her. Before Zara could react, Ellie threw out a hind leg, cow-kicking at the closer of the two horses.

"Hey, watch it!" the rider exclaimed, glaring at Zara.

"Watch it yourself," Zara shot back.

"Isn't that Zara Trask?" the second girl asked her friend as they rode on.

They were already too far away for Zara to hear any more. But she saw both riders glance back at her, then turn away again. A moment later they caught up to another rider, and all three of them stopped in the center of the ring and watched Zara ride by.

From then on, Zara could feel more and more eyes on her, watching her every move. She was so distracted that she screwed up her next jump, running Ellie at it way too fast. Then she overcorrected the next time around, crawling to the base so the mare had to lurch her way over from a near stand-still. That seemed to make Ellie testy, and things went down-hill from there. Ellie ended the warm-up much more agitated than when she'd started, overjumping everything and looking for any excuse to spook.

Finally Jamie pulled Zara over to the rail near the gate. "Listen, Zara, I can tell you're trying to hold things together," he said kindly. "But it's starting to look like this just might not be Ellie's day."

"She's fine." Zara gave a tug on the reins as the mare slung her head around restlessly. "I'm sure she'll chill once she's in the ring by herself."

"Maybe. But she's still a little green, and we don't want either of you to have a bad experience your first time out. How about if we scratch, regroup, and maybe try again tomorrow?"

His eyes were already turning toward the next rider, and Zara could tell he was expecting her to nod, say he was right, and agree with the plan. She was sure that was what any of his other riderbots would do. Jamie Knows Best, right?

But she was no bot. "We'll be fine," she said firmly. "I want to show today."

"I understand," Jamie said, just as Tommi rode toward them. "But if you're not ready—"

"I'm ready," Zara interrupted loudly. "I mean, it's a Children's Hunter course, right? Not the Grand Prix at Spruce Meadows. What's the big deal? So we had a less-than-perfect warm-up, so what? That's no reason to scratch. I want to show."

She stared at him, daring him to say no. Jamie hesitated, then shook his head.

"I'm sorry, Zara," he said. "I really think—"

"Excuse me, Jamie," Tommi put in, dropping Toccata's reins on his neck. "I don't mean to butt in or anything, and you can totally tell me to shut my noisehole if you want. But if Zara wants to show, why not let her? It's not like she's some newbie at this. I'm sure she can handle a bad warm-up."

"Yeah. I'm not some pony brat who's going to fall apart if I don't win a pretty blue ribbon." Zara frowned at the trainer.

Jamie hesitated, glancing from Zara to Tommi and then back again. Finally he shrugged.

"Fine," he said, obviously not fully convinced he was making the right decision. "If you still want to show, let's show. You've got about ten minutes, and I think any more jumping in here would be counterproductive. Just walk her along the rail and try to keep her calm."

With that, he hurried off toward the young rider on the bay pony, who was waiting for him in the center. Zara sent Ellie into a walk along the rail, and Tommi and Toccata fell into step beside them.

"Thanks for that. He was totally going to make me scratch." Zara shot the other girl a curious look. "But why'd you butt in?"

"Couldn't help it." Tommi sat relaxed in the saddle, her body swaying gently with her horse's long, flowing walk. "I think it's a cop-out to scratch just for nerves or whatever. I thought you might feel the same way." She turned her head and met Zara's eye. "Jamie's the best, but he's a little too cautious sometimes. I hated to see him treating you like some wimpy Adult Amateur who has a panic attack if her horse, like, stomps at a fly or something."

Zara couldn't help being surprised. She and Tommi barely knew each other. Probably the longest conversation they'd had was that time Tommi had reamed her out for supposedly inviting the entire staff of Daily Scandal Dot Com to the barn. So how come Tommi seemed to get her so well all of a sudden?

It was weird. Unexpected. Maybe a little nice, too. But mostly weird.

"Okay, well, thanks," Zara said. "Hope I don't fall off over the first fence and make us both feel stupid."

She didn't fall off over the first fence. Ellie settled down once she was alone in the ring, just as Zara had predicted, and actually seemed to remember her job. Zara could hear Jamie's voice in her head as she steered through the opening circle: *Easy, keep it quiet. Less is more with this mare.*

They met the first jump smoothly, and the next one, too. Ellie changed leads at the barest whisper of a leg aid, cantering softly down toward the next line. As they rounded the turn, Zara knew they were kicking ass. Okay, so it was only a Children's round, but still. Jamie would have to eat his words if they ended up with a ribbon, right?

The thought distracted her just enough for her to lose

focus. It was time for another lead change, and she gave the mare a firm nudge to ask for it. That was what her old hunter, a lazy sort, had needed.

But this was Ellie. Taking offense at Zara's overly strong aid, the mare raised her head a little and kicked out, speeding up as she rounded the turn. She did make the swap at the same time, but the bobble was just enough to screw up their approach to the next line, resulting in a minor chip at the first fence and a gappy spot at the second.

Okay, could've been worse, Zara told herself as she completed her final circle. Despite that one sketchy line, she figured she hadn't done too badly for what was basically her fourth ride ever on her new horse.

"Good girl," she murmured as they slowed to a walk and turned to exit the ring. "Sorry about the brain fart."

Then she heard it. One of the spectators standing at the rail nearby, whistling a catchy tune.

Not just any tune. Zara instantly recognized one of her father's best-known songs, "Golden Girl." Specifically, the distinctive melody of the bridge, the part with the lyrics that went *"Everything he touches/it always turns to dust/He's the butt of every joke/his whole life's just a bust."*

Her jaw clenched as several people laughed, obviously recognizing the tune—and the rider. She glared at the people lined up on the rail, trying to catch the douchebag who'd whistled. Whoever it was had gotten to her. This time she couldn't totally hide it. She hated that. She hated it a lot.

She was still totally distracted as she rode back in for her next jumping round. Was the jerkwad whistler still here, watching her, hoping to see her screw up again? She couldn't resist searching the faces at the rail.

Realizing Ellie was picking up the canter on her own, Zara steered her into their opening circle. As she aimed toward the first fence, an inviting gate, she shot one more look at the spectators.

This time her moment of distraction really cost her. Ellie felt her rider's lack of attention and took advantage. Her stride wavered and then she surged forward—and darted to the side, running right past the fence!

A moan of sympathy went up from the crowd. Maybe hiding a few nasty giggles? Zara strained her ears as she felt her cheeks go hot. She spun Ellie around hard and fast, nearly unbalancing her. Kicking hard, she sent the mare into a ragged canter that was closer to a hand gallop.

Narrowing her eyes, she glared at the fence as they reapproached it. One stride out she kicked hard again, daring Ellie to try to run out this time.

The mare tossed her head, bobbling the final stride but flinging herself over anyway. They landed hard, and it took them a stride or two to recover. Zara could feel Ellie thinking about stopping at the next jump, but once again she booted her forward and the mare went over.

After that, there was no danger of a stop. Ellie raced around the rest of the course as if it was a jump-off, her ears flattened against her head.

Zara barely managed to pull her up at the end. Ellie was prancing and blowing as they left the ring.

Jamie was waiting for them just outside, his face an

emotionless mask. Still, Zara could feel the waves of disapproval wafting off of him.

"That was fun," she said, loudly enough for half the crowd at the ring to hear. "I always liked the jumpers better than the hunters anyway."

A few bystanders laughed, but Jamie didn't look amused. "Let Javier take Ellie," he said, waving the young groom forward. "You come with me."

Moments later they were in a quiet spot behind the food stand. "Okay, let's get it over with," Zara said. "I suck, right? And you knew I should've scratched, and blah blah blah."

"You don't suck, Zara. But you do need to understand something. Ellie is a talented horse with a world of potential. But she's no packer. If you want to do well with her, bring out that potential, you're going to have to put in some hard work to get there. Not just rely on your natural talent. Be a real partner to her."

Zara shrugged. "Okay," she muttered sullenly. He made riding sound like a chemistry test at school or something. All work and no play. Who needed that?

Jamie had more to say, but she'd pretty much stopped listening. What was the point? Showing was supposed to be fun. Wasn't that why she did it?

🏇

"Anybody home?" Tommi called as she entered her family's town house on Sunday afternoon.

She'd finished showing early. Normally that wouldn't stop her from hanging out for the rest of the day, watching Kate and her other friends ride, cheering on the barn and helping out as needed.

But today she had something important to do.

She heard a shout from the back of the house and smiled. Good. Her father was home. That was one miracle. Could she hope for two?

Hurrying through the house to her father's spacious and sunny home office, she found him shuffling through the paperwork on his massive mahogany desk. He glanced at her over the top of his reading glasses as she entered.

"Back so soon?" he asked. "Everything go all right?"

"Yeah, fine," Tommi said. "Great, actually."

"Good, good." Mr. Aaronson grabbed another sheaf of papers. "Callie really enjoyed watching you ride yesterday. She mentioned it right before she left for the airport."

"So she's on her way back to DC?" Tommi asked.

Her father nodded. "Wish she could've stayed longer. But they can't spare her any longer down there."

Tommi smiled tightly. She wasn't going to get distracted by verse 962 of her father's Ode to Callie's Perfection. Not right now. This was too important.

"Listen," she blurted out before she could lose her nerve. "I need to talk to you about something. You know Legs, that horse you saw me ride yesterday?"

"Of course." Her father's gaze was already wandering back to his papers. "Nice-looking animal."

"I'm glad you liked him." Tommi took a deep breath. "Because I want to buy him."

Her father looked up. "Oh, I see." He set down the papers

he was holding. "All right, I'm in a good mood, so why not? Tell Jamie to call me, and I'll see if we can make a deal."

"Wait," Tommi said. "This isn't like the others. I don't want Legs as my own personal horse. I want him as a business investment." She rushed on, not daring to look directly at her father; knowing that if he started laughing at her, she'd either fall apart or start yelling. And neither of those things would gain her any points. "See, I know I could finish his training myself—well, with Jamie's help, of course, but doing all the riding and the work myself. Then when he's ready, I could sell him on, and hopefully clear a nice profit. Enough to buy another greenie and start again."

She finally had to stop for breath. Her father didn't say anything for a moment; actually, he appeared to be speechless, a very unusual state for him.

"I see," he said at last. "Is this about that talk at dinner the other night?"

"Sort of," Tommi admitted. "But I'm really serious about it. I want to find a way to make a career out of showing, and this is one way I think I could do it."

Her father sighed and rubbed his forehead. "Why insist on a career in this nonsense?" he said. "There's nothing wrong with riding on the side once you've finished college and established yourself in business or law or something practical."

"But I'm not interested in those things. *You* are. Callie is. But not me. *I'm* interested in riding. You're not going to talk me out of that, Dad." Belatedly remembering the sheet of paper she'd been clutching since she entered, she shoved it across the desk at him. "Here—I typed this up on my laptop in the hotel last night, so it's a little rough. It's a business plan for how this could work."

Her father took the paper and scanned it. "I see," he said again. "Well, I'll have to take a closer look and think about it."

Tommi let out a breath she hadn't even realized she was holding. Okay, he still seemed skeptical. Verging on dismissive. But he said he'd think about it. She figured that was as good as she was going to get.

"Thanks, Dad," she said. Then she hurried out of the office before he could change his mind.

TEN

▬ ▬ ▬ ▬ ▬

Kate couldn't believe how crowded the mall was on Monday evening. She had to circle the parking lot twice before she found a spot. By the time she made it to the entrance courtyard, Natalie was already waiting.

"About time!" Nat exclaimed when she spotted her, jumping to her feet. "I was starting to think you were ditching me."

"I know, sorry I'm late. But I've got a good excuse." Kate reached for the door, looking forward to the cold blast of AC. It had been one of those hot and humid summer days when every move felt like swimming through butter. Even the fans in front of the horses' stalls barely seemed to move the hot air around much.

"Okay, let's hear it." Natalie walked into the mall behind Kate, her trendy ribbon flip-flops slapping the tile floor. "It better be something about how you were making out with that cute rich guy you were telling me about."

Kate's face was already flushed from the heat, but now

it went a little redder. Why had she ever even mentioned Fitz to Natalie? Nat had obviously jumped to the exact wrong conclusion, as usual.

"Don't be ridiculous," she said. "I told you, Fitz and I are just friends. Anyway, he wasn't even at the barn today—it's Monday."

"So?"

"So the barn's closed to customers on Mondays." Kate bit her lip, stopping herself just in time from what she was about to add next: *All the big barns around here are.* That was exactly the kind of comment guaranteed to piss Nat off, make her think Kate was looking down on her.

And she definitely didn't want to start that kind of fight right now. Tonight was supposed to be about the two of them hanging out, reconnecting. That was why Kate was at the mall, even though all she'd really wanted to do after her long day out in the heat was jump into a cool shower and then into bed.

"Anyway, I was totally going to be on time until one of the ponies got loose from the farrier," she told her friend. "I had to help chase it down."

"What, is that fancy-ass trainer of yours too good to get his hands dirty?" Natalie said. "I swear to God, Kate, they work you like a dog at that place."

Kate didn't bother to remind her that she'd worked just as hard at Happy Acres back in the day. "Jamie wasn't around. Otherwise he would've been right there with us."

"Okay, if you say so." Natalie stopped in front of a trendy clothing store. "Let's go in here. I need some new shorts."

Soon they were flipping through racks of clothes. Natalie

started chattering about guys and parties and the usual, but Kate wasn't really listening. Her mind was already jumping ahead to tomorrow—lesson day. Her lesson on Fabelhaften, to be specific.

"I'm going to try these on," Nat's voice broke into her thoughts. "Grab something for yourself and come with—here, like this. It'll look great on you! Totally bring out your eyes."

She shoved a blue spandex minidress into Kate's hands. Kate stared at it.

"Um, I'm not really planning to buy anything tonight. Besides, I don't have anywhere to wear something like this."

"So what? Try it on anyway. It'll be fun." Nat grabbed her hand and dragged her toward the dressing rooms in the back of the store. "Come on!"

Soon the two of them were crammed into one of the boxy dressing rooms. Nat had already wriggled into a pair of denim shorts so short and tight that Kate felt a little uncomfortable looking directly at them. Then she'd insisted that Kate try on the dress she'd picked out for her. Kate was a little surprised when she checked out her reflection in the full-length mirror on the dressing room wall. The dress actually looked pretty good, even with her bare feet and messy ponytail. If Fitz thought she was cute in pilled breeches and a polo covered in horse slobber, what would he say if he ever saw her in something like this?

"Kate? Yo, Ground Control to Major Distracto!" Natalie waved both hands in front of Kate's face. "I know it's a shock to see yourself in an actual dress for a change, but try to stay in this dimension, okay?"

Kate smiled weakly, already reaching for the zipper to take the dress off. "Sorry, guess I'm a little distracted."

"Dreaming about strutting your stuff in this for your cute rich so-called friend?" Natalie smirked playfully.

"Not even close," Kate lied. "I'm just distracted 'cause Jamie wants me to start doing the Big Eq, and tomorrow I have a lesson on the horse he's letting me ride. Guess I'm a little nervous."

"Letting you ride?" Natalie echoed as she peeled off one pair of shorts and reached for another. "What do you mean?"

"There's this horse named Fable at the barn—his owners sent him to Jamie to be sold. He's not stylish enough to be a top hunter and he's too slow to make it as a jumper, but Jamie thinks he'd be perfect in the eq. Just needs some mileage. So that's where I come in."

"Kind of weird to ride a sales horse in eq, isn't it?" Natalie wrinkled her nose as she stared into the mirror, though Kate wasn't sure if it was in reaction to what she'd said or to the current pair of shorts, which bunched at the thighs in an unflattering way.

"Actually, it's pretty common," Kate said. "People do it all the time. Tons of people even end up at finals with borrowed or leased horses."

"Really?" Natalie shrugged. "Still sounds pretty weird to me. I don't think I could do it."

Kate didn't bother to point out that Natalie had never been anywhere near a show with Big Eq classes, so she probably didn't have to worry about it. She wasn't that bitchy, even if Nat kind of deserved it sometimes.

"Anyway," she said instead, "Fable can be a handful, so I'm

a little nervous about tomorrow. I mean, I've ridden him in a few lessons before this, but now it's different. You know how barn gossip is. Everyone's probably heard he's my new eq ride, so they'll all be watching us."

"Yeah." Nat let out a snort of laughter. "You've never been good with people watching you. Remember your first show? They'd just brought that bratty Appaloosa pony home from the auction and everyone was scared of him except you, so you volunteered to take him in the student show. But as soon as you rode into the ring and realized people were looking at you, you totally froze and he bucked you off."

Normally that memory made Kate laugh. She'd come a long way since then, that was for sure.

But today, for some reason, her mind flashed to that embarrassing moment when she'd spotted Zara's father and crashed Ellie through that fence. Come to think of it, maybe she hadn't come quite as far as she'd thought. She only hoped she'd be able to survive tomorrow's lesson, or her Big Eq dreams would be over before they'd begun.

"Hold still, would you, you brute?" Kate muttered. It was Tuesday afternoon, and she was tacking up Fabelhaften for the group lesson. Or trying to, at least. The big gray gelding kept slinging his head, shifting his weight, and chewing on the cross-ties. He was full of energy and seemed to have an opinion on everything she did, from currying his neck to picking his feet. And with him being every inch of 17 hands, his opinions were difficult to ignore.

"Need any help?"

Kate spun around and saw Fitz standing there watching her. She'd been so busy with the horse that she hadn't heard him approach. His reddish hair was a little rumpled and damp, as if he'd just jumped out of the shower.

"Hi!" she blurted out. "Um, thanks. Fable's being kind of—"

"A big butt-head?" Fitz grinned and gave the gelding a fond pat. "Yeah, that's him. Likes to throw his weight around."

Kate smiled. "Usually his goofing off doesn't bother me, but I guess today it's getting to me a little."

Fitz shot her a sympathetic look. "I feel you. I know what this barn is like. Everyone's going to be looking at you, wondering if you and Fable will turn out to be the next Big Eq stars."

"I don't know about that." Kate wrestled the cross-tie out of the horse's mouth, and immediately had to duck as Fable swung his huge head around to stare at a barn cat slinking past. "They'll probably just be wondering if I can stay on."

Fitz chuckled. "Get real. Everyone knows you can ride the hair off anything in the barn, Kate. Even if some people are too jealous to admit it."

Kate didn't answer. She never knew what to say when someone complimented her. Especially someone like Fitz. For a second her mind jumped back to herself in that blue dress. But no—she wasn't going there. Especially not now.

"Um, thanks," she said. "But I seriously doubt anyone here would ever be jealous of someone like me."

"Don't be so sure." Fitz reached over to hold Fable's head as she tightened the girth. As he did, his arm brushed against hers, making her skin tingle. "And not just because you're gorgeous, either."

Kate was about to roll her eyes to disguise her blush. But when she glanced at Fitz, his eyes were uncharacteristically serious.

"For real, Kate," he said softly. "I mean, all the money in the world can't buy what you've got. I'm not even sure what it is— just something really special, like, um . . ." He let his voice trail off and turned away abruptly, giving Fable such a hearty pat on the neck that the big gelding jumped in place. "Anyway, you can't put a price on sexy, right?" He checked his watch. "Oops, guess I'd better go find my horse. Need any help with this brute before I go?"

"No, I'm fine. You'd better get going—you know how Jamie gets if we're late."

"True. And I'm already on his shit list for running over that brand-new bottle of fly spray with the golf cart last week." Fitz laughed, then hurried off down the aisle.

Kate watched him go, feeling confused. What had that been all about?

Then Fable nudged at her impatiently with his big nose, bringing her back to her senses. Fitz was a distraction, and she couldn't afford any distractions today.

🐎

Zara's head was pounding as she walked into the barn. Freaking hangover. She'd stayed out until dawn partying with some new people she'd met at one of her dad's press things. Fun, but she was paying for it now.

Miguel was walking Ellie up and down the aisle. The mare was tacked up in Zara's Antares saddle and Eskadron open-front boots.

"You're late, miss," the groom informed her. "The others started warming up twenty minutes ago."

"I'm here now, okay?" Zara muttered, grabbing the reins.

She led the mare out of the barn and up the hill to the huge main jumping ring. The rest of the riders were already warming up their horses. Zara spotted Tommi, Summer, Marissa, Dani. And of course Fitz, who was looking especially hot in his custom chaps. For a second she didn't recognize Kate, who was on some big gray Zara hadn't seen before.

Jamie was perched on the portable mounting block in the center of the ring, talking on his cell phone. He hung up when he saw Zara enter.

"You're late," he informed her. Like most trainers Zara had encountered, he had a voice that didn't seem very loud when talking face-to-face, but that really carried across a ring.

"Yeah, I can tell time." Zara pushed her sunglasses up her nose. "Sorry, my bad. It happens, so let's get over it, okay?"

She was aware that most of the other riders were watching her. Out of the corner of her eye, she saw Dani roll her eyes. *Bitch.*

Jamie frowned at Zara. "Enough," he snapped. "Every word you say just wastes more time, and you don't have any to spare. You'll have to warm up at the far end and join us when you're ready. I don't know how things worked at your previous barn, but here we don't hold up the whole class for one rider."

"Burn!" Dani whispered loudly, and Marissa giggled.

Zara scowled. Who the hell did Jamie think he was? He was her trainer, not her nanny. She was just about ready to turn around, march right back out of the ring, and just keep going.

Then Fitz rode past. "Hurry up, Zara," he called with a grin. "You don't want to miss all the fun!"

Zara got a little distracted as she watched him trot off. He looked even hotter with those long legs wrapped around a horse. It would be nice to have some eye candy in a lesson for a change.

Jamie stood up to clear the mounting block. But Zara ignored him, yanking down her stirrups and then swinging on from the ground. She hadn't done that in a while, and Ellie was taller than her old hunter, so she had to grab some serious mane to pull herself up. Ellie danced around a little, tossing her head, but by then Zara was aboard.

"Come on, mare," she muttered, turning Ellie's head toward the far end. "Let's get this show on the road."

Ellie resisted, setting her neck against the rein. But Zara wasn't in any mood for her antics. She gave her a sharp kick with both heels, which sent the mare flying forward with her head up.

"Easy!" Jamie chided. "We talked about this last time, Zara. Ellie likes a soft hand and a light seat until she loosens up, or you'll end up fighting each other the whole time."

Zara just scowled, not bothering to answer. But as soon as the trainer turned away to watch the others, she gave the mare a quick scratch on the withers. "Sorry, girlie," she whispered under her breath.

Twenty minutes later, Kate was near tears. She'd had a disastrous lesson so far, starting with Fable nearly dumping her at the mounting block when a couple of the barn dogs had raced past outside the ring. And things weren't getting any better. She was having trouble controlling the big, strong gelding, who was in an especially frisky mood. He ran through her aids, overjumped easy fences, and bucked through almost every lead change.

"Try it again, Kate," Jamie called as she brought Fable back to a trot after their latest attempt. "Shoulders back, and stay focused. See if you can get him a little softer this time."

Kate braced herself as she saw Fable's ears perk toward a four-foot vertical farther down the ring and felt him start to drag her toward it. Somehow she managed to get him turned toward the first jump in the current exercise, all too aware of six pairs of eyes watching her. Normally they would have moved on to doing courses by now, or at least some more challenging gymnastics or something. Kate had the sick feeling that she was one of the main reasons they were sticking with the current easy exercise, making her feel like a beginner who'd never ridden anything more challenging than the mechanical horse outside the local supermarket.

"Stay cool, you're doing fine," Tommi whispered as Kate rode past. She was sitting on Legs, who was standing calmly on a loose rein despite his reputation as a firecracker.

Just then Kate heard a commotion somewhere behind her. Glancing back, she saw that Zara's mare was acting up again. She was the other reason they hadn't moved on; Ellie was tense and resistant and had actually refused a fence or two. Now the mare was backing up rapidly, shaking her head against Zara's hands.

"Hold up a second, Kate!" Jamie called.

Kate turned off the track to the fence, circling back around to where the others were waiting. Summer was sitting on her horse beside Tommi and Legs. "You need to relax, Kate," Summer said. "Your shoulders look really tense. You should try counting your strides out loud to keep yourself calm."

Kate didn't answer. She was breathing deeply, trying to stop herself from totally melting down.

"You okay?" Tommi asked.

Kate just nodded, afraid to speak. She bent to fiddle with her stirrup leather to avoid having to meet her friend's eye. Summer was still blabbing her stupid advice, something about her heels this time.

But Kate barely heard her. As she sat up, she caught Fitz looking at her. He smiled and shot her a thumbs-up. *You can do it*, he mouthed.

Luckily Jamie had things under control with Ellie already. He turned back to the others. "Sorry about that," he called. "Try again, Kate."

Sucking in one last deep breath, Kate sent Fable into motion, Fitz's smile giving her back a little of the confidence she'd found before the lesson. This time she was determined to do it right.

Zara watched sullenly as Kate and the big gray she was riding cleared the line. They looked a lot better this time. Great. That meant Zara was the only remedial case in the lesson, thanks to her hyper mare.

"What's wrong with you, anyway?" Zara muttered as Ellie tried to yank the reins out of her hands.

"Your turn, Zara," Jamie called. "Nice and easy. Trot a circle first to make sure she's accepting your aids."

Zara squeezed Ellie into a trot, sending her around in a big, loopy circle in front of the line. Or at least that was what she tried to do. The mare veered off the circle when she saw the jump, popping her shoulder and trying to pull toward it.

"Quit it!" Zara exclaimed, tugging at the mare's mouth to get her back on the circle.

Ellie protested by flinging her head straight up, fighting to escape the bit. She ended up scooting sideways with her head twisted to the side.

"Easy with your hands!" Jamie called.

Zara let out a string of curses as she tried everything she could to get Ellie back under control. But the mare kept going, skittering sideways like some demented dressage horse.

"Watch it!" Dani exclaimed as Ellie almost crashed into her Thoroughbred, who was always a little amped. He responded by jumping forward, then letting a hind leg fly in Ellie's direction.

The kick didn't connect, but it spooked Ellie. She leaped suddenly in the opposite direction, jerking Zara along with her and making her lose both her stirrups and her balance. Before she could recover, the mare yanked her head down and bucked like a rodeo star.

"Oof!" Zara hit the ground hard, landing flat on her back.

Jamie was at her side in seconds. "Don't move," he ordered.

She ignored him, shoving herself into a sitting position. "I'm fine," she muttered, grabbing her sunglasses. They'd landed in the dirt beside her, miraculously still in one piece.

"Oh my God!" Summer exclaimed. "Zara, are you okay? That was sooo scary!"

Jumping to her feet before the trainer could stop her, Zara shook off the arena dirt. She was going to have one hell of a bruise on her ass tomorrow, but otherwise nothing was hurt except her pride. Coming off in her first group lesson? Yeah, really epic way to introduce herself to her new barn.

Ellie had stopped nearby. Zara hurried over and grabbed the mare's flapping reins. "Hold still, horse," she ordered. Running on adrenaline, she launched herself up into the saddle.

"Zara, wait," Jamie said. "I think you'd better—"

Zara didn't give him time to finish. Jamming her feet into the stirrups, she kicked Ellie into a trot. Aiming her at the largest jump in the ring, a four-footer that Jamie had been ignoring, Zara sent the mare into a brisk canter.

"Zara!" Jamie yelled.

But they were already at the jump. Ellie pricked her ears as they approached, and for a second Zara thought she might stop. She gave her a nudge and a growl, and the mare gathered herself and flew over.

There, Zara thought as they landed. That should show everyone that she could ride in spite of that stupid fall.

"Zara, stop!" Jamie ordered, striding forward to grab Ellie's bridle as they circled back around.

"Uh-oh. Wave good-bye, Zara," Dani whispered to Fitz, probably a little more loudly than she'd intended.

Zara shot the other girl a glare. Fine. So what if Jamie

kicked her out of the lesson? The important thing was that she'd made her point—on her own terms.

She glanced down at the trainer, trying to hide her emotions. Jamie stared back, looking strangely thoughtful. Finally he let go of the bridle.

"That really wasn't necessary," he told her calmly. "Let's not pull anything like that again—consider this your warning. Now get back in line."

For a second Zara wasn't sure whether to tell him off, laugh in his face, or jump Ellie right out of the ring and never come back. But something in Jamie's eyes made her think that none of those things would be a good idea right now. Sure, she was already pretty sure he was too uptight for her. But if she left this place, she wanted it to be on her terms. Not get kicked out for mouthing off. The last time that had happened, her parents had grounded her from riding for over a month.

"Whatever," she muttered under her breath, riding over to take her place with the others.

🐎

"That was quite a lesson, huh?" Marissa commented to Tommi, shooting a look in Zara's direction as they all walked their horses back to the barn.

Tommi was watching Kate, who was leading Fable a few yards ahead. The big gray had finally calmed down a little toward the end of the lesson. Still, Tommi knew Kate well enough to be sure she wasn't happy with their performance.

But Kate would recover and learn from the bad ride, like she always did. Zara was another story. Tommi wasn't sure what she'd do next. She'd blown into the quiet, professional atmosphere of the barn like a tornado, and seemed just as unpredictable.

"Yeah," Tommi said to Marissa. "I'm surprised Jamie's putting up with her garbage. Any of us would've been grounded for pulling a stunt like that."

Marissa shrugged. "Maybe he's afraid to get after her 'cause she's a celebrity."

"Doubtful. Since when is Jamie afraid of anybody?" Tommi had no idea why Jamie was cutting Zara so much slack. Maybe he was just giving her a chance to settle in before he whipped her entitled little ass into shape.

Whatever, Tommi figured it wasn't her business, so she tried to forget about it as she took care of Legs. He'd performed well, mostly ignoring the craziness. That made Tommi more anxious than ever to find out what her father thought of her business plan. He'd been at some kind of meeting in White Plains for a couple of days, leaving town before she got up on Monday. But he was due back sometime that afternoon.

Half an hour later Legs was settled in his stall. Tommi gave him one last pat, slipped him a peppermint, then headed around the corner to the main aisle.

Most of the others from the lesson group were hanging out near the tack room. Fitz waved as Tommi approached.

"Ready for pizza?" he asked.

Tommi had almost forgotten about their summertime tradition of Tuesday-night post-lesson pizza. For a second she was tempted to beg off, wanting to head home and wait for her father. But why bother? He'd call or text her when he was ready to discuss it. Might as well distract herself in the meantime.

"Sure," she said. "I'm in."

"Cool." Fitz grinned. "I was just telling Zara about it. She's not sure she wants to hang out with us losers, but I think I've almost convinced her to give it a try."

Tommi knew he was just joking around, but that didn't stop her stress from spiking as she glanced at Zara. "I don't know, doesn't really seem like her kind of scene," she said. "The press won't be there to cover it or anything."

"Funny," Zara shot back with a scowl. "That the best insult you could buy with all your daddy's billions, Tommi?"

"Shut up." Tommi glared back. "You don't know anything about me."

"Ditto."

"Guys," Kate spoke up, sounding nervous, "take it easy, okay?"

"Yeah," Marissa put in. "Let's just order the pizza and have fun."

Fitz nodded. "Zara, you like mushrooms?"

Zara didn't answer right away, and for a second Tommi thought she was about to storm out. But then her mouth twisted into a humorless half smile. "Yeah, but not on my pizza," she said. "Pepperoni for me."

Tommi rolled her eyes. However long it took for Zara's antics to get her kicked out of the barn, it couldn't be too soon.

ELEVEN

Kate was thinking back over everything she'd done wrong in the lesson when Fitz slid onto the bench beside her. "What's up?" he asked, nudging her with one elbow. "Something wrong with your pizza?"

"Huh?" Kate blinked at him, then glanced down at the untouched slice in her hand. "Um, no. Just not very hungry, I guess."

She set the pizza down on the bench and wiped her hand on a napkin. The tack room had turned into a party. The pizza boxes sitting on the big bandage trunk in the center of the room were half empty. Summer and Marissa were over by the bridle wall laughing at something Zara was saying, while Dani was leaning against a saddle rack talking to Tommi. Hugo, Chaucer, and a couple of the other dogs were circling like sharks, hoping for their share of the pizza.

Fitz crammed the rest of his slice into his mouth. "Food of the gods," he pronounced after he'd chewed and swallowed. "So you and Fable ready to kick the eq world's ass, or what?"

Kate grimaced. "If I keep riding like I did today, I couldn't even win a short-stirrup class."

"Come on." Fitz licked tomato sauce off his fingers. "You did fine. Even Jamie would've had his hands full when Fable was in that kind of mood."

"I don't know about that." Kate stared into space, in too serious a funk to pay much attention to the way Fitz was leaning toward her, their shoulders almost touching. "I feel like Jamie has all this faith in me, but I'm not sure I can live up to it, you know?"

"Jamie's not a moron," Fitz said, tossing a stray bit of crust into Hugo's eager mouth. "If he thinks you can do this, who are you to question him?" He grinned.

Kate forced a weak smile. "I guess. But everybody's wrong sometimes, right?"

"Ah, Kate. So beautiful and yet so down on yourself. It's tragic." Fitz shook his head. "I think maybe it's time for a reality check. You weren't around yet when I started doing the eq, which means you didn't get to see me the time the judge called for us to ride without stirrups in the flat phase and I fell off. At the walk."

"Really?" Kate stared at him, not sure whether to believe him or not. "What'd Jamie say?"

"He pretended he didn't know me. For like a week." Fitz grinned and stood up just long enough to grab himself another slice of pizza. "Then there was the time I had to do a rollback to a skinny vertical. My horse decided it would rather swerve past the second jump and jump the first one again, backward this time. I ended up hanging halfway off his neck over the top, and on the other side he bucked me off into a bunch of flower pots that were decorating another jump."

This time Kate was pretty sure he had to be exaggerating at the very least. But Marissa had turned to listen. "I remember that," she said with a laugh. "You looked like some kind of cartoon character with those flowers on your head."

"No way. I looked sexy. Daisies are totally masculine." Fitz took another bite of pizza. "But wait," he said through a half-chewed mouthful, "I almost forgot about the time I mounted my very first Short Stirrup pony backward. Rode half the course before I realized my mistake."

By now everyone else in the room had turned to listen, too. Kate laughed along with the others. Okay, so she was pretty sure that last story wasn't true. But weirdly enough, Fitz's tall tales were already making her feel a little better.

Yeah, she'd been less than stellar today. So what? It wasn't the first time she'd felt like she didn't know what she was doing. And it wouldn't be the last. That was life with horses. She'd just have to work harder and ride better next time.

Halfway across the room, Zara wasn't thinking much about riding. She'd put the bad lesson out of her head as soon as it ended. Why dwell?

"Fitz is a riot, isn't he?" Dani said as they listened to him start another long, humorous story about embarrassing himself in the ring. "Only like half of what he says is true. But all of it's usually pretty entertaining."

"Yeah, he's pretty cool." Zara watched Fitz gesture wildly

along with his story. She noticed he was sitting awfully close to Kate and wondered if he had something going with her. "Do you know if he's seeing anyone?" she asked Dani.

Dani rolled her eyes. "Always," she said. "He's a total player."

"Oh, yeah? You know that from personal experience?"

Dani giggled. "You could say that. He's a lot of fun as long as you aren't looking for anything serious."

"Interesting."

Dani shot her a sidelong look. "Go for it, Zara," she said. "It's practically, like, a rite of passage to ride here." She giggled again. "Once you've been Fitzed, you'll totally be one of us!"

Zara laughed. Okay, maybe this girl wasn't a bitch after all. In fact, everyone was being pretty nice to her. Maybe trying to make up for Tommi's freak-out before the party.

She shot a look at Tommi, who was standing by herself sucking on a soda. Her eyes were a million miles away. Zara shrugged and tuned back in on Fitz.

". . . so after that disaster, I had to lie low for a while, since nobody here would talk to me, or admit they rode with me," he was telling Kate.

Summer's eyes opened wide. "Seriously?" she said. "That's sooo mean!"

Marissa giggled. "He's lying, Summer," she said. "You know how you can tell when he's lying?"

"His mouth is moving!" Dani called out. She traded a high five with Marissa.

"I'm hurt, ladies." Fitz put a hand to his chest, clearly enjoying every second of the attention. "Truly wounded to the core."

"So how long have you all been riding here, anyway?"

Zara asked. "I mean, the way you guys are talking, it sounds like most of you have been with Jamie since you were still making wee-wee in your diapers."

"Just about," Marissa said. "I think Fitz and Tommi have been here the longest, right?"

"Almost ten years," Fitz confirmed.

"I started a couple of years after that, and then Dani came," Marissa went on, stroking Chaucer's big round head as she talked. "Summer and Kate have been here about two or three years."

Summer nodded. "I used to ride at this totally lame barn on Long Island," she said. "But Jamie's way better. You'll love it here, Zara."

Zara shrugged. "Well, the pizza's pretty good," she said. "But I'm not sure about the trainer yet."

"Don't be too hard on Jamie, Zara," Kate said with a smile. "He can be tough, but only because he wants us all to be our best."

"Hmm." Zara wasn't too sure about that. But she had to admit it was kind of sweet to hear the way they all talked about Jamie and the barn. Different. Maybe sort of weird. But sweet.

Dani wandered off to get another soda, and Zara walked over to join Marissa and Summer. They were talking about some show that was coming up soon.

"If Jamie makes me do the eq at that one, I'll probably die," Marissa moaned. "I get soooo nervous at the bigger shows! Hunters is about all I can handle. At least there I know the judge is looking at the horse, not me."

"Don't worry. If you fall off, I'm sure your boyfriend Javier will be there to pick you up." Summer smirked as Marissa blushed.

"Javier?" Zara said. "You mean that groom who, like, never has anything to say?"

"He's probably just not totally comfortable speaking English yet," Marissa said. "He only moved up here from Mexico like three months ago."

"Marissa's taking Spanish in school, so that means they share two languages," Summer said. "Español, and the language de amor!"

"Hey, go for it." Zara shrugged. "He's not exactly Señor Personality, but he's cute."

Marissa sighed happily. "I know, isn't he adorable?"

Zara was distracted by seeing Fitz leave the room. "Yeah. Be back in a bit," she told the other girls. "I need to make a pit stop."

"You know where the bathroom is, right?" Summer asked eagerly. "I can show you if you don't."

Zara shook her head. The girl was such a puppy dog it was pathetic. "Stay put," she ordered before Summer could get up. "I'll find it."

Slipping out of the tack room, she looked up and down the aisle. No sign of Fitz. She wandered toward the bathroom, figuring he was probably making a pit stop himself.

While she waited, she found herself looking around the barn, which somehow seemed very different at this time of the evening. It was getting late; the horses had been fed, and most of them were turned out for the night. Jamie had long since disappeared to his house on the hill behind the grass jumping field.

She could hear an occasional burst of laughter drifting out of the tack room halfway down the aisle, but otherwise the barn had a quiet, peaceful feel to it. Not like her old barn. There had been so many people at the busy, crowded equestrian center that it was never still and empty like this. Sort of like New York City—it was the barn that never slept.

But this place was different from that one in a lot of ways. Some of them good, some not so hot. Some she wasn't sure what to think about yet.

She heard a door swing open and snapped out of her reverie. Glancing down the aisle, she saw Fitz emerge from the bathroom.

Zara smiled as he looked up and saw her. Okay, this was one way her new barn had it all over her old one. Wetting her lips, she sidled toward him.

$\cdot \textit{\large k}$

"What do you think, Tommi?"

Tommi blinked and stared at Marissa, realizing she had no clue what the girl had just said. "Um, what?" she asked. "Sorry, guess I spaced out for a sec."

Marissa shrugged. "We were just talking about the Hounds Hollow show," she said. "Think they've improved the footing in the warm-up rings?"

"Oh. I dunno, probably. A lot of people complained last time." Tommi couldn't care less about the footing at the upcoming show. All her focus was still on her talk with her father. Had it been a mistake to propose buying Legs for resale? Could she really pull off something like that?

Tommi wasn't the type of person to doubt herself. In fact,

she got frustrated with Kate sometimes for being so wishy-washy and insecure about her own abilities.

But right now, she had an inkling of how Kate must feel when she got like that. Because Tommi had never felt so uncertain about anything in her life. Was she being silly to think she could do horses as a career? Wouldn't it be easier to go off to some great college like her family expected and just ride on the side? She wasn't like Callie—she could make it all work if she was devoted enough.

She realized Marissa was talking to her again. But by now Tommi was too worked up even to fake interest. "Excuse me," she blurted out. "I just remembered I—I think I left my gloves in the wash stall."

Soon she was out in the quiet of the main aisle. She wandered along without any particular destination in mind, wishing that Legs was in so she could go visit him, remind herself what this was all about. But he was turned out in the cool night air along with the rest of the horses.

Most of the other horses, anyway. Tommi heard a sudden thump from a stall up ahead. That was a little weird. Especially when it was followed by another thump, and then a weird groaning sound. Was a horse in there colicking or something?

Suddenly worried, Tommi hurried forward. The door to the stall in question was standing open, and she glanced in, expecting to see one of the grooms or maybe the vet in there with the ailing horse.

But no. There was no horse in the stall at all. Just Fitz and Zara making out like porn stars!

Tommi stepped back quickly, not wanting them to see her. But it was too late for her not to have seen them. The image of the two of them was burned into her retinas, and she couldn't help feeling kind of sick about it. Not because she'd expected any better of either of them, necessarily. And she was certainly no prude. But she'd actually started to believe that Fitz might be seriously interested in Kate. Maybe even as something more than a fling.

"Guess not," she whispered as she ducked around the corner.

Just then her cell phone buzzed, and she grabbed it out of her pocket. It was a text from her father. "CALL ME," it read.

Tommi rushed down the aisle to a more private spot in one of the equipment rooms. She was embarrassed to notice that her fingers were trembling as she quickly punched in her father's cell number.

"Dad?" she said when he picked up. "It's me."

"Tommi. Good, you got my message." He sounded brisk and businesslike despite the late hour. "I've been thinking about your proposal. Even discussed it with your mother."

"Oh?" Tommi was a little surprised. Her parents were amicably divorced, but the two of them didn't chat very often. Especially since Tommi's mother had moved to Florida with her new husband.

"I was pretty skeptical at first," her father went on. "But I was also impressed with your initiative. So I've got a proposal for you—if you're really serious about this idea of yours, I'll chip in for half of this horse's purchase price, and allow you to withdraw the other half from your trust fund."

"Cool!" Tommi exclaimed. "I'm totally serious. I really think I—"

"Hold on, I'm not finished," her father warned. "This isn't

a free ride, Thomasina. I expect you to prove you're serious by training this horse up and getting him sold for a profit within two months."

"Two months?" Tommi cried. "That's nuts! I can't—" Then she stopped herself, taking a deep breath. "I mean, that seems a little, um, ambitious as a schedule. I was thinking more like six or eight months to really get him showing and winning so he'll be marketable, maybe taking him to Florida for the winter shows and getting him sold there."

"That fancy barn of yours ain't cheap, you know," her father said. "If you're paying board for six or eight months along with all those entry fees, not to mention shipping to Florida and so on, where's your profit?"

Tommi had to admit he had a point. Still, if she pushed Legs too hard and fast, she could ruin him and not be able to sell at all.

"How about we say he needs to get sold by the last of the big indoor shows in the fall?" she said. "That's a good way to get a horse seen."

"Hmm." Her father was silent for a second or two. "All right, I suppose that makes sense. But if the horse is still on the books after that, you have to agree to cut back your hours at the barn and focus more on academics. If you don't have the grades, there's no guarantee Georgetown'll take you."

Tommi was pretty sure that wasn't true. She was no academic superstar, but her grades were respectable enough. And her father's name was on a building and a couple of scholarships at his alma mater; she would get in if she wanted to. But she didn't bother to point that out.

"And if I sell for a profit by then?" she asked.

"Then I'll keep supporting this little business venture of yours at least through your senior year, and we'll see what happens after that."

"It's a deal," Tommi said.

"Good. I'll give Jamie a call in the morning and work out the details. See you at home."

"See you. Thanks, Dad."

Tommi hung up and just stood there for a moment, clutching her phone and feeling kind of stunned. Her father was a master negotiator—she knew this was the best offer she was likely to get from him. But could she really do it? What if she failed? Was she ready to gamble her riding dreams on one quirky horse—and her own skills in handling him?

Then again, she'd never backed down from a challenge before. She would make this work. She had to. There was no other option.

TWELVE

When Zara woke up, she wasn't sure where she was for a second. She'd been dreaming she was back in LA, chilling at one of her favorite nightclubs, only then she'd looked over and noticed that Jamie was the DJ. He'd started yelling at her, something about not living up to her potential, but Zara couldn't hear him over the pounding music. Then Fitz had appeared and told her he and Tommi were getting married, and she was invited, but he needed to know how many slices of pepperoni she wanted on her pizza. She'd tried to tell him she didn't like pepperoni, only she had to yell to get him to hear her because Jamie kept turning the music up even louder.

Then the obnoxious music had morphed into the blare of a truck horn on the street outside and she was awake, blinking in the harsh sunlight blasting in through the double-height windows along one side of the room. Now she remembered. She was in New York, in her family's new penthouse loft in Soho.

"But I *do* like pepperoni," she muttered right before the last remnants of her dream slipped away.

Sitting up and stretching, she looked around her new room. It was kind of bare and colorless compared to her room in the old house in the Hollywood Hills. But she liked it. It was clean, simple—no muss, no fuss. White walls, polished black wood floors, no moldings or other adornments. Maybe someday she'd add some color, paint one wall hot pink or something. But for now, she was okay with the minimalist look.

Pulling on a pair of shorts along with the tank she'd slept in, she padded out onto the landing in her bare feet. Glancing out over the metal-and-cable railing, she was surprised to see her father in the huge main living area below. He was lounging on one of the sleek retro vinyl sofas, sipping a cup of coffee while paging through the *New York Times*. Bo the bodyguard was reading a magazine nearby, but the rest of the posse was nowhere in sight.

"What's the matter?" Zara asked as she walked down the stairs. "Finally run out of publicity crap to do?"

Zac glanced up at her and smiled. "Morning, Little Z." Then he checked his watch and corrected himself. "Afternoon, I mean. You out late last night?"

Someone had laid out a full coffee-and-bagels extravaganza on the white lacquered console table near the bottom of the stairs, and Zara grabbed the coffeepot and poured herself a cup. Her mother hated when she drank coffee, claiming it would stunt her growth or give her zits or something. But Gina wasn't here—she'd be stuck in Vancouver for most of the summer.

"Not really," Zara told her father. "Just hung out at the barn for a while, then came home and watched TV."

Zac sat up and stretched. "How are things going at your new barn? You liking it there?"

Zara thought back to last night's pizza party. Hanging out with the whole gang had made her feel like a character in some lame-ass teen TV drama or something. But it had been kind of cool, too. Nobody did that kind of thing at her old barn.

Then there was Fitz. Just as she'd thought, that preppy exterior hid a wild streak. She was looking forward to finding out just how wild he could get. They'd made an interesting start yesterday, though Fitz had cut things short, saying someone would notice they were both gone. Zara wasn't sure why that should matter, but she'd gone along with it.

"The new barn's okay, I guess," she told her father, blowing on the hot coffee as she sank down onto a leather club chair. "The people are totally East Coast. But most of them are tolerable."

"And the new horse? That working out?"

"Mostly." Zara grimaced when she thought about yesterday's pathetic lesson. She still couldn't believe she'd fallen off. At least the others hadn't rubbed her nose in it. Nobody had even mentioned it, at least to her face. "Jamie thinks I need to, like, take more lessons or something so I can ride her better or whatever. But I bet we'll get used to each other. Mares can take a little longer to warm up to a new person sometimes, and I think . . ."

She let her voice trail off when she noticed that Zac's eyes were already straying back to the paper. Typical.

"So I have some cool news," he said, pretty much confirming that he'd just been getting the small talk over with so he could turn the conversation back to its usual topic—himself. "The band and I got invited to this big charity rockfest thing in Amsterdam next month."

"Amsterdam? Really?" Zara looked up from her coffee, suddenly at least marginally interested.

Zac rubbed his hands together. "Yeah," he said. "And while we're over there, we figure we might as well extend the visit with a few shows around Europe. Marv and the guys are still figuring out the details, but it's looking like we'll be over there through August, probably." He grinned at Zara. "So what do you say? Your mom'll have to miss it, but how about the two of us hit the road together? We'll probably leave right after that downtown benefit concert week after next."

Zara couldn't help smiling at his enthusiasm. Her dad loved touring—he pretty much lived for it. He wasn't truly happy unless he was out on the road, living out of a bus or a hotel room, eating bad food and drinking good champagne, chain-smoking and stopping in strange bars for jam sessions in the middle of the night.

It had been a long time since he'd invited her along on tour, at least to anywhere good. And Amsterdam was one of Zara's favorite places in the world. Hot European guys, legal drugs—what wasn't to like? She opened her mouth to say she was in.

Then she noticed her riding boots, which she'd dropped by the bottom of the stairs last night. That reminded her that show season was really just gearing up. There was the big, prestigious Hounds Hollow show coming up soon, where she was planning to let Keeper show these East Coasters how the jumpers should be done. Then a couple of other major shows next month. If she went on this trip, she'd miss all of it. Not to mention tons of time at the new barn in between.

So what? Since when did that bother her? The barn would still be there when she got back. Jamie could keep her horses tuned up, maybe get Ellie some more show mileage so she'd be easier to ride when Zara returned. Wasn't that the whole point of a full-service barn? To keep riding from interfering with the rest of her life?

All that made sense. But she couldn't shake the feeling that she'd be missing too much if she left now.

"I don't know," she told her father slowly. "Maybe. I'll have to think about it."

Zac looked surprised. "Fair enough, Little Z," he said. "You let me know." Picking up his coffee cup, he headed toward the kitchen.

Zara just stood there for a second, kind of weirded out by her reaction to her father's invitation. Then she shook it off.

"Hey, Bo," she called to the bodyguard as she headed back toward the stairs. "Call Mickey and tell him I need a ride to the barn. I'll get dressed and meet him downstairs in half an hour."

When Zara got to the barn, she spotted a lone rider in the closest outdoor ring. She took a few steps that way, wondering if it was Fitz—it looked like a guy.

Then she realized it was Jamie. He was riding a flashy bay large pony, which had made him look a lot taller than he was. Zara stood there for a moment, watching the trainer school the pony, which appeared to be young and a little green. This was the first time she'd seen him ride, and she had to admit she was impressed. The guy knew what he was doing. He was totally focused on his mount and hadn't noticed her watching.

When he brought the pony back to a walk and gave it a pat, Zara moved on. Inside the main barn, she spotted Kate wielding a bottle of fly spray. She was doing her best to spray it on a tacked-up horse that Marissa was holding in the aisle. The dark bay warmblood was objecting by dancing around like an elephant avoiding a mouse.

"Guess your horse doesn't like fly spray, huh?" Zara said as she stopped to watch.

Both girls stopped what they were doing and smiled at her. "Hi, Zara," Kate said. "Yeah, Miles is a wuss about fly spray."

Marissa nodded, giving the gelding a pat. "Which is weird, 'cause he's totally bombproof about everything else."

"That's horses for you, right?" Kate said with a laugh.

"Guess so," Zara agreed. She was a little surprised they were being so friendly. Sure, they'd all hung out yesterday. But these girls barely knew her.

Just then Summer appeared, clutching her ratty-looking little brown-and-white dog in her arms. "Zara!" she squealed, rushing over. "OMG, I just saw your dad on TV."

"Oh?" Zara said.

Summer nodded eagerly, brushing past Kate. "He was talking about that charity concert thing in Tribeca next week," she said breathlessly. "Are you going? It sounds like it's going to be sooo fun! Too bad it's sold out, or I'd definitely go!"

Summer was *definitely* angling for an invite to Zac's benefit concert. The girl just kept finding new ways to get on Zara's nerves.

"No, it doesn't sound fun," Zara said bluntly. "It sounds like a total drag. I'd rather stab myself in the eye with a hoof-pick than go to that thing."

Summer looked startled. "Really? Um . . ."

"Gotta go," Zara said. "I want to check on my horses."

She made her escape before Summer could protest, then walked over to the aisle where Fitz's horses lived. His eq horse and his older Appendix were in their stalls, but his big gray jumper was missing. Okay, so he was probably riding. Zara took a few steps in the direction of the indoor, wondering if she should tack up one of her horses and join him, or maybe just hang out and wait for him to finish so the two of them could pick things up where they'd dropped them last night.

She smiled as she thought about the way he'd looked at her after she'd kissed him the first time. Surprised, turned on, and kind of amused all at the same time. Things had only gotten better after that. The guy definitely knew what he was doing.

But the nice feeling faded a little when Zara remembered how he'd backed off so suddenly, even though they could've easily hidden behind the stall door until Summer walked by. What was that about? It wasn't as if she was discouraging him, giving any hint that she wasn't ready to go as far as he wanted.

A sudden clang broke into her thoughts, and Zara noticed a wheelbarrow sitting in the aisle just ahead. As she watched, another chunk of manure flew out and landed in the wheelbarrow.

Zara hurried over and glanced into the stall. A horse was dozing along one wall as Sean the stall mucker cleaned around it.

"Hey," Zara called loudly enough for him to hear over his iPod.

He glanced up, and a slow grin spread across his face. "Hey," he replied, yanking the earbuds out of his ears. "What's up, Zara?"

"Not much." She leaned on the partly open stall door. "Having fun in there?"

"Yeah, shoveling shit is a real party." He slid his gaze down to her cleavage. "But at least the scenery just got a lot better."

Before Zara could respond, she heard someone calling her name. Glancing over her shoulder, she saw Jamie hurrying toward her with a serious look on his face.

"Uh-oh," she whispered to Sean. "Speaking of shit, I think I might be in some deep stuff."

She stepped away from the stall, not wanting Sean to get in trouble for talking to her while he was supposed to be working. Especially after the last time Jamie had caught them together.

"What up?" she said when the trainer reached her. He was still in his riding clothes, his helmet tucked under his arm.

"Zara," he said. "I wanted to talk to you about yesterday."

"Yesterday?" Her mind flashed immediately to Fitz. Did Jamie have video cameras in the stalls or something? She wouldn't put it past him.

But he was already saying something about the lesson. ". . . and I realize you're still new here, but I can't have you disrupting things the way you did yesterday," he said sternly.

Zara had been feeling pretty good since arriving at the barn, Summer aside, but her mood suddenly plummeted. "Well, excuse *me* for having the nerve to fall off," she said. "I didn't realize I had to be perfect to freaking ride here."

"I'm not talking about the fall," Jamie said. "I'm talking about what happened afterward. Taking that jump was incredibly reckless and irresponsible—what if you or Ellie had been hurt? Not to mention the example it sets for other people. If you were to pull something like that at a show, it would reflect badly on me, your fellow riders—the whole barn. I can't have that."

Zara felt her whole body tightening up. Who did this guy think he was? He was treating her like some bratty pony that needed remedial schooling to remind it not to run away with its rider.

She was ready to go off on him, tell him exactly what she thought of him and his uptight attitude and his freaking barn rules. He wasn't worth it. Neither was this stupid stuck-up barn. Maybe she should just tell him to shove it, that she was done with riding—or at least riding at prissy Pelham Lane Stables. Tell him she'd be spending the summer partying in Europe and finding a new barn when she got home.

But something made her hold back. Clenching her fists at her sides, she avoided his eye.

"Fine, I hear you, okay?" she muttered.

He gave her a long, searching look with those cool blue eyes of his. "All right," he said. "As long as we have an understanding."

She shrugged, staring fixedly at the horse in the stall across the way until Jamie left. A moment later she was aware of Sean sidling out of the stall to stand behind her.

"Whoa, the boss was pretty heinous to you just now," he said.

Zara rolled her eyes, still not sure why she hadn't told Jamie off. He'd definitely deserved it. "Tell me about it," she muttered to Sean.

He nudged her in the side. "Don't sweat it, babe, the guy's a tool," he said. "But listen, if you're interested, I've got just the thing to help you relax . . ."

"Good boy," Kate murmured as she tightened Fable's girth.

As she stepped around the horse to grab the bridle, she saw Tommi coming. "Hey," Tommi greeted her. "Taking Fable for a hack?"

Kate nodded. "After yesterday's lesson, I figure we need all the saddle time we can get together."

"Come on. You guys did fine yesterday."

That was the kind of thing Tommi always said. But this time she had a weird look on her face.

"What?" Kate asked, suddenly suspicious. Had she done even worse than she'd thought in the lesson? Nah, that probably wasn't possible.

"What what?" Tommi asked.

"You look weird." Kate brushed a hand over her face. "Do I have something hanging out of my nose or something?"

Tommi laughed. "No way, I'd tell you if you did." She hesitated, uncertainty flitting through her eyes.

"Seriously, what? Are you trying to figure out how to tell me I'm not cut out for the eq and I should take up tennis instead?"

"No, nothing like that." Tommi bit her lip, glanced around, then smiled. "But actually, I do have some news. It's about Legs . . ."

Kate listened as Tommi told her about her new deal with her father. The more she talked about it, the more excited Tommi got, waving her hands and grinning as she outlined her plans.

". . . so of course I'm already totally panicking that I'm going to screw this up," Tommi finished breathlessly. "I just hope I haven't bitten off more than I can chew, you know?"

"You'll do great. This kind of thing is right up your alley, and Legs is an amazing horse." Kate smiled. But her stomach churned with conflicting feelings. On the one hand, it was great that her friend was so happy. Tommi was so even-keeled, so all about keeping her game face on. Seeing her so openly excited and nervous was different, and kind of nice.

At the same time, Kate couldn't help feeling a twinge of resentment. Did Tommi even realize how lucky she was to have this kind of opportunity? To have a father who could buy and sell horses that cost more than Kate's family's house? Sure, Tommi had worked hard for every bit of her success in the saddle—Kate knew that as well as anyone. But what did she really have to be nervous about now? How much of a gamble was this, really? If she succeeded, she got to try again, maybe building things up into a nice little business eventually. If she "failed," she ended up at some fancy college. Boo freakin' hoo.

Almost as soon as the thoughts flitted through her mind, Kate wished she could take them back. How could she think such things? Of *course* Tommi knew how lucky she was. Kate should realize that as much as anyone, since she was *supposed* to be one of her best friends.

"Just let me know what I can do to help you, Tommi," she said. "You know I'm here for you."

"Thanks. I know, and I really appreciate it." Tommi smiled. "Good thing, too. I'm sure I'll need tons of help to make this work."

"Hey, buddy," Tommi said as she reached Legs's stall. The gelding was nosing at his hay, but came over to see her with his ears pricked forward.

She patted him, looking him over with a shiver of nerves. Was she doing the right thing? Should she have stuck with the status quo, or was this gamble worth it?

She decided to try not to think like that. What was done was done—she'd made the deal, now she had to make it work.

"Come on, let's celebrate," she told the horse. "I'm taking you for a nice hand graze."

Minutes later they were out on the grassy lawn between

barn and rings. Tommi watched the gelding as he wandered around with his head down, searching out the tastiest patches of clover.

As they came within view of one of the outdoor rings, she saw Kate leading Fable in through the gate. Tommi watched her mount, wondering if she should have told her about seeing Fitz with Zara. She'd almost spilled it just now. But at the last second, she'd decided to keep quiet. Kate was so focused on horses that Tommi wasn't sure she knew what a guy was for. She probably hadn't even noticed Fitz flirting with her. Maybe Fitz had realized that, too, and decided to move on to easier pickings. It certainly seemed like it, based on what she'd seen last night.

A buzz interrupted Tommi's thoughts. Shifting Legs's lead to her other hand, she dug her phone out of her pocket. She didn't recognize the number, but decided to live dangerously by answering anyway. What the heck? Maybe it was some top European jumper rider looking to drop a wad of cash on the perfect prospective Grand Prix horse.

She was still smiling at that thought when she said hello.

"Tommi?" the voice on the other end of the line said. "Hi. It's Grant. Your dad gave me your number."

Of course he had. Nobody had ever accused Rick Aaronson of being subtle.

"Hey, Grant," Tommi said. "What's up?"

"Dinner was fun the other night. But we didn't have much chance to talk. Want to get together tomorrow night? You can help reintroduce me to good old NYC."

Tommi hesitated. With this new business venture on her

plate, she wasn't going to have much spare time for hanging out or partying. Besides, she didn't want to lead anyone on—Grant *or* her father. She'd been glad to see her old friend again, but there definitely hadn't been any romantic sparks between them. Now or ever.

"Um . . . ," she began.

"It's cool if you're busy or whatever," Grant added, clearly catching on to her long pause. "Just figured I'd ask."

"No, that's okay," Tommi said quickly, feeling a flash of guilt. "I was just, um, trying to remember if I was doing anything tomorrow. I'm pretty sure I'm free."

"Great!"

He sounded so happy that Tommi was glad she'd said yes. Grant might not be her dream guy, but he was a good friend. Why not get reacquainted now that he was back in town? Besides, her father liked him. And it wouldn't hurt to stay on his good side right now.

They made plans to meet up the following evening. After she hung up, Tommi stayed out with Legs for a good long time, daydreaming about the future.

Finally she headed back to the barn. As she was passing the small six-stall quarantine barn where Jamie kept new imports or sick horses, she smelled something. A certain familiar sweet, smoky smell.

Tommi's heart started pounding. No way. Nobody would be stupid enough to do that *here*, inside one of the barns.

She peered inside. "Oh, you have got to be kidding me!" she blurted out.

Two sets of eyes looked back at her—guilty ones belonging

to Sean the stall mucker and defiant ones belonging to Zara. The two of them were passing a half-smoked joint between them.

"Yo, Tommi." Zara held it out. "Want a hit?"

THIRTEEN

— — — — —

Kate stared in the front window of the swanky SoHo boutique, wondering what could possibly possess someone to buy six-inch metallic sandals. "So then what happened?" she asked Tommi.

Tommi shrugged. "I started yelling as soon as I realized what was going on," she said. "Sean tried to take off, but Miguel happened to be nearby and saw them, too, and he called Jamie. I had to take Legs back to his stall, so I'm not sure what happened after that."

"I heard Sean got fired," Kate said.

Tommi shot her a look. "Even on your day off, news travels fast, huh?"

"Yeah." Kate ducked a guy trying to shove an advertising leaflet in her face. West Broadway was crowded with shoppers, tourists, and vendors hawking everything from handmade jewelry to bootleg DVDs. Definitely a different world from the peace and quiet of Pelham Lane.

Kate never quite knew what to do with her day off. After the first few times she'd come to the barn anyway, Jamie had officially banished her. The juniors had a lesson that afternoon, so she was allowed to turn up then. But she knew better than to show her face too early.

The last place she wanted to hang out was her house. Her brother had skipped his first day of summer school, which meant World War III was in full cry between him and their father. That in turn meant her mom was sinking even deeper into her rituals. Tommi's invitation to come into the city for lunch and shopping had offered a welcome escape, and Kate had rushed out to the train station without even stopping for breakfast.

"Guess we won't be seeing Zara at the lesson this afternoon," she commented as the two of them wandered on down the sidewalk.

"Guess not. No big loss there."

"Come on. She wasn't that bad." Kate felt a pang of sympathy as she thought about Zara's short time at the barn. Sure, she hadn't exactly gone out of her way to fit in. But Kate knew that sometimes a person's exterior didn't show the whole story. Zara seemed so guarded, almost angry, and yet so lonely somehow.

"Are you kidding?" Tommi sounded incredulous. "Look, it's none of my business if she wants to light up a fatty at home, in the barn parking lot, in the middle of Times Square, wherever. But smoking *in the barn*? Risking the lives of however many zillions of dollars worth of horseflesh, not to mention Jamie's entire livelihood? Talk about selfish!"

"Good point, I guess." Kate shivered, her all-too-vivid imagination immediately latching on to what Tommi had said. Concocting horrible images of horses screaming in terror, their eyes rolling back in their heads as their stalls went up in flames around them . . .

"Anyway, Jamie's already given Zara enough second chances," Tommi went on as they paused at the corner, waiting for the light to change. "She didn't walk into a barn yesterday—she knew what she did was stupid and did it anyway. I doubt we'll see her again."

Kate nodded, knowing her friend was right. Jamie was the biggest of Big Name Trainers. He wasn't afraid to kick someone out of his program. He'd done it before, and with much less provocation. Still, she couldn't help feeling sorry for Zara. What would it be like to be kicked out? Kate hoped she'd never, ever find out.

They window-shopped for a while longer, though Kate's heart wasn't really in it. What was the point? She'd never be able to afford most of the stuff she saw at the mall with Nat, let alone anything in these shops. Not that she cared. Fashion wasn't really her thing. If she couldn't wear it to the barn, she didn't need it.

Finally Tommi checked her watch. "We should eat," she said. "What do you feel like?"

"I don't care, I'll eat anything. You decide."

She regretted her words when Tommy led her into a busy, chic little café on Mercer Street. "Seems kind of pricey," Kate said as she peeked at the menu the intimidatingly glamorous waitress had handed her before rushing off.

"Don't worry about that." Tommi was scanning the menu, too. "I invited you to lunch, remember? It's my treat."

Kate bit her lip, knowing better than to argue. Tommi could be funny about stuff like that. Maybe because it was no big deal for her to make such an offer—or to accept one, either. Why should it be? In her world, expensive lunches were the norm, just like six-figure horses, four-figure monthly board bills, $350 bridles, and name-brand breeches. She couldn't be expected to understand that in Kate's world, any lunch that cost more than ten bucks had better be celebrating something important, like a birthday or a graduation.

"Um, okay," Kate said. "Thanks. I had a huge breakfast, though. I'll probably just have a salad or something."

As they waited for the waitress to come back, Kate found herself wondering what it would be like. Having that much money. Enough so you could eat anywhere, order anything, shop in any store.

It took her a moment to realize that Tommi was talking to her. Something about Fitz.

"Huh?" Kate asked.

"I said, I noticed Fitz has been hanging around you a lot lately." Tommi sipped her water. "And it seems like you don't really mind having him around. True?"

Kate felt her cheeks go pink as she avoided her friend's gaze. "He's cool, I guess," she said. "I mean, we're just friends, if that's what you're implying."

"I'm not implying anything. I'm asking."

"Okay, then I'm telling you. Fitz isn't my type. As if you had to ask."

"Good." Tommi sat back in her seat, looking oddly relieved.

"Because you're way too good for him. I'm glad his ridiculous ninja flirting hasn't overwhelmed you like it seems to do with everyone else. I hope you keep it that way."

Kate grabbed her own water glass, taking a long drink to avoid responding. Yeah, she could tell that Tommi thought she was looking out for her. And that made sense—Tommi had a lot more experience with guys, which wasn't difficult, since Kate had practically, oh, none. But still, who was Tommi to tell her who was "good enough" for her to date?

Or could it be *Kate* who wasn't good enough? The thought slipped in before she could stop it, slippery as an oiled snake. Fitz came from serious money. Tommi didn't seem to care about stuff like that, but maybe . . .

No. Kate did her best to shake off the notion. But the sick little knot in the pit of her stomach was still there when the waitress returned to take their order, making it easy to stick to her plan of ordering nothing but a small salad and another glass of water.

"Zara's horses are still here," Dani announced, stopping at the end of the aisle with her horse trailing behind her. "At least Ellie is. I didn't see her jumper, but there's hay and fresh shavings in his stall, so he's probably in turnout or something."

Kate shrugged as she tightened Fable's girth, dodging the big gelding's annoyed nip. "It only happened yesterday," she pointed out. "I'm sure Jamie gave her time to arrange to take the horses somewhere else."

Summer was leaning against the wall with Whiskey in her

arms, watching Javier adjust her horse's saddle in the next set of cross-ties. "Yeah," she said. "I wonder where she'll go?"

"I'm sure we'll find out. We'll probably still see her at shows." Tommi glanced up briefly, then returned to fiddling over Legs's jumping boots.

At that moment Fitz rushed in, breathless and dressed in shorts and flip-flops. "Am I late?" he cried. "My watch stopped, and I overslept, and then there was this heinous traffic on the bridge."

"Chill, you're okay," Dani said. "We've still got plenty of time. I don't think Marissa's even here yet."

"Whew!" Fitz collapsed against the wall. Noticing Kate looking his way, he grinned and waggled his eyebrows playfully. "Hey, sexy."

Kate smiled tightly and turned away, feeling self-conscious. She was all too aware that Tommi was standing nearby, probably watching for any signs of her succumbing to Fitz's nefarious flirtation.

Fitz didn't seem to notice her reaction. His eyes had turned to Tommi's horse. "So hey—is it official, Aaronson?" he asked, stepping over to give Legs a rub on the neck. "You a for-reals horse wheeler-dealer now?"

"If you want to call it that." Tommi rolled her eyes. "Yeah. My dad wired Jamie the money this morning. Legs is officially mine—for better or for worse."

"Congrats!" As Tommi straightened up, Fitz grabbed her arm to look at her watch. "Whoa! I'd better hustle. If I'm late one more time, Jamie threatened to make me ride without stirrups for the entire summer."

A few minutes later Kate, Tommi, and Summer were leading their horses up the path toward the main ring. They weren't exactly late, but they weren't early, either, thanks to Summer's stubborn refusal to move out of the way until Javier found the polos that *exactly* matched the shirt she was wearing that day. Glancing forward, Kate saw that Jamie was already perched on the fence watching three riders warm up. Dani and Marissa were two of them.

"Who's that?" Summer asked, staring at the third.

Kate's eyes widened as she recognized the horse. "I think it's—"

"Zara!" Tommi finished for her. "What the hell?"

Zara kept her gaze on Keeper's neck as the other riders filed into the ring. She could feel the stares hitting her like shrapnel, though nobody said a word. Probably only because Jamie was right there. None of his loyal little riderbots would ever dare to question him.

But Zara could imagine what they were all thinking.

Then Fitz rushed up to the ring with his horse trotting along behind him. "Zara!" he blurted out when he spotted her. "Um, hi?"

"Hi," she muttered as she walked Keeper past the gate.

"Wow," Fitz said, for once clearly at a loss for words. "I, um . . ."

"Are you here to ride or to chat?" Jamie asked him pointedly.

Fitz shot Zara another glance and shrugged. "I'm here to

ride," he said, yanking his left stirrup down and swinging aboard.

If Zara thought she'd feel less self-conscious once the lesson started, she'd thought wrong. She might as well have had a neon sign hanging over her head reading LOOK AT ME. Or maybe CLASS LOSER. At least she was riding Keeper today instead of Ellie, and the big chestnut gelding was a saint as always. Still, by the third time Dani shot her a curious look as she rode by, Zara almost wished Jamie had kicked her out of the barn after all.

Almost.

Why had he let her stay, anyway? She still wasn't sure. He claimed it had nothing to do with who her parents were. Right. It *always* had something to do with that.

With Jamie, though, she wasn't sure that was the whole story. He'd spent an awful lot of time talking about her potential as a rider. Raving about her natural gifts. And she was pretty sure he didn't mean the natural gifts most people noticed on her. For one thing, he obviously didn't roll that way.

So what *did* he mean? She spent so much time brooding over it that she almost missed when everyone started to canter. Luckily Keeper was paying more attention than she was. He stepped into a smooth depart, swinging along on the rail after Marissa's horse.

"Easy, Tommi!" Jamie called.

Glancing back, Zara saw that Tommi was having trouble with her horse, the lean, fiery-looking bay she'd been riding at the shows lately. He was tossing his head, trying to bolt away from her at the canter.

So Little Miss Perfect wasn't having a perfect ride for a

change. Zara allowed herself the smallest of smirks. Served her right for narcing her out.

But she couldn't blame Tommi for this. Not really. Why had Zara let that idiot Sean talk her into toking in the barn, anyway? She knew better. Risking her own neck was one thing. She never had a problem with that. But endangering all those innocent horses—not cool.

Jamie called for a halt. Keeper stopped promptly and Zara gave him a loose rein, staring moodily out over the ring fence at Summer's bratty little dog. It was wandering around with its nose to the ground, probably looking for some expensive tack to chew on.

But Zara wasn't really paying attention to the dog. She was wondering if she was going crazy. So she'd made a mistake. Big whoop—the barn *hadn't* burned down, no horses had been hurt, it was over. Why was she still worrying about it? It wasn't as if she'd never been on probation before.

The difference was, this time she was pretty sure Jamie meant it. Not like all those other trainers, teachers, even her parents, who rarely followed through on their threats. No, Jamie had made it pretty clear that this was her last chance. That she'd better not screw up again or she was out, no matter who her parents were.

And so the hell what? She wasn't even sure she liked it here anyway. So why had she put up with Jamie's lecture? Maybe she shouldn't have told her dad she'd be skipping that trip to Europe. This place wasn't worth all the drama. Was it?

"Okay, everyone," Jamie said. "Sitting trot on the rail. I want to see those butts hugging the saddle."

The flatwork portion of the lesson continued. Zara was

vaguely aware that Tommi was still having trouble with her horse, though she was too focused on her own problems to pay much attention.

Jamie decided to end with a gymnastic exercise. He set up a series of four low jumps, then sent them through one by one. Keeper nailed it the first time through, but a couple of the other horses had some trouble, including Tommi's.

"Let's try that again," Jamie said after everyone had taken a turn. "Tommi, you're up first this time. Make sure Legs comes in at a steady pace and then just let him find the distance to the second jump."

Tommi had a determined look on her face as she rode the horse toward the first obstacle. He was wriggly going in, but she kept him balanced between her hands and legs and got him over the first element. He landed and tried to spook and bolt forward as he'd done the first time. This time Tommi was ready for him, though, steadying him with a firm half-halt and then letting him go forward.

"Nice," Zara murmured as she watched the bay meet the second fence perfectly.

As the horse landed after the second jump, ears pricked toward the third, there was a sudden flurry of barking from just outside the ring. Zara glanced over just in time to see a small, furry creature dash into the ring followed by a slightly larger furry creature. Summer's dog chasing a squirrel.

"Whoa!" Marissa cried as her normally placid horse pricked his ears and took a quick couple of steps backward. Some of the other horses reacted as well, though Keeper barely flicked an ear.

Tommi's horse was another story. Flinging up his head, he spooked hard to the left and then bolted again, clearly too panicked to see the next jump just ahead. He crashed into the standard, then belatedly tried to jump, twisting his body awkwardly in the air and ejecting Tommi right into the next fence.

FOURTEEN

━━ ━━ ━━ ━━ ━━

"Tommi! Are you okay?" someone cried. Tommi was too shaken up to notice who, though she thought it might have been Kate.

Jamie was already running toward her. "Stay still," he ordered, kicking aside one of the fallen rails. "Can you feel all your limbs?"

"I'm okay. I didn't hit my head or anything." Tommi started carefully wriggling various body parts, checking that everything was still in working order. She'd clocked one of her shoulders on the jump standard and landed on her hip on a rail, but she was pretty sure nothing was broken. "Is Legs all right?" she asked.

She glanced across the ring. Fitz had jumped off, leaving Dani holding his horse while he went after Legs. The bay gelding pranced nervously, his nostrils flared and his eyes rolling, but allowed himself to be caught without much trouble.

"Take it easy," Jamie warned, putting out a hand to steady

Tommi as she climbed to her feet. "You want to sit out the rest of this one? I can hop on Legs for you."

"No, I'm fine." Tommi did her best to shake it off. That was the hardest fall she'd taken in a long time. Adrenaline was still pumping through her, but she knew when it wore off she was going to be sore.

Fitz led Legs over. "I think he's okay," he offered. "I jogged him a few steps."

"Thanks," Jamie said, taking the reins. As Fitz headed back to his own horse, the trainer glanced at Tommi. "Sure you don't want me to get on first?"

For a fraction of a second, Tommi wanted to say yes. Wasn't that what a trainer was for? To help you through the tough moments?

But no. Legs was supposed to be *her* project now. If she let Jamie take over every time things got tricky, what was the point?

"I'm fine," she said firmly, pasting on her game face as she grabbed the reins. "I want to do it."

Jamie stared at her for a second, then nodded. "Show's over, everyone," he said briskly, striding to the center of the ring. "Kate, you're up next."

Tommi walked Legs over to the mounting block, checked the girth, then swung aboard. The gelding jigged a little but settled quickly. When Tommi asked him for a trot, she held her breath for the first few steps. He felt a little tense, but otherwise normal. Sound. Thank God. What would she do if that crash had made him lame?

But it hadn't, she reminded herself. Everything was fine.

The best way to handle it—for her and the horse—was to move on and act as if nothing had happened. Act normal, even if she wasn't feeling it.

That turned out not to be so easy. As soon as the rest of the class had their chance at the gymnastic, Jamie moved on to more flatwork. That was weird, and Tommi had the distinct feeling that she was the reason for it. Didn't he know by now that he didn't have to take it easy on her? It was almost insulting—like she was one of those Adult Ammies who were half scared of their horses and needed Jamie to hold their hands after every spook or snort.

As she trotted along the rail, she shot a glance at the jump she was passing, a good-sized oxer left over from a different lesson. For one crazy second she was tempted to pull out of line, gallop over, and take it just like Zara the other day. She could picture the shocked look on Jamie's face if she did it . . .

But no. She was no Zara. Shaking off the stupid little fantasy, she focused again on her work.

"I *still* can't believe she's still here," Kate whispered as Zara walked past the end of the aisle where Kate and Tommi were untacking their horses after the lesson.

Tommi glanced that way and saw that Zara had already changed out of her riding clothes into a strapless sundress and beaded sandals. Interesting fashion choice for the barn, and probably not the best way to get back in Jamie's good graces if he noticed.

But Tommi was too distracted by her fall to care much about

Zara. "*I* still can't believe I came off today," she told Kate with a sigh. "I'm going to be one huge walking bruise tomorrow."

"That dog of Summer's shouldn't be allowed anywhere near a barn," Kate said with a frown.

"Probably true." Tommi shrugged. "But shit happens. It's not like Legs won't ever have to deal with spooky stuff at a show. I should have handled it better."

Kate tossed her a sympathetic glance as she pulled Fable's saddle off his broad back. "Don't be so hard on yourself. Everyone comes off sometimes. Even Jamie."

"I know." Tommi sighed and rubbed her face. "It just seems like kind of a bad omen, you know? This was literally my first ride on Legs since he officially became mine."

Before Kate could respond, Zara reappeared. This time she turned down the aisle and walked toward them.

"Hi," she said, her voice a little brusque and her face unsmiling.

Tommi wondered if she was there to ream her out for ratting on her yesterday. If so, she wasn't in the mood.

"Hi," she retorted cautiously.

Zara shifted her weight from one sandal to the other. "So you okay?" she asked. "That looked like a hard fall."

Okay, that wasn't the comment Tommi was expecting. But she tried not to let her surprise show. "Yeah, I'll live," she said. "Thanks."

Zara nodded. She glanced over at Kate. She'd been staring, but quickly busied herself with her horse's saddle pads. After that Zara just stood there for a few seconds as the awkward silence grew.

"Um, okay," she said at last. "See you."

"That was weird," Kate said as soon as Zara was gone.

"Yeah. It's almost like she was trying to be human."

Kate smiled. "Be nice. Jamie must see something in her or she wouldn't still be here."

"You're right. I wonder what it is?" Tommi bent down to unhook Legs's boots. "All I can see in her so far is some spoiled celebrity's kid who's only out for fun and doesn't care who she hurts on the way. What happened yesterday was just Exhibit B."

"Really? What's Exhibit A?"

Oops. Tommi realized she'd been thinking about Zara's little makeout session with Fitz. But Kate still didn't know about that.

"Um, just the way she took that jump after her fall that time," Tommi said, thinking quickly. "She could have hurt her horse with a stunt like that."

Kate wasn't looking at her anymore. She was staring down the aisle. "Hey, it's your cute friend who came to the show last weekend," she said. "Is there something you haven't told me, Tommi?"

"What friend?" Tommi glanced back. "Grant!" she exclaimed when she saw who was coming. "What are you doing here?"

Grant grinned as he reached them. Hugo, who was always the first to greet any newcomer to the barn, was frisking eagerly around his feet. "Surprise!" Grant said, reaching down to rub the dog's ears. "I was in the neighborhood, so I decided to stop in and check out the place where you spend all your free time."

"In the neighborhood?" Tommi echoed.

"Yeah. Buddy of mine wanted me to come check out his new Lexus. I took the train up this morning to Larchmont." Grant took a step closer. "I figured since we were planning to hang out tonight, you wouldn't mind giving me a ride back to the city, so I had him drop me off here."

Tommi felt a jolt. She'd almost forgotten about their plans that night. After that fall, the only thing she'd had in mind was soaking her aches and pains away in a hot bath, followed by an early bedtime.

She was tempted to ask Grant if they could reschedule. But she hated to disappoint him, especially now that he was already here.

"Sure, no problem," she said. "I just need to finish up a few things here before we go."

"That's cool. I don't mind hanging around as long as you want." Grant noticed Kate watching from nearby and smiled. "Hi," he said. "It's Kate, right? I'm Grant. We met at the show, remember?"

"Sure, of course." Kate returned his smile shyly.

Just then Summer careened around the corner. "Kate!" she yelled. "Where are you? I need you to clean off my—Oh! Hello!" she interrupted herself, her entire demeanor changing as she spotted Grant.

"Hi," Grant said.

"Summer, this is my friend Grant," Tommi said. "Grant, Summer. She rides here, too."

"Nice to meet you, Grant," Summer said sweetly. "So you and Tommi are friends, huh? I haven't seen you around here before."

"That's because he's never been here before." Tommi quickly snapped a lead onto Legs's halter and unclipped the cross-ties. "I was about to give him the grand tour. Come on, Grant."

"Right behind you," he said agreeably. He tossed a smile toward Kate and Summer. "Later, ladies."

"Bye!" Summer called as Tommi led Legs and Grant away around the corner.

Tommi hurried into the living room of the town house, freshly showered and dressed in her favorite Free People tunic and skinny jeans. Grant was leaning against a distressed leather sofa chatting with her stepmother. He looked like something out of the J. Crew catalog, and for a second Tommi wondered if she'd been too quick to write him off as a romantic prospect. Maybe she was just out of practice—she'd broken up with her last boyfriend almost two months ago . . .

But no. She'd seen this guy at age seven in his Spiderman underpants and been there when he'd puked his guts out over the edge of his uncle's sailboat at age ten. Not exactly the stuff of romantic legend. Let Summer drool over Grant if she wanted; Tommi was happy to keep things friendly.

"Ready to go?" she asked.

Grant turned toward her. "Wow, you look great!" he said, taking in her outfit.

"Thanks." Uh-oh. Tommi might be comfortable with keeping it casual. But she was going to have to make sure Grant didn't get the wrong idea.

"Have fun, kids!" Tommi's stepmother trilled as they headed for the door.

"Thanks, Mrs. Aaronson," Grant said. "I'm sure we will."

"What now?" Tommi asked as she and Grant walked out of the restaurant into the steamy night air of downtown Manhattan. "Feel like catching a movie or something?"

Now that she was out, she was glad she'd come. Why stay home and be miserable just because of some stupid fall?

Instead, she was having a great time. The two of them had lingered over dinner, catching up on both their lives over the past couple of years. Tommi had forgotten how easy Grant was to talk to, how quick and funny he was. How he was one of the few people she knew who seemed to get her—her competitiveness, her sense of humor, everything. Kind of like the brother she'd never had, she figured.

Grant checked his watch. "I told some friends we might meet them at the new club over on Eleventh Avenue," he said. "James and some of the gang from the Hamptons. You up for it?"

"Wow, I haven't seen most of those guys for eons!" Tommi laughed. "Is Duckface going to be there?"

"If we're lucky." Grant grinned, already stepping toward the curb to hail a cab.

A few minutes later they were flashing their fake IDs at the entrance to the club. It was still early, barely ten o'clock, but the place was already packed. People were six deep at the bar, and hip-hop blared out over the crowded dance floor.

"Wow, it's going to be hard finding the guys in all this." Grant looked around. "See them anywhere?"

"Not yet," Tommi said, standing on her tiptoes to get a better view. "I . . ."

Her voice trailed off. She didn't see the friends they were supposed to meet. But she'd just spotted two other familiar figures dancing at the edge of the floor, limbs intertwined and bodies grinding to the throbbing music.

"What?" Grant asked, noticing her look. "Spot them?"

"Nope, just some other people I know. Last time I saw them together they were in almost the same position, minus the music."

Grant looked confused. "Huh?"

"Never mind. It's just some people from the barn. I should go say hi."

She pushed her way through the crowds, heading toward the couple. Fitz saw her first.

"Tommi!" he exclaimed, peeling his hands out from beneath Zara's skintight tank top. "Hi there."

"Hi. I thought that was you two." Tommi glanced at his partner. "Hey, Zara. Is Fitz showing you around New York?"

Zara smirked. "Something like that," she said, smoothing down her shirt. She cast an interested eye over Grant. "Who's your friend?"

"This is Grant." Tommi introduced both the others. "Fitz, you probably remember Grant from back in the day. He went to Dalton until he left for Europe a couple of years ago."

"Sure. Good to see you, dude." Fitz stuck out his hand, and the two guys shook.

"Europe, huh?" Zara tilted her head, gazing up at him. "Where were you?"

"Mostly Germany and Switzerland," Grant began. "My grandmother's parents were from Geneva, and . . ."

Tommi didn't hear any more. Fitz had just given her a tug on the arm, pulling her slightly away from the others.

"Whoa, thanks for rescuing me," he muttered, shooting Zara a look. "That girl is relentless!"

Tommi gave him a skeptical look. "Since when does the mighty Fitz Hall need rescuing from a woman?" she asked, only half joking. "Usually they're the ones who need rescuing from you."

"Ha-ha." He smiled weakly. "Seriously, Zara and I didn't come here together or anything, if that's what you're thinking. I had plans to meet up with some buddies of mine, and I guess maybe she overheard me talking to them on the phone back at the barn. Because I turned up, and wham! There she was, like some kind of Fitz-seeking missile." He laughed self-consciously, shooting Zara another look to make sure she wasn't listening.

"Hmm." Tommi wasn't sure whether to believe him or not. And normally she wouldn't really care. But she couldn't help remembering the way she'd caught him looking at Kate.

But Kate had no interest in him. She'd said so. So why stress about it?

Just then she heard a shout. Several people were rushing toward them, waving wildly. Tommi grinned, forgetting about Fitz.

"Duckface!" she shouted.

For the next few minutes, she was lost in the chaos of their gleeful reunion. By the time she looked around again, Fitz and Zara were gone.

Then a new song started, and one of the girls in the group let out a squeal. "I love this one!" she cried. "Let's dance, people!"

Tommi laughed as the other girl dragged her out onto the dance floor with the guys following. Soon she was grooving to the music—her fall, her new business deal, Zara and Fitz, and everything else forgotten as she just let herself go and had fun.

FIFTEEN

It was one of those mornings. Zara slept so late that she felt light-headed when she finally woke up. Then again, that might have had something to do with the six or seven mojitos she'd sucked down last night.

"Ugh," she mumbled as she glanced at herself in the mirror over her dresser. Good thing Fitz couldn't see her now.

Then again, so what if he did see her with one eye crusted shut and her hair frizzed halfway to Connecticut? Even looking her best, she couldn't seem to close the deal with him. Once again, he'd seemed into her for a while last night, then pushed her away before things could go too far.

But whatever. She wasn't too shy to throw herself at a guy if she thought he was hot. But if he decided not to catch her, she wasn't going to beg. There were too many guys out there to waste her time with that crap.

By the time she showered and got dressed, her stomach was grumbling. She padded downstairs in her bare feet.

Several people were sprawled around the main room—Zac's head roadie, a couple of record company interns, a backup bodyguard or three. The usual.

"Where's my dad?" she asked Zac's assistant publicist, Phil, who was puttering around with the TV remotes.

Phil glanced up. "Oh, you're up," he said. "Zac's at a photo shoot up in Chelsea."

Figured. The one day she had nothing to do, he hadn't bothered to wake her up and invite her along.

Zara wandered into the kitchen, which reminded her of Frankenstein's lab—all industrial stainless-steel appliances and pressed concrete. She opened the huge custom fridge and stared inside, waiting for inspiration to strike.

She was still standing there when Vic slouched in. He was in his midtwenties and a constant presence in the entourage, though Zara wasn't sure what he did, exactly, other than smoke pot practically 24-7.

"Zara," Vic said, tapping his cigarette over the sink and flipping back his lank blond hair. "You're here."

"No, I'm not. Dude, you must've smoked something extra potent this morning."

An easy grin spread across Vic's ruddy face. "Good one, dude," he said.

Zara rolled her eyes. Vic was a walking stereotype. "Isn't there anything to eat in this place?" she complained. "I can't wait till Zac gets over this dumb-ass macrobiotic phase. A girl can't live on sprouts and brown rice."

"Bo hid some Fruity Pebbles behind the miso," Vic offered. "Don't tell him I told you."

"Score!" Zara yanked open a cabinet and found the cereal. "Thanks, Vic."

Vic leaned against the counter, watching her pour herself a bowl. "Going to that horse barn of yours today?" he asked, taking a drag on his cigarette.

"Nah. No point. Nothing going on today. We're taking the weekend off from showing, since there's this big-deal show coming up next week."

"Cool. Doesn't that mean you should be, like, practicing or whatever?"

"Got better things to do," she muttered, digging into her cereal.

Vic shrugged, tamped out his ciggie, and wandered out. But his comment had started Zara wondering. Were the other junior riders at the barn today, even though there was no show and no lesson?

Probably, she figured. Kate would be making like a busy little bee, since it was her job and all. And it was pretty obvious that Tommi took riding überseriously. She wouldn't win so much if she didn't, expensive rides or no. She was probably there schooling one of her horses, or maybe one of Jamie's.

Then there were people like Fitz and Summer. Did they really get off on riding the way the other two did? Or were they just passing time, having fun showing until something better came along?

She chewed her cereal, thinking about that. Which category did she fit in to? She knew what most people would guess. Were they right?

Frowning into her bowl, she wondered if she should head

out to the barn just to see what was going on, maybe take Keeper for a quick hack or something. Had to be better than moping around here all day.

Just then she felt her phone vibrate in her pocket. Pulling it out, she checked the number. She didn't recognize it, but answered anyway.

"Zara? It's me, Kalindi."

It took Zara a second to place the name. Oh, right. Kalindi was a girl she'd met at a party a few nights ago. NYU student. Weird but cool, with rich parents and an encyclopedic knowledge of NYC hot spots.

"What's up?" Zara said.

"I'm fiending for some new shoes," Kalindi said with a laugh. "Want to go shopping?"

Zara smiled, feeling oddly relieved. "Hell yeah," she said. "Where should I meet you?"

"Steady, pal," Kate murmured as the horse she was holding shifted its weight. The barn's regular farrier, Burt, was pounding a horseshoe into shape on his portable anvil nearby. Burt was a fireplug of a man with arms the width of Kate's thighs, a hearty laugh, and a relaxed way with the horses. He'd just taken a break from a long, funny story about the latest horse-purchase-gone-awry at another show barn to reshape one of the bar shoes that helped keep this particular horse comfortable and sound. Traveling constantly from barn to barn as he did, Burt was a font of mostly reliable gossip.

"So then the client told the trainer she wasn't paying her

commission unless she got the thing resold within the week," Burt said as he lifted the horse's right front leg and checked the fit of the shoe. "Trainer hit the roof, of course—and who could blame her? We're talking her next three or four farm payments, probably."

"Wow." Kate was still amazed sometimes when she realized how much money there really was in the A circuit world. The horse she was holding, for instance—he was getting older now, and Jamie was trying to convince his owner to step him down from the 3'6". But in his prime, the gelding's sale price could have paid Kate's college tuition for four years at any school in the country. Easily.

Burt had moved on to the horse's hind shoes—and another story—when Kate saw Fitz walking down the aisle toward them. He had one hand behind his back and a playful grin on his face.

"Hi," she greeted him. "You here to get some extra schooling in before we leave for Hounds Hollow?" The upcoming show was on her mind. For one thing, it was the reason Burt was here today instead of his usual Monday appointment. Plus the big, ultra-prestigious show would be her first time riding Fable in the Big Eq. Nothing like diving in headfirst.

"Partly," Fitz replied, stepping over Burt's rolling shoeing box. "And partly to give you these." He pulled his hand from behind his back, presenting her with a bouquet of dandelions. "I picked them specially for you."

Kate accepted the humble bouquet, not quite sure whether he was teasing her or flirting with her. Knowing Fitz, probably both.

"Um, thanks," she said. The horse she was holding turned his head to sniff at the flowers with interest.

"Hey! Don't eat Kate's flowers, you pig!" Fitz chided.

Kate glanced up as Javier appeared at the end of the aisle. The groom was leading one of Fitz's horses, fully tacked up in his jumper gear. "Looks like Chip is ready for you," she told Fitz.

"Wow, that was fast. If I didn't know better, I'd think Javier wanted to keep me from talking to you." Fitz shrugged. "Could be true. What guy wouldn't have the hots for Kate the great?"

Luckily Kate didn't have to come up with a response to that. Fitz was already loping off down the aisle, tossing a quick "See you, buddy" to Burt on his way.

Burt finished tacking the shoe on and straightened up, watching Fitz disappear. "Uh-oh," he said.

"Uh-oh what?" Kate had gone back to watching the horse she was holding.

Burt shook his head. "You better watch out for that one, Katie. That boy has a rep already. What I hear, he's loved 'em and left 'em at barns and shows all over Zone 2. Parts of Zone 1, too."

Kate shrugged, feeling uncomfortable. "Fitz and I are just friends," she mumbled.

"Really? Good." Burt stared at her closely for a moment. "'Cause you're too nice a girl to get mixed up in that business."

He went back to his work—and his story—and didn't mention Fitz again. But Kate was still thinking about the farrier's comments as he finished for the day and packed up. As she led the last horse toward its stall, she passed Tommi coming out of the tack room, carrying a saddle.

"Hi," Tommi said with a smile. "What are you looking so thoughtful about?"

Kate hesitated, instantly flashing back to their chat over lunch the other day. Why was everyone suddenly so interested in her love life these days, anyway? Didn't they think she could handle herself?

Besides, what she'd told Tommi—and now Burt—was true. She wasn't interested in Fitz as more than a friend. Was she?

For a second she allowed herself to picture it. Her and Fitz a couple. Going out on dates. Hanging out together at the shows. Holding hands as they walked down the barn aisle, then maybe ducking into an empty stall to steal a quick kiss . . .

She immediately shut down those thoughts, feeling foolish. Burt was right; Fitz had a reputation for going through girls like a horse went through sweet feed. Fast and hungry. How could she even imagine she might be anything more to him than yet another conquest?

"It's nothing," she told Tommi, forcing a smile and jiggling the horse's lead to keep it from barging ahead. "Just thinking about Hounds Hollow, that's all. Speaking of which, I'd better get going—I'm supposed to be helping Elliot clean out the trailer right now."

"Tommi! Over here!"

"Excuse me," Tommi murmured. She eased her way around a pair of twentysomething hipsters who were arguing with the hostess of the popular Upper East Side bistro she'd just entered. Grant was sitting at a tiny table along one wall, waving at her. She held her breath as she squeezed between tables, customers, and bustling waiters to reach him. "Wow, this place is packed!" she exclaimed as she sat down.

"Yeah, so much for missing the Saturday crowds by doing a late lunch." Grant glanced at the oversize clock on the wall above the kitchen door. It read a few minutes past 2:00 p.m. "Guess everyone was out till the wee hours just like us."

Tommi winced. "Yeah, I'm still paying for that."

"Hangover?" Grant grinned.

"Maybe a tiny one." Tommi smiled back. "But it's worth it. That was fun last night, wasn't it? It was great seeing the old gang. Duckface is as crazy as ever. And I can't believe Parker and Court are an item now!"

"I know, right? I didn't even think Parker liked girls." Grant chuckled. "But yeah, it was a blast. It's been way too long since I got to hang out with such fun people. Especially you."

At that moment a waitress rushed past, pausing by their table just long enough to drop a couple of menus. Tommi was grateful for the interruption. She recognized that look Grant had just given her. It meant maybe she hadn't done such a hot job of keeping things casual.

Then again, she hadn't been focused on that last night. After an intense week at the barn she'd needed a chance to blow off some steam, and she'd done just that. That hadn't left much mental energy for worrying about her relationship with Grant.

She would have to deal with that. But not now.

"So how late did you sleep in this morning, anyway?" Grant quipped after the waitress raced off again. "You sounded a little funny when I called you at ten thirty. I was afraid I woke you up."

"Not even close," Tommi said. "I was already at the barn by then. If I sounded a little distracted, it was probably because I was riding."

"You mean right then, when I called?" He looked surprised. "Like, you were talking to me from the saddle?"

She had to laugh at his astonishment. "I do still get reception way up there," she teased. "Anyway, yeah. I was riding Legs, my new training project."

"Your what?"

Tommi realized that despite all their conversation last night, she'd never quite gotten around to telling him about Legs. She hadn't mentioned her fall, either. She still didn't feel like going into that, but found herself telling Grant the rest—about Legs, the deal with her father, and her plans for the future.

He listened without comment until she was finished. "Wow," he said. "Have to admit, I didn't think you were serious about going into the horse business."

"What do you mean? I said I was at dinner that night."

"I know. It's just . . ." He shrugged. "I don't know. Seems like a tough life. You have so many other options."

She unfurled her napkin, avoiding his gaze. "Now you're sounding like my dad."

"Sorry." He laughed sheepishly. "I guess I just don't get it. You can still ride and show without going pro, can't you?"

"Sure."

"So why not do that? Skip the grunt work and the early mornings and all the other stressful crap, and just enjoy the fun parts."

Just then the waitress finally returned. "Thanks for your patience," she said, sounding harried. "What'll it be?"

Tommi skimmed the menu and ordered something pretty much at random. Her mind was focused on what Grant had said. Not that she hadn't heard it all a million times before—from her father, her sister, her mom.

But hearing him say it made her wonder. *Was* it weird to want to do this with her life? Did all her nonhorsey friends secretly think she was crazy?

Suddenly it all just seemed too hard and complicated to figure out. Maybe Grant was right. Maybe she should just go with the flow, ride for fun, accept that she'd never make the Olympic show-jumping team. Go to college, get a job, get married—maybe to someone like Grant. Okay, so he didn't exactly make her drool with lust when she looked at him. But he was a good friend and a nice guy, and there was a lot to be said for that. Hadn't her own father learned that lesson the hard way? He'd married her mother after some whirlwind romantic two-week courtship, and look how that had turned out.

When the waitress left, Grant sat back in his seat. "So how was your ride this morning on the Invest-o-horse, anyway?" he asked.

"Fine. He was a good boy." Tommi thought back over the schooling session. There had been at least half a dozen other riders in the outdoor ring. No surprise on a summer Saturday right before an important show, but Tommi had wished it was a little quieter. Legs had done his best, but he'd been more distracted than she would have liked.

She played with her fork, wondering if she should ask Jamie to hop on Legs once or twice before they left for Hounds Hollow. The last thing she wanted was screw up the talented gelding's training, especially now that she had her father's deadline to meet.

But she immediately shook her head. It was tempting, but she couldn't do it. This was her thing now; she was the one who was supposed to be training her new investment horse. If she backed off after one bad ride, she might as well hang up her Vogels and start perusing the Georgetown course catalog.

And that thought scared her way more than galloping down to a five-foot oxer ever could. A life filled with nothing but shopping and charity luncheons or some boring office job or whatever everyone else thought she should do? No way, that wasn't for her. She belonged in the saddle, bringing out the best in her horse.

How could she ever imagine doing anything else?

SIXTEEN

━━ ━━ ━━ ━━ ━━

Kate's days at the barn were always long. But that Monday was even longer than most. The barn was leaving for the Hounds Hollow show early the next morning, and there was a ton to do before then.

"Did you pack the extra lead ropes?" she called to Javier as he flew by with an armful of haynets.

"*Sí*, already in the truck," the groom replied without slowing down.

Kate checked that task off her mental to-do list and headed toward the tack room to make sure nothing was still on the racks and hooks that shouldn't be. Most of the clients were supposed to take care of packing their own tack trunks for shows, but Jamie never took any chances. Kate was checking everything against the list in her pocket when her phone rang.

"Hello?" she answered without bothering to check the number.

"Kate? That you?"

"Nat?" Kate blinked, her friend's voice catching her by surprise. "Oh, hi. What's up?"

"I was going to ask you the same thing. Haven't heard from you since that day at the mall."

"Sorry." Kate wedged the phone against her shoulder, her fingers flying as she rearranged a stay-behind bridle into a proper figure eight. "I've been kind of busy, I guess."

"What else is new?" Natalie laughed. "But listen, I have the perfect way to help you chill out. Party at the barn this Friday. Wanna come?"

For a second Kate was confused. How could there be a party when the entire barn would be away at the Hounds Hollow show?

Then she caught up. Duh. Natalie was talking about *her* barn—Kate's old lesson barn, Happy Acres.

"Oh," she said. "That sounds like fun, but—"

"It's going to be totally fun!" Natalie interrupted, sounding excited. "The Tanners are going out of town and leaving Marc in charge of the farm, and you know what that means. So what do you say? We can down a few, then hop on a couple of ponies bareback and race them across the field—just like old times."

Out of the corner of her eye, Kate saw Miguel hurry past the tack room door, struggling under the weight of a large grooming box. "Wish I could," she told Natalie hurriedly. "But I'll be at a show all week until Sunday."

"So take one night off." Natalie's voice took on a steely edge. "What's the big deal? Can't that fancy barn run without you for one measly night?"

"I can't," Kate said. "The show's like four hours away, plus

Friday night Jamie's riding in the Grand Prix and I really want to see him go."

"Whatever." Nat sounded pissed off now. "I forgot you've got more important things to do than hang out with the little people."

Kate saw Miguel rush past again. She bit her lip, knowing she could probably jolly Natalie out of being mad. But that would take time that she didn't have right now.

"Sorry," she said again. "I really have to go. I'll call you when I get home from the show, okay? Maybe we can do something then."

"Don't do me any favors, big shot."

Kate winced as the line cut off. But she didn't have time to worry about it. She'd just have to make things right with Natalie after the show.

She spent the next few hours working like crazy to get everything done. Finally Jamie found her sorting polo wraps and ordered her to go home and get some sleep.

Kate yawned as she headed out to the parking lot. There were only a couple of cars still there—the grooms mostly lived on-site and those who didn't parked over by the equipment shed.

She blinked as she saw a tall, shadowy figure leaning against the back of her car. For a second all her father's grim warnings leaped into her mind.

Then the figure straightened up so she could see his face in the light leaking out of the barn buildings. "Fitz!" she blurted out. "What are you still doing here?"

"Waiting for you." He smiled and took a step toward her. "I know you've been busting your ass getting ready for the show. I wanted to show you that at least one guy appreciates it. Let me take you out for something to eat."

"I—um . . ." Kate checked her watch. Almost ten o'clock. She really needed to get home and to bed.

"Come on," Fitz wheedled. "You've got to eat, right? And the diner's close."

A hollow rumble from her stomach made her realize he was right. She hadn't eaten a bite since breakfast. There hadn't been time. And who knew what the food situation would be at her house? The way her mom had been lately, she might have decided to toss anything that wasn't divisible by four.

"Okay," Kate said cautiously. "I guess that would be okay."

Tommi dropped another pair of Ariat breeches into her suitcase. She'd be showing in all three divisions at Hounds Hollow—hunters, eq, and jumpers. That meant three times as many show clothes to pack. Not to mention almost a whole week's worth of regular hanging-around clothes. Normally she probably wouldn't go up on Tuesday and stay the whole week, since most of the junior divisions didn't go until the weekend. But this time, with Legs her responsibility, she wanted to be there. Besides, there was a warm-up class she thought would be perfect for her and Legs to do to get comfortable with the venue.

As she was debating whether to bring a dress in case everyone went out for dinner somewhere nice, her father stuck his head into her room. "Still packing?" he said. "You'd better get to bed soon if you're getting up at the crack of dawn."

"Almost done." Tommi added the dress to the suitcase, then flipped the cover shut.

Her father watched as she struggled to get the zipper closed. "So how's our horse doing?" he asked. "Making progress?"

Tommi hesitated, flashing back to that disastrous first lesson. True, things had been going better since then. How could they not? But it hadn't exactly been all smooth sailing, either. Jamie said she was doing fine, but Tommi was finding it kind of daunting to be the one in charge of the training plan. Not that she was about to admit it to her father. That would probably be all the excuse he needed to withdraw his not-so-enthusiastic support.

"Legs is great," she said, forcing a smile. "He's really coming along. I'm expecting good things from him at this show."

"Fantastic." Her father shot her a thumbs-up. "Good night, Tommi."

"Night, Dad."

She held her smile until he disappeared, then let it go with a sigh. She didn't feel guilty about the lie, because it really wasn't one. No more than Jamie was lying whenever he assured his less successful Ammies that they'd do better next time after a disappointing show.

It was all just part of the game.

Zara hated being nervous. It usually made her angry and kind of aggressive.

Sometimes that worked out for her. Like when she was stepping into the ring for a challenging jumper course.

But right now, in her empty loft without a horse in sight, it wasn't doing her much good, and she wished there was someone around to talk her down. For a second she missed her mother so intensely that it hurt.

But Gina was still on location and hard to reach even when she wasn't actually working. Zac might pretend to listen, pasting on that serious-artist expression that had served him so well over the years. But Zara sometimes wondered if her father ever really heard anything she said.

Besides, he wasn't an option at the moment, either. He was off somewhere with his whole posse, probably making plans for the European minitour.

Zara wandered over to the floor-to-ceiling wall of windows, staring moodily out at the lights of downtown Manhattan. Why was she so nervous, anyway? She wasn't even leaving for the stupid show until Thursday, though Jamie and the horses were heading up in the morning. She was looking forward to finally getting Keeper back in the ring now that he was all settled in. She liked the hunters well enough, but jumpers was the thing that really gave her the rush she was after. Then there was Ellie . . .

She closed her eyes, thinking back to their last lesson. It had gone pretty well—she and Ellie were starting to reach an understanding, at least most of the time. Jamie had even complimented their steady pace through the last course, saying he thought they were ready for their 3'6" debut together.

Still, Zara could tell that everyone at the barn was watching her. Remembering what she'd done. Waiting for her to screw up again.

"It's not fair," she said aloud as she opened her eyes.

Nobody answered. She was all alone. Another thing she hated. It made her feel restless and irritable.

She thought about calling some of her old friends in LA. But she dismissed the idea even before she'd figured out the time difference. None of them had bothered to call or text much since she'd left; it was as if she'd ceased to exist as soon as she crossed the Rocky Mountains.

Her mind jumped next to the girls at the barn. They all seemed really tight; she could imagine them all calling each other when they had problems, talking each other through stuff like characters on some TV show.

But she couldn't quite picture herself as part of the scenario. She was still an outsider—the crazy bitch who'd almost burned down the barn and killed all their horses. No way could she just call up any of them out of the blue, though for one crazy second she was tempted to give it a try.

"Shit," she muttered at last, turning away from the window. She had to do something to distract herself, or she'd really go crazy.

Heading to the liquor cabinet over near the stairs, she yanked open the doors. She spotted her father's beloved bottle of forty-year-old Glenfiddich and smiled. Perfect. Her dad would freak when he realized it was gone. Talk about two birds with one stone.

Pulling out the bottle, she uncapped it and took a chug. The stuff burned going down, but that was okay. No pain, no gain.

"What's the matter?" Fitz glanced across the Formica table at Kate's plate. "Something wrong with your sammy?"

"No, it's fine." Kate forced herself to pick up the tuna melt she'd ordered and take a bite. Ever since they'd arrived at the diner, she'd been too nervous to do more than pick at her food.

What was she doing here? She wondered if the exhaustion had gone to her head, made her think it was any kind of good idea to accept Fitz's invitation.

Fitz tossed a french fry into his mouth. "So you're heading out to the show tomorrow with Jamie, huh?" he said. "Almost makes me think it's worth going early myself, even though I don't show until Thursday."

"Why are you doing this?" Kate blurted out, finally too confused and tired to try to figure it out on her own.

"What?" He blinked at her across the table. "Doing what? Talking? Eating fries? Having dinner with a gorgeous girl?"

"Yeah, that last one." She frowned, knowing her face was probably bright red but actually not caring that much. "It's flattering and all, but I don't have time to waste being, like, a notch on your belt or whatever, if that's what you're thinking."

"Kate, stop." His smile faded. "Look, I know I've messed around a lot in the past. But that's not what this is about. I know you're not like that."

"What is it, then?"

He shrugged, his eyes suddenly uncertain. "It's different this time, with you," he said, poking at his burger. "I'm not sure why. I guess I just see something in you—something different from all those other girls."

Kate wasn't sure what to say to that. There was a look in his eye that she'd never seen before, and it made her more uncomfortable than ever. She grabbed her glass and took a gulp, but her hands were shaking and she ended up dribbling iced tea down her chin.

Fitz looked up in time to see it and grinned. "Looks like

you're developing a pretty serious drinking problem there," he quipped, sounding much more like his normal self. "Let me give you a hand."

He reached out and dabbed her chin gently with his napkin. Kate didn't move as she felt his fingers brush her face. She would be the first to admit she wasn't used to getting up close and personal with guys very often. But she couldn't remember ever feeling that quiver before when one touched her.

"So how about it?" Fitz asked, dropping his napkin and leaning forward. "Will you give me a shot, see what happens?"

Even under the fluorescent lights of the diner, he looked handsome and sincere staring at her like that. She couldn't help smiling.

"Um, sure," she said. "I guess. Why not."

"Cool!" He flopped back in his seat, grinning. "Then I guess this is our first official date, huh?"

"Okay." Kate sneaked a peek at her watch. "But I'd better cut it short. Sorry. But I need to be back at the barn in like six hours."

Fitz looked disappointed, but shrugged. "Okay. Don't want to get you in trouble with the boss."

He paid the check and they headed back to the barn. Fitz had driven to the diner, and pulled his racy red convertible in right next to Kate's car.

"Thanks for dinner," Kate said, suddenly feeling shy again.

"You're welcome." Fitz unhooked his seat belt and leaned toward her. Kate closed her eyes, knowing what was coming and not sure if she was ready for it.

She felt Fitz's hand touch her arm and then his lips gently

brush hers. "Good night," he murmured. "Sweet dreams. I'll see you on Thursday."

Kate opened her eyes, her heart beating faster. "Good night," she whispered. Then she climbed out of the car and hurried to her own, fumbling with her keys. She was very aware of Fitz watching her until she'd started her car, then he revved his engine and followed her down the winding drive. Glancing into the rearview as she paused at the end, she saw him wave as they prepared to turn in opposite directions down the quiet country highway.

Soon she was speeding toward home, her mind buzzing with everything that had just happened. Fitz thought she was special. He wanted to be with her, see what might happen between them. Was he for real, or was that just another line? She had no idea, and suddenly didn't really care. She spent way too much time worrying and wondering and trying to figure things out ahead of time. Maybe this time she just needed to go with it for once, be a little more daring. Kind of like Zara seemed to be—going for what she wanted without worrying about the possible consequences, or what anyone else might say.

She liked Fitz, and he seemed to like her. So what was the worst that could happen?

SEVENTEEN

━━ ━━ ━━ ━━ ━━

"Bag, boots, helmet case," Kate muttered under her breath as she dashed out of her bedroom and took the stairs two at a time. "Bag, boots, helmet case . . ."

It was very early the next morning, and Kate was rushing to get out of the house and over to the barn. She was trying hard not to forget anything important—always a difficult task on four hours' sleep. Today it was made extra challenging because every time she slowed down, she caught herself thinking about Fitz. Had last night really happened? She was pretty sure it had, because she was even more sleep-deprived than normal for a show morning. But it was still hard to believe someone like Fitz could really be interested in her.

As she reached the first floor, she heard her brother's voice shouting in the kitchen. Uh-oh. That couldn't be good.

She stepped into the room just in time to see Andy slam his hand down on the counter. "I don't care what you say!" he yelled. "I can do what I want!"

Their mother shuddered as if he'd physically slapped her. "Keep your voice down, Andrew," she said. "You'll wake your father, and he needs his sleep. He worked the late shift last night."

"What's happening?" Kate asked, since neither of them had noticed her standing there.

Andy whirled around and glared at her, as if whatever had wounded his fourteen-year-old being to the core *this* time was somehow her fault. "Mom's being a Nazi, that's all," he spat out.

"Andrew!" Their mother looked shocked. Stepping over to the sink, she touched a glass sitting in the drying rack. Once, twice, three, four times. Then she moved on to the next glass. And the next.

"Seriously, what'd you do?" Kate asked her brother, mostly for an excuse not to watch her mother's rituals.

Andy shrugged. For a second she thought he wasn't going to answer.

"Went out with my friends, lost track of time," he muttered at last. "Got in a little late. So sue me."

His mother paused in her rituals long enough to shoot him an accusing look. "A *little* late? You only got home ten minutes ago."

Kate felt her stomach clench. Now Andy was staying out all night? Who knew what kind of trouble he was getting into with those loser friends he'd been hanging around with lately.

"What's going on out there?" Kate's father bellowed from the master bedroom. "Some people are trying to sleep!"

"Gotta go." Kate grabbed a banana out of the bowl on the

counter and her boots from their spot beside the back door. "Don't forget, I'll be at the show all week. Back Sunday night."

"Have fun, sweetheart," her mother said without looking at her. "Don't forget to leave your phone on in case we want to reach you."

"I always do. Bye." Hearing her father's grumbled curses coming closer, Kate slipped out the back door quickly, relieved for the excuse to escape.

"So what divisions are you doing?" Marissa asked.

Zara leaned on the fence of the warm-up ring, watching the usual chaos in there. "Junior Hunters with Ellie," she said. "Jumpers with Keeper. You?"

"Hunters and maybe Eq," Marissa said. "If I don't die of nervousness first. I hate doing eq at huge shows like this—it totally freaks me out for some reason."

Zara glanced around and shrugged. Yeah, the show was bigger than the first one she'd done with Jamie's barn. There were three rings going full-time, hundreds of horses, tons of vendors. But it was nothing compared to some of the biggies out on the West Coast.

"I thought you guys did all the big shows," she said. "This one doesn't seem that huge to me."

"I know, right?" Marissa laughed, rolling her eyes. "Ignore me. I do this every time. Dani says I should, like, buy stock in Xanax."

Zara shrugged again. If Marissa got so freaked out by show-ing, why did she bother? But she didn't ask. People usually got offended by questions like that for some reason.

It was Thursday morning, and Mickey had dropped her off a little while ago. She'd run into Marissa within minutes and been hanging out with her ever since. The girl talked too much, laughed too much, and seemed a little clingy. But hanging with her was better than feeling invisible like last time.

Zara's eyes stopped on one particular rider in the crowd. "Hey," she said, "I heard Tommi bought that horse she's riding right now."

"You mean Legs?" Marissa turned to scan the ring. "Yep, that's him. She and her dad bought him together. Like a business deal, or something."

"Really? Wow, how totally Wall Street of her." Zara watched as Tommi trotted past them, dodging an out-of-control pony rider.

She was pretty sure Tommi hadn't noticed her and Marissa standing there. Every bit of her attention appeared to be on her horse. Not that it was doing her much good. Legs looked majorly tense. He kicked out every time she asked for a transition and tossed his head every few seconds.

"Looks like she's having some trouble with him today." Marissa sounded sympathetic. "Maybe he doesn't like all these other horses so close."

Zara had a feeling that wasn't it. Legs wasn't the only one who looked tense—Tommi did, too. Zara could see that she was riding defensively. No wonder, after that fall she'd taken in the lesson last week. That one would take a while to shake off.

"Hi, guys. Have either of you seen Max?"

It was Kate, looking harried and freaked out as usual. Zara was pretty sure she hadn't seen the girl stand still for more than two seconds since she'd met her.

"Haven't seen him," she said as Marissa shook her head.

Meanwhile Kate had spotted Tommi. "Legs looks cranky," she commented. "What happened?"

"Nothing that we saw," Marissa said. "Maybe he's just having a bad day."

Zara shook her head, though she didn't say anything. She could see why the gelding was acting up. Tommi was sitting way too deep, and it was pissing him off. Zara recognized all the signs, mostly because Jamie had gotten after her about the exact same thing a couple of lessons ago.

Still, none of her business. Tommi was a big girl, and pretty much the barn superstar from what Zara could tell. Let her figure it out for herself. Why should Zara help the girl who'd busted her, gotten her in deep doo-doo with Jamie?

She watched as Tommi brought the gelding back to a walk, then asked for a canter depart. Legs planted his front legs, shaking his head. Then he popped up in a half rear and jumped sideways, almost crashing into a girl on a fat bay gelding.

"Watch it!" the other rider exclaimed.

"Sorry," Tommi muttered, wrestling Legs over to the rail, then letting him walk on a long rein. Her expression was fierce and frustrated, and Zara felt a twinge of sympathy. She'd been there.

"Hey," she called when Tommi and Legs neared the spot where she and the others were standing. "Ellie was doing the same thing with me last week. Try lightening up your seat a little and let him stretch his neck and relax, see if that helps."

Tommi shot her a dark look. "When I need a riding lesson from you, I'll let you know, okay?"

Zara scowled. "Whatevs," she snapped. "Sorry I said anything." She spun on her heel and stormed away, ready to go back to being invisible.

Tommi barely noticed Zara's departure. The last thing she was in the mood for right now was riding advice from Miss Rebel Without a Clue. She half-halted strongly as Legs started jigging.

"Stand, dammit," she muttered, keeping her hands firm as the horse flung his head all over creation.

Only when he finally stopped for a second did Tommi realize that Marissa and Kate were standing at the rail, too. Kate had a troubled expression on her face. The girl was pretty much an open book.

"What?" Tommi snapped.

Kate bit her lip. "Don't kill me, okay?" she said. "But Zara might be right. You're the one who's always saying Legs needs a soft touch until he gets into the groove. Sort of like Ellie. It looks like you're sitting pretty heavy right now, and he's getting frazzled."

Tommi scowled, ready to bite her head off, too. But she forced herself to stop and think. Kate wasn't Zara. She actually knew what she was talking about. Could she be right?

As soon as she asked herself the question, the answer was right there staring her in the face. "Duh," she said, more to herself than to Kate. "How stupid am I?" She shot Kate a rueful smile. "Thanks, I'll give it a try."

Tommi gave Legs a pat as she slipped out of his show stall. "Sorry about before, buddy," she said, fishing in her pocket for a peppermint. "Good thing you aren't the type to hold a grudge."

She'd taken Kate's advice and relaxed, giving Legs the freedom to loosen up his back and neck—and his restless mind—before picking up more contact again. They'd done fine after that, ending the warm-up on a much better note than they'd started it.

But it wasn't really *Kate's* advice, Tommi reminded herself. It had been Zara's first. Zara might not be her favorite person in the barn, but she deserved an apology. She'd seen what Tommi herself had been missing. Thanks to the change in plans, Tommi hadn't had to scratch from their first class as she'd been seriously considering. She and Legs hadn't gone in and made a spectacle of themselves, either. An unlucky rail had blown their shot at a ribbon, but overall Tommi was pleased with the way the gelding had risen to the occasion. She smiled as she glanced back at his head hanging out over the stall guard, suddenly looking forward to seeing what they could do together when they took it to the next level.

Tommi checked Zara's horses' stalls, the tack stall, and everywhere else she could think of. But Zara was nowhere to be found. Nobody had seen her since she'd left the warm-up ring.

"What do you want with her, anyway?" Summer asked.

"Nothing. It can wait." Maybe the middle of a busy show wasn't the ideal spot for an apology anyway. Tommi could find a moment to talk to her back at the hotel.

Just then her phone buzzed. It was a text from Grant, asking what time she was riding the next day.

"Who's that?" Summer asked, as tactless as always.

"A friend of mine. He wants to come watch me ride tomorrow."

"A friend?" Summer's eyes lit up. "You're not talking about that yummy dark-haired guy who came to watch you at the last show, are you?"

"I'm not sure who you mean," Tommi lied. The last thing she wanted was to get some ridiculous rumor started about her love life. "I'd better go get ready for my next class. See you later."

After putting a safe distance between herself and Summer, Tommi stopped and stared at the text message. She couldn't believe Grant wanted to drive four hours to see her ride. Yeah, it was time to let him down easy. Past time. But she'd fix that tomorrow.

EIGHTEEN

━━ ━━ ━━ ━━ ━━

It was Friday afternoon, and Zara was feeling good. She leaned on the door of Ellie's stall, allowing the mare to delicately lip small pieces of carrot off her hand while Jamie's big bulldog watched and drooled.

"You're a superstar," Zara told the horse. "I knew it the first time I rode you."

The mare seemed much more interested in the treats than the compliment. But Zara didn't mind.

Jamie had ridden Ellie in the pro classes earlier in the week, and when Zara had ridden her into the ring for the Small Juniors the mare had been perfect. For once Zara didn't even wonder if they'd pin as she left the ring, because it didn't matter. They'd kicked ass, and whether the judge used them or not was almost beside the point. Nobody would be whistling "Golden Girl" at her today!

It had been icing on the cake when she'd discovered that they had, indeed, pinned in one of their three jumping rounds. Only sixth place, but still. On top of that, they'd gotten third in the hack despite a couple of sloppy transitions. Score one for fancy gaits!

"I'm back in the game, baby," she whispered. She couldn't wait to take Keeper in the jumpers the next day.

Just then Jamie hurried down the aisle. "Nice job today, Zara," he said, pausing for a second to smile at her. "Keep it up, and you and Ellie'll be bringing home the tricolors before long."

"Thanks." Zara smiled back, even though the trainer was already moving again. As annoying as the guy could be, she was starting to realize that Jamie really knew his stuff. Her riding had improved more in the past few weeks than it had in the six months before that. Her performance today proved it. Maybe this barn was going to work out after all. She tossed Chaucer a piece of carrot, feeling good.

She heard voices coming her way and glanced around. Tommi was walking toward her with a guy at her side.

"Hi, Zara," Tommi said. "Remember my friend Grant? You guys met at the club that time."

"Nice to see you again, Zara." The guy actually stuck out his hand.

"Hi," Zara said, already checking him out as they shook. She hadn't really paid much attention to him before, but now she saw that he was worth a second look. Tall, broad-shouldered, good-looking in a straitlaced preppy kind of way. Pretty much exactly the type Zara would expect a Wall Street tycoon's daughter to date.

Tommi elbowed him. "Hey, Grant, feel like making a run to the food stand? I could use a soda." She glanced at Zara. "Want something?"

"Yeah. A Scotch on the rocks."

Grant chuckled. "Iced tea close enough?"

"Guess it'll have to do."

As he headed down the aisle, Zara enjoyed the back view for a second. "Not bad if you like the type," she commented. Shooting a sidelong look at Tommi, she added, "And I'm guessing you do."

"Grant and I are just friends," Tommi said, giving Ellie a pat as the mare nosed at her, hoping for more treats. "But listen, while he's gone, I need to talk to you about something."

"Yeah?" Zara was instantly on guard.

"Yeah. I was kind of a jerk to you yesterday, and I'm sorry."

Whatever Zara had been expecting, that wasn't it. "Oh. Um, okay," she said cautiously.

"Seriously," Tommi said. "I was on edge, and I took it out on you. I know you were only trying to help. And it turns out you were right. I tried what you said, and Legs went way better."

Zara shrugged. "Thought so."

Tommi laughed. "Yeah. So thanks, and sorry again, okay?"

"It's cool." Maybe it was just her good mood making her feel generous. But at that moment, for the first time, Zara could almost picture hanging out with this girl. Maybe. If she didn't have anything better to do.

Yeah, it was turning out to be a hell of a day.

⸭

Grant pulled into the parking lot of the hotel where Jamie's barn was staying. "Thanks for the ride," Tommi said as she unbuckled her seat belt. "And thanks for being so understanding."

"No worries." Grant smiled. "Can't say I'm not a little bummed, but hey."

Tommi smiled back. She'd pulled him aside after her final class of the day and let him down easy. He'd taken it really well, which somehow had made her feel even worse.

"Anyway," she said, relieved that he'd be gone soon and she wouldn't have to think about it, "you've got a long drive back, and it's getting late, so I guess I'll let you—"

"Hey!" a loud voice interrupted before she could finish. "There's some more of my Pelham Lane peeps!"

Zara raced up to the car and leaned in the window. Her face was only inches from Tommi's, making it impossible to miss the smell of beer on her breath.

"Hi," Tommi said. "I was just saying good-bye to Grant."

"No way, dude, you can't leave!" Zara leaned in even farther. She was wearing shorts over a bathing suit, and her boobs were almost spilling out of her bikini top and into Tommi's lap. *Lovely.*

"Sorry, I've got to head back. Long drive." Grant didn't sound very convinced as he stared at Zara's cleavage.

Zara pouted. "But we're having a party! Everybody fun is there. And I want to celebrate my awesome rides today. Just stay for a while, okay?"

It was pretty obvious that for Zara, the party had already started. But Tommi wasn't in the mood. She was already stressing over tomorrow's jumper division with Legs. Sure, they'd recovered from that disastrous warm-up yesterday. But were they ready to show? A bad performance at a show like this could give the horse a reputation it would be tough to shake.

But Grant was already grinning at her hopefully. "What do you think?" he asked. "I guess I could stay for a little while if you want to hit this party. I don't have to get up tomorrow."

Tommi wanted to say no. But she still felt guilty about the whole Grant situation. Why not go along with it? Maybe then he'd feel like his drive up here hadn't been a total waste of time.

"Sure," she said. "I guess. I can't stay too late, though. I need to be back over at the showgrounds early to lunge Legs."

"Cool! Then get your asses out to the pool." Zara shot Grant a wicked grin. "Maybe later we can do some skinny-dipping."

Soon Tommi was perched on the edge of a lounge chair, a barely touched beer in her hand, watching her barnmates party. It was almost ten o'clock, and the pool was officially closed, though all that really meant was that there was no lifeguard on duty. The pool was located some distance away from the hotel building, on the far side of the parking lot and tennis courts. That was probably a good thing, considering the loud music and the shrieks of laughter.

"Quite a party, huh?" Grant said.

Tommi glanced over at him. He was lounging in the next chair, shirtless and bopping his head to the music. They'd barely spoken since they'd arrived, mostly because her mind kept wandering back to Legs. She'd already moved on from stressing about tomorrow's jumper class. They'd just do their best and take it from there. If they did well, great. If not, there were plenty of other big shows coming up where they could prove themselves.

"Yeah, I guess," she said, realizing Grant had to be kind of bored. "You don't have to sit here with me if you want to go dance or something."

"It's okay, I don't mind."

There was a sudden ear-piercing shriek of laughter. Glancing over, Tommi saw Zara racing down the diving board.

"She's the life of the party, isn't she?" Grant commented as he watched her cannonball into the pool.

"Yeah, guess so."

A couple of guys tried to grab Zara and dunk her, but she escaped and climbed out of the pool. Noticing Tommi and Grant watching her, she danced over to them.

"Okay, at first I thought this barn was hardcore boring," she said, her voice a little too loud as she squeezed water out of her curly hair. "But hey, I've been wrong before."

"Great party, Zara," Grant said, sitting up and taking a swig of his beer.

"Yeah. Where'd you find so many guys at a horse show?" Tommi asked, only half kidding. She recognized the show farrier's cute young assistant, the source of gossip among the female population of the barn all week, and also spotted one of their own younger grooms, Max. And she was pretty sure the two guys over there doing body shots with Dani were from the barn in the next aisle of stalls. But there were several guys she'd never seen before.

"Call it a talent." Zara smirked. "As soon as Jamie and the other tight-asses left for dinner, I rounded up everyone cool I could find." Her smile faded slightly. "The only one who blew me off was Javier. I don't know what his problem is."

"He's shy, plus I think he's kind of self-conscious about his

English," Tommi said. "Anyway, the grooms all work really hard. He probably just wanted to sleep."

"Whatever." Zara took a swig of her beer. "His loss."

Suddenly Tommi realized someone else was missing. "Where's Fitz?"

"Dunno. Couldn't find him. I left a message."

"Then I'm sure he'll be here soon. Fitz never misses a party."

"Me neither. But you two look like you've never been to one before. You need another beer."

Grant lifted his beer and shook it. "I think you're right. Get you one, Tommi?"

"No thanks, I'm good," Tommi said.

"Come on, big guy. Let's get you liquored up." Zara grinned and grabbed Grant by the hand. He let her pull him out of his chair, then followed her over toward the cooler by the diving board.

Tommi was kind of relieved. Now she wouldn't have to feel as if she needed to entertain him for a while, and she could go back to planning out the rest of Legs's show season in her head.

Kate checked her watch and winced. Eleven o'clock. Her 4:00 a.m. wake-up call wasn't going to be fun.

It had been a long day, and she was so exhausted that her head was spinning. But she could never let herself leave until everything was done, even though she knew Jamie and the grooms probably thought she'd headed back to the hotel hours ago. They were all long gone themselves except for Elliot and

Javier. Security at this show was notoriously lax, and the grooms were taking turns sleeping over at the showgrounds to keep an eye on things. Kate could hear the sounds of snoring drifting out of the tack stall right now. There was never any mistaking when Elliot was sleeping nearby.

Then she heard another sound: footsteps. Good. Maybe Javier could finish tidying the meds cabinet, and she could head back to the hotel and get at least a few hours' sleep before she had to get up and do it all again.

"Javier?" she called. "In here."

But it wasn't the groom's face that appeared around the corner of the equipment stall. "Kate? That you?"

"Fitz!" Kate couldn't help smiling despite her exhaustion. "What are you doing here? I thought everyone went back to the hotel ages ago."

"They did. But when I realized you weren't there, I came back to find you." He stepped in and gently pried the bottle of Banamine out of her hand, shoving it back into the cabinet. "Come on, even *you* can't work twenty-four-seven without keeling over."

"Yeah, maybe you're right." Kate allowed him to take her hand and lead her out of the room, though she felt a guilty twinge when she noticed that the supplement shelf was a mess. Oh, well. Maybe she could come back a little early tomorrow and take care of that.

Out in the aisle, Fitz put his arm around her. "Wow, you're tense," he said. "Here, let me see if I can help."

Kate had just started to yawn, but she swallowed it when he spun her around and started kneading her shoulders. Even as exhausted as she was, his touch sent an electric current through her. She was so focused on the feel of his hands pressing into her that it took her a moment to realize he was steering her across the way and into one of the hay storage stalls.

"Um, what are we . . . ," she began uncertainly.

"Sh," he whispered, his breath tickling her ear. A second later she felt his lips brushing the side of her neck.

"I, um . . . ," she murmured, her heart beating faster as his soft kisses traveled down to her shoulder. "We shouldn't . . ."

But he was already turning her to face him. His eyes were close, staring into hers with an intensity that made her shiver. Then his lips were on hers, gentle at first, then hungry and searching. His hands started on her back then wandered downward, and before Kate knew quite what was happening she was on her back with stiff, scratchy hay poking her through her clothes and Fitz's weight on top of her.

"You're so freaking beautiful, Kate," Fitz said, his voice husky as he nuzzled her cheek.

Kate tried to answer but gasped instead as she felt his hand slide up under her shirt. This was all moving way too fast, but she wasn't sure how to stop it. She wasn't even sure if she *wanted* to stop it . . .

🐎

"Ow! Hey!" Tommi's eyes flew open as someone crashed into her chair, almost tipping it over. Sitting up, she realized she must have dozed off for a second. No wonder. It was getting late, and she'd been up since dawn.

She saw that Summer was the one who'd bumped her. The

younger girl was a sloppy drunk, and as she staggered around trying to figure out which way she was going, she kicked over Tommi's half-full beer.

"Oops!" Summer squealed with a loud giggle. "This party is epic, isn't it?"

Without waiting for an answer, she raced over and flung herself—literally—at some guy, knocking them both into the pool. Tommi rolled her eyes and smothered a yawn. Once upon a time, she would've had fun at a party like this. But right now it just seemed like a waste of time.

She looked around for Grant, hoping he hadn't downed too many beers to drive home tonight. The last thing she needed was him sleeping it off in her hotel room.

It didn't take her long to spot him. He was in the middle of the pool, stripped down to his boxers, making out with Zara. Her legs were wrapped around his waist, and his hands were all over her.

Tommi felt a weird pang as she watched them. She wasn't into Grant, and he was a big boy—so what if he wanted to have some fun with Zara, or anyone else for that matter?

But she couldn't shake the feeling that something was wrong here, even if she couldn't quite pinpoint why. She hated that feeling, and was relieved when the sudden buzz of her phone distracted her.

Checking the number, she saw that it was Kate. "Hey, what's up?" Tommi said into the phone, turning her back to the scene in the pool. "You're not still at the showgrounds, are you?"

"Tommi?" Kate's voice sounded shaky, and Tommi instantly knew that something was wrong.

"Kate? What is it? What happened?" she demanded, pressing the phone to her ear and stepping a little farther away from the music.

There was a long pause, and for a second Tommi thought she'd lost her connection. But finally Kate sniffled, then spoke.

"It's Fitz," she blurted out. "He was here, and we started kissing, and then, well . . . Stuff happened."

"Stuff?" Tommi echoed. "What do you mean? Oh my God, did you guys—you know, do it?"

She held her breath as she waited for the answer. As far as she knew, Kate was still a virgin. Why hadn't she pressed harder when she'd asked her about him that time? Kate was so weirdly private about certain stuff; Tommi should have known she wasn't telling her the whole story. She should have known better than to ignore her own instincts about the situation.

"N-no," Kate whispered. "Not quite. But he seemed kind of mad when I stopped him, and I really need to talk to someone . . ."

"I'll be right there. Stay put." Tommi hung up and spun around, striding toward the pool. This time she hardly noticed what Grant was doing as she called his name. "I need your car keys," she told him when he finally peeled his lips off Zara long enough to look over.

He blinked, looking surprised and a little embarrassed. "Um, what?"

"I need to go back over to the showgrounds," she said. "Let me borrow your car, okay?"

He waded toward her with Zara still clinging to him, nibbling on his earlobe. "I'll drive you, Tommi," he said.

Tommi rolled her eyes. "No way. You're in no condition to drive." Realizing his keys had to be in his pants, she wished she'd thought to just find them and sneak off without saying anything. It wasn't as if he would have missed her.

Zara finally seemed to notice what was going on. "Wait, we're going back to the showgrounds?" she said loudly. "Whoo-hoo! Party at the barn!"

A few people nearby heard her and cheered. Tommi wasn't quite sure how it happened, but somehow all the partyers ended up piling into several cars for the short trip back to the showgrounds. Tommi was less than thrilled about that, especially since the farrier's assistant kept trying to reach over from the backseat and grope her while she was driving and Max insisted on singing some tuneless song at the top of his lungs. But she was too worried about Kate to care much.

The showgrounds were dark and silent when they arrived. Leaving everyone else milling around in the parking area trying to figure out if anyone had remembered to bring the beer, Tommi hurried straight to the stall tents.

"Kate?" she called as she entered Jamie's section. "It's me! Kate, where are you?"

She paused outside the tack stall. Elliot and Javier were both in there, sound asleep and snoring away in two-part harmony. She moved on, checking the equipment and hay stalls and then the feed area. But Kate wasn't in any of them. She also wasn't at Fable's stall or out by the Porta-Potties. Where could she be? Worry stabbed at Tommi's heart as she stopped and stared around. She tried to text Kate, but there was no response.

It wasn't until her fourth or fifth time around the place

that she heard a muffled sob from one of the stalls. "Kate?" she called softly, stepping closer.

The stall's resident was Sir, a sweet, steady older gelding belonging to one of Jamie's longtime adult clients. He was currently leased out to a ten-year-old who was learning the ropes in the Pre-Children's, but Tommi immediately recalled that Kate had ridden him when she first came to Jamie's barn. The patient old packer had helped Jamie undo some of the bad habits Kate had developed learning to ride by the seat of her pants. It hadn't been long before she'd moved on to more challenging mounts, but Tommi knew that Kate had a special place in her heart for Sir.

She peered inside and saw Kate huddled in the back corner of the stall with Sir standing over her, dozing. Tommi let herself in, giving the horse a pat on her way past.

"Kate," she said softly, kneeling in the soft shavings to wrap her arms around her friend. "It's okay. It's going to be okay."

Kate leaned into her with a sob. "He said it was different with me," she whispered. Then she started crying, and Tommi just sat there rocking her.

Ten or fifteen minutes later, Kate finally seemed to run out of tears. She pushed away from Tommi, sat up, and wiped her face with her shirt.

"Thanks for coming," she told Tommi with a sniffle. "Sorry if I woke you up."

"You didn't. There's a party back at the hotel." She grimaced as she heard a muffled giggle from somewhere nearby. Probably some drunken couple looking for privacy. "Actually, they seem to have moved it over here now."

Kate didn't seem too interested in that. "I feel like such an idiot," she said sadly.

"So what happened, anyway?" Tommi asked. "Last I heard, you and Fitz were just friends."

"We were," Kate said. "At least I thought we were for a while. Then we went to the diner the other night, and started talking . . ." She let her voice trail off as they both heard the sound of a horse's shrill whinny.

Tommi sat up straight. This wasn't the movies, where directors seemed to think that horses whinnied as often as dogs barked. This was real life, and that horse sounded upset.

"Was that coming from our stalls?" she asked.

"I don't think so." Kate jumped to her feet and hurried to the front of the stall, her problems pushed aside for the moment. "It sounded like it was coming from over toward the jumper ring, maybe?"

"Great. If a horse is loose, the lame-ass security company will probably never notice." Tommi frowned. "And the last thing some poor panicked horse needs is for the drunken dorks from party central chasing it down."

Kate was already letting herself out into the aisle. Tommi followed, hurrying after her friend as she rushed for the exit.

The jumper ring was the closest one to Jamie's show stalls. Even before she got there, Tommi could see activity inside the ring. There were no lights on at this hour except a few security lights. But the moon was up, allowing her to see several horses and riders in the ring along with a bunch of spectators on foot.

"What's going on out there?" she exclaimed as she and Kate jogged closer.

"Next!" one of the riders shouted with a laugh. "Come on, Mikey—you're up!"

"That's Zara," Tommi said.

"Who's she riding?" Kate sounded confused.

Tommi hurried closer. Some of the spectators were leaning on the rail. A college-age guy she didn't know glanced over as she stopped beside him.

"Hey, babe," he said, taking a swig of his beer.

"What are they doing?" she asked.

He grinned. "Bareback high jump," he said. "John already knocked it down, but the others are still in it."

Tommi had no idea who John was, and didn't much care. It was sinking in that this was bad news. All of the riders were drunk, none were wearing helmets or even shoes, and the horses looked confused and agitated.

"Oh my God—isn't that Mrs. Walsh's mare?" Kate had joined her by now. She pointed to a big bay horse with a crooked blaze, which had just picked up a choppy canter.

Tommi realized she was right. "And Zara's riding Ford," she said, recognizing the flashy chestnut Irish sporthorse, a promising young show hunter that Jamie had recently taken in to sell for its wealthy owner/breeders, who had been hoping for a foxhunter. She shook her head grimly. "Looks like they just grabbed random horses."

"We need to stop this before someone gets hurt." Kate glanced back toward the barn. "Should I go wake up Elliot?"

Tommi couldn't believe the grooms hadn't heard the commotion by now. She held her breath as Mike—a pretty good jumper rider from another local barn—aimed the bay mare at one of the jumps in the ring. The horse cleared it easily, and Tommi let out her breath. The spectators—Summer, Dani, Marissa, Max, random others—let out a cheer.

"If Jamie hears about this, they'll all get kicked out, not just Zara, and Max will definitely get fired," Tommi told Kate. "Let's try to deal with it ourselves first."

"Raise it!" Zara was calling out at the same time, pointing to the jump. "Let me show all you bitch-ass punks how it's done, West Coast style."

Giggling, Dani and Summer hurried over to the jump. They fumbled with the top rail, almost knocking it onto their own heads before Dani managed to get one of the pins out.

Tommi ducked through the rails, striding over to them. "Don't be morons," she said. "Come on, you've got to help me get these horses back in before someone notices they're gone."

"Chill out, Tommi." Dani's words were slurred. Tommi had seen her drunk before, but never *this* drunk.

"Yeah," Summer said with another giggle. "I want to see who wins."

They both had their jump cups raised by now. Zara rode by, steering the chestnut gelding with her bare legs, her reins loose.

"Higher!" she ordered.

"Okay, if you say so." Dani raised her cup another hole.

Tommi turned to Zara. "Hey!" she called. "Listen, Zara . . ."

But it was too late. Zara had kicked the horse into a trot, then a canter, circling it back around toward the jump.

"Wait!" Summer squealed. "I'm not ready yet!"

Dani's side was set at about 4'9", but Summer was still

struggling to raise hers from its old mark several inches lower. Zara was coming back around now, so Summer gave up and scurried out of the way. Tommi thought about stepping in front of the jump, forcing Zara to pull up. But she didn't quite dare. In her current condition, who knew if Zara would see her—or stop even if she did?

She jumped aside, hurrying back to Kate, who'd ducked into the ring but was standing back by the rail. "This is crazy!" Kate cried.

"I know. And she's running him at it too fast—he's all strung out," Tommi said, watching the horse. "Maybe he'll run out and she'll fall off on top of Summer." Her mouth twisted into a smirk at the thought, even though the situation was far from funny.

But the horse didn't stop. He galloped wildly at the crooked jump and flung himself at it from an awkward long spot. Tommi wanted to close her eyes, guessing what was coming. But they stayed open, watching helplessly as the horse's front legs hit the top rail and he somersaulted over the jump, landing on his back with a crash on the far side.

NINETEEN

━━ ━━ ━━ ━━ ━━

Zara saw the world turn upside down a couple of times, like some kind of bad trip. Then she hit the ground hard, landing on her back. All the breath left her body and she struggled to breathe. In, out, in, out . . .

Finally, after what seemed like half a lifetime but was probably just a second or two, her lungs started working again. Only then did she become aware of shouts, screams, and lots of running around.

Marissa dropped to her knees beside her. "Are you okay?" she exclaimed, practically sobbing. "Oh God, Zara, speak to me!"

Before Zara could answer, she saw Tommi shove the other girl aside and crouch down. "Don't move," she ordered, sounding so much like Jamie that Zara would've laughed if she hadn't been pretty sure it would hurt too much.

"I'm fine," she said, pushing herself up into a sitting position with a groan. "What happened?"

"The horse flipped over the jump." Tommi shot a look across the ring. "Luckily for you, you got thrown clear."

Zara followed her gaze. A small crowd was gathered around the snazzy-looking chestnut she'd been riding. Kate was at its head, leading it around at a walk, but Zara couldn't see much else.

"Oops," she said. "He okay?"

"Well, he got up. That's a start."

Dani came running over. "He's lame," she reported breathlessly. "Kate wants you to call Jamie and the vet."

Tommi nodded and pulled out her cell phone. "Wait!" Zara said. The fall had knocked most of the buzz out of her, and her brain was clicking along at top speed as she worked out what had just happened—and what was probably going to happen next. "You can't call Jamie."

"We have to." Tommi was already scrolling down her numbers list.

Zara lunged over and grabbed the phone out of her hand. The movement made her bare thigh scrape across the footing, grinding more of it into her raw skin. Ouch. That one was going to leave a mark. No more short shorts for a while.

"Give that back!" Tommi said, grabbing for the phone.

"Just listen." Zara hid the phone behind her back. "You can't let Jamie know about this. I'm already on probation, remember?"

"Yeah, well, you should've thought about that before you pulled a stupid stunt like this." Tommi's eyes were cold and completely lacking in sympathy.

"Tommi!" Kate was coming toward them, leading the chestnut horse. "Did you get Jamie yet?"

"Trying." Tommi glared at Zara. "Give me back my phone."

Zara was watching the horse. "He doesn't look lame to me."

"I just jogged him out," Kate told her. "He was head-bobbing from the first step. I think it might be his left front suspensory."

"Oh, man!" Marissa shook her head. "That sounds bad. My aunt had to retire her good hunter because of a suspensory thing."

Zara glanced around, feeling desperate. Over half the party-ers had melted away after the crash, along with the other horses. Those remaining were gathered around Zara and the injured horse. Kate, Marissa, Summer, Dani, Max, that hot friend of Tommi's . . . all of them staring at her. Judging her. Probably knowing it was their last chance to do so before Jamie kicked her out so fast and hard she wound up back on the West Coast.

"Don't call, or else!" she blurted out.

Tommi rolled her eyes. "Or else what?" she said, taking another swipe at her and grabbing the phone this time.

"Or else, um, I'll tell Jamie that Javier's in the country ille-gally," Zara blurted out.

It was the only thing she could think of, and a total stab in the dark based on the kid's heavy accent and general air of anxiety. But when she saw Max's eyes widen, she guessed she'd hit the mark. Score.

"That's right," she said, embellishing. "I know his papers are forged. And if you guys tell anyone what happened here tonight, Jamie'll know it, too."

She saw Tommi shoot a look at Max, then at Kate. For a second there was silence as everyone stared at one another.

Finally Max spoke. "I'll take Ford back to the stall and rub him down," he said. "He'll probably be okay with some rest."

"Yeah," Marissa said quickly. "He might've just stung himself on the rail. He'll probably be fine in the morning."

Dani and Summer were already nodding. Zara looked at Tommi and Kate. They were exchanging a long stare.

Finally Tommi shrugged, and Kate spoke. "I guess it wouldn't hurt to wait and see how he is in the morning," she said softly.

Tommi's head was pounding when she arrived at the show-grounds the next morning, and she doubted any amount of caffeine would help much. She'd tossed and turned all night, wondering if it had been wrong to give in to Zara's blackmail. But what other choice did they have? Jamie was a stickler about immigration status—always said the horse world had a bad enough rap for that sort of thing without him adding to it. If he found out Javier was illegal, the kid would be back on the bus to Mexico before he could say *adios*. It was too late to take back what had happened to the horse; why should both of them pay for Zara's bad judgment?

Still, the decision didn't sit easy with her. She was so distracted that she was almost on top of the injured horse's stall before she noticed the vet stepping out of it with Jamie right behind him.

"I'll stop back later this morning to check on him," the vet said. Nodding to Tommi, she hurried off.

"What's going on?" Tommi asked Jamie.

He sighed and ran one hand down his face. "Ford managed to injure himself last night somehow," he said. "Torn suspensory and possibly a wither fracture. Best we can guess is he must've gone down in his stall and gotten cast."

"Wow." Tommi's stomach lurched. Even worse than she'd thought. She couldn't believe Jamie and the vet actually thought the horse could've hurt himself so badly just thrashing around on his side, wedged up against a stall wall trying to get his feet under himself. Then again, horses could injure themselves in all sorts of crazy ways. And if everyone assumed the horse hadn't left the stall . . .

"Yeah. Horse was peachy when I left last night. Miguel discovered there was a problem when he went to get him for his morning lunge." Jamie shot her a look. "You didn't hear anything last night, did you? A little bird told me you kids came back over here after hours."

Figured he'd hear about that somehow. Not much got past Jamie.

"Nope, sorry." Tommi hated lying to Jamie's face like that. Hated it almost enough to tell him the truth—Zara be damned. But then she saw Javier scurry past at the far end of the aisle with a saddle over each arm, and that reminded her again why she was doing this.

But she still really, really hated it.

"Thanks, Javier," Kate said as the young groom tightened Fable's girth another notch. She didn't look him in the eye as he nodded and turned to hurry off to his next task—she was afraid he'd read the guilt written all over her. Had Max or anyone else told him about Zara's threat? She couldn't tell. He was as quiet and efficient as ever, his face an emotionless mask.

She was trying not to obsess over everything that had happened last night, but it wasn't easy. Her mind skipped back and forth from the incident in the hay stall to the accident in the ring and back again, both events growing larger and more horrible every time she thought about them. She'd managed to avoid both Fitz and Jamie so far that morning, though Tommi had told her what the vet had said.

"Ready, big guy?" she whispered as she slipped on Fable's bridle.

The horse snorted and nudged at her, almost knocking her back against the wall. She gave him a pat and a tug on the reins to get him moving. At least freaking out over Fitz and the accident hadn't left her much time to get nervous about her first Big Eq class on Fable.

But as soon as she mounted to start her warm-up, her show nerves came screaming out of hiding, crowding out the rest of her problems, at least for now. Could she do this? She and Fable had been doing much better since that first disastrous lesson. But were they ready for the big time?

She stayed in the warm-up ring for as long as she dared, half tempted to skip the class entirely. But no. She couldn't do that. Jamie had gone out of his way to make this happen for her, and she couldn't let him down.

"Okay, buddy," she told Fable with a sigh, giving him a pat. "Here goes nothing."

As she rode toward the show ring, Kate picked out Jamie's slim form near the gate. Even from the back she could tell from the tense set of his shoulders that he was totally focused on what was going on in the ring. When she got closer, Kate could see why. Fitz had just started his course.

Seeing him made the feelings from last night flood through her all over again—the good ones as well as the bad. She stopped her horse near the gate and watched as Fitz rode. He was relaxed but aggressive—and totally hot, which made Kate feel flustered and angry at the same time. He attacked each fence, each challenge, with a keen focus, making the tough course look easy.

Fitz was smiling as he rode out of the ring. He tossed a grin and a quip at Jamie, then turned his head and saw Kate sitting there on her horse.

"Kate!" he blurted out. "Where have you been? I've been trying to—"

"Kate, you're up," Jamie called at that moment, cutting him off. "Warm-up go okay?"

She nodded, not trusting her voice to respond.

"Good. Just remember what we worked on last week—rhythm, impulsion, just keep things flowing and look for your spots, and Fable can handle the rest. Okay?" He patted the horse on the neck, then stepped back and waved her past him.

Kate's mind felt numb as she rode into the ring. Luckily her body was pretty much on autopilot, sending Fable into a trot and then a canter, steering him into the beginning of their opening circle.

She knew she had to snap out of it. Fable wasn't an overly

sensitive type of horse like Ellie or Legs; he wasn't likely to get upset if she wasn't paying attention. But this wasn't a hunter course. There were several tricky elements to it, a tight rollback and some other twists and turns, along with the usual funky distances. He was going to need some guidance from her at some point if she didn't want to make a total fool of herself.

For a second she felt dizzy with helplessness. Maybe she should just pull up, excuse herself, leave the ring.

She glanced over at the gate as she came out of the circle. Jamie's face jumped out at her from among the crowd of people standing there; he saw her looking, smiled, and gave her a thumbs-up.

That was when she knew she couldn't give up. Couldn't let him down—or herself, either. Couldn't let Fitz ruin this for her.

What would Tommi do if she were me? she asked herself as she aimed Fable at the first fence. She knew what she *wouldn't* do. She wouldn't let some stupid guy throw her off her game. She'd pick herself up, dust herself off, and ride.

Doing her best to channel her friend's strength, Kate shortened Fable's stride slightly, aiming at the first obstacle, an inviting vertical. They met it perfectly, and just like that, the course snapped into sharp focus and Kate stopped thinking about anything else.

By the end of the course, Kate had stopped thinking completely. She and Fable were like one creature, communicating without words, moving together flawlessly. It was the best feeling in the world.

Jamie was grinning when she rode out. "See?" he called to her. "Told ya you could do it! Outstanding!"

"Thanks." Kate beamed at him, then leaned down to give Fable a pat as she rode out through the gate. "And thanks for Fable. He's amazing!"

Her smile froze on her face as she turned and saw Fitz. He must have handed off his horse to one of the grooms, and now he was standing there with his helmet tucked under his arm. "Congrats," he said. "If you don't pin after that round, the judge is either blind or clueless."

Kate didn't answer, shifting her gaze to some point on the horizon as she urged Fable on past him. Jamie had already turned to give Summer some last-minute advice as she got ready for her go.

"Kate, wait!" Fitz hurried to catch up with her. "I want to talk to you."

"There's nothing to talk about." Kate had been about to dismount, but instead she nudged Fable into a walk, riding him in the direction of the show stalls.

Fitz had to jog to keep up with the long-strided horse. "Come on, aren't you even going to let me apologize?" he said. "I'm sorry about last night. I shouldn't have pushed you like that—it was totally uncool. I wanted to get closer to you, that's all. I just got carried away."

By now they were well beyond the in-gate crowd at a relatively private spot between rings. Kate halted the horse and glared down at him, unable to listen anymore. "How stupid do you think I am?" she cried. "I fell for your crap once; I'm not going to fall for it again."

"It's not crap! Not this time. I told you—you're different, Kate." He put a hand on her leg.

She kicked it off so ferociously that Fable tossed his head and skittered to one side. "Don't touch me," she hissed at Fitz.

"Please, Kate." He kept his hands to himself, but took a step closer. "You really are different. That's not just a line, I mean it. You're probably the sweetest, most amazing person I've ever met, and it kills me to think I hurt you this much. I never meant to do that. What do I have to say to convince you? What do I have to do to prove it?"

"You can't," she said. "You blew your chance last night."

"Aargh!" He grabbed his hair with the hand that wasn't holding his helmet. "This is so . . . Seriously, Kate. Do you need some kind of big dramatic gesture or something to convince you I'm for real here? Because I'll do it, whatever it takes. Boom box outside your window, tattooing your name on my face, you name it."

"I don't want anything from you." She gave Fable another nudge, sending him ambling along again. "Why should I believe anything you say?"

"Because it's all true," he insisted, still keeping up with her. "I'm ready to do anything. Make whatever sacrifice you want. Seriously."

She stopped again and shot him a look, her anger bubbling up anew. "Are you kidding me with this?" she exclaimed. "You've never been serious about anything in your life. You just float through without ever putting much effort into anything. Except maybe riding and scamming girls. Your two true talents." Her face twisted in a humorless smile. "Everyone knows how you are. *I* know how you are. You don't even know what sacrifice is. And you definitely don't know anything about what I really want."

"Kate . . . ," he began, looking surprised. And maybe a little hurt?

Whatever. She couldn't look at him anymore; couldn't take it anymore. If she stayed here any longer, she was afraid she might burst into tears. She kicked Fable forward, heading back to the barn at a brisk trot.

TWENTY

So far, the best part of Zara's morning was the hangover. Her pounding head and the queasy feeling in her stomach occasionally managed to distract her from how everyone was treating her like a turd in the punch bowl. The grooms had been shooting her dirty looks every time they saw her, along with most of the other juniors. Even freaking Summer was staying away from her, which somehow irked her even more than the rest.

The only one acting normal was Jamie. Well, normal for him, anyway. She would take what she could get.

"I should probably just blow out of here early," she murmured to Keeper as she stopped by his stall to give him a pat. "You don't care if we skip your jumper division, do you?"

It was tempting. Why not bail? It wasn't as if anyone wanted her here.

But she knew she couldn't do it. Jamie would be mad if she ditched the jumper class she'd been talking about all week.

And maybe suspicious. She'd heard that the horse she'd ridden last night was in kind of bad shape. Not that anyone had told her, since nobody was talking to her. But she'd heard a couple of people whispering about it.

She spent the rest of the morning hanging around near the rings watching a bunch of boring unrated classes, then had lunch—by herself. After that she wandered back to the stabling area to see if Keeper was ready yet. Javier had him in the cross-ties waiting for her.

"He's almost ready, miss," he said in his soft, polite voice.

Zara just nodded, not daring to look him in the eye. Did he know? Had anyone told him what she'd done?

"Listen, Javier," she began.

Then she stopped. What was she supposed to say next? *Sorry I threatened to get you deported, nothing personal, I didn't mean it?* She couldn't say that, even though it was kind of true. If she let anyone call her bluff, that would be it. She'd be out of here for good. There was no easy fix this time.

Before she could figure out what to do, Jamie hurried in. "There you are," he said, pointing at Zara. "Come on, get your bridle on and let's go. The others are already warming up."

Soon Zara was riding into the crowded warm-up ring. Several of her barnmates were in this division—Fitz, Dani, Tommi. But she was careful not to look at any of them, keeping her attention on her horse when she wasn't looking at Jamie.

When Tommi and Dani left with Jamie to head over to the ring, she relaxed a little. Fitz hadn't been there last night as far as she'd noticed, though he had to know all the sordid details by now. She shot him a look or two as they both rode around, and once she caught him looking back at her. But he didn't make any move to ride over to her, so she made sure to keep her distance.

Then it was her turn. Keeper felt good as they entered the ring—loose, alert, focused. He flicked his ears at one of the more colorful jumps at this end of the ring and she smiled, feeling better than she had all day.

"Let's show them how it's done, babycakes," she whispered, adjusting her reins. "If we're going to go out, at least we can do it with a bang."

Keeper flowed over the first jump like a hunter. As soon as they landed Zara closed her legs, asking for more speed. The horse responded instantly, ears already pricked toward the next obstacle

By the fifth jump Zara was smiling, everything else forgotten in the sheer joy of galloping and jumping. Keeper felt even better than usual and seemed to be enjoying himself as much as she was.

She steadied him around the turn and looked for her next fence. Her heart started pounding as she realized it was the same jump she'd crashed the night before. It looked different today—a little lower, a little more filler. But seeing it made her tense up as it all came rushing back—the horse hurtling at the jump, the moment she'd realized they weren't going to make it, her bare legs losing their grip as she flew through the air, the poles crashing down all around her, the thud of the horse landing flat on its back a few feet away . . .

For a second she froze. Keeper felt it, hesitating even as he locked on the fence, waiting for her to make an adjustment.

When it didn't come, the experienced horse shrugged it off and jumped anyway, but he put in an extra stride and took off a little too close. A second later the top rail clattered to the ground, eliciting a moan of sympathy from the spectators.

Keeper was already galloping on, looking for the next fence. But Zara had started to shake. She hauled on the reins, pulling the horse to a walk. Then she raised a hand toward the judge, signaling that she was withdrawing.

Jamie was waiting for her at the gate. "What happened?" he asked, sounding confused. "It was only one rail."

Zara just shook her head, too aware of dozens of sets of eyes on her. She wasn't going to let herself break down in front of all these people. No way. Tossing Keeper's reins at the nearest groom, she took off at a run.

When she reached the barn, she almost ran into Tommi and Kate, who were standing in the middle of the aisle. Tommi was still in the clothes she'd just showed in, though her horse and helmet were nowhere in sight. Kate looked like a mess as usual, her T-shirt and jeans splattered with hoof polish and horse slobber.

Zara tried to dart past them, but Tommi blocked her path.

"We were waiting for you," she said.

"I'm kind of busy right now," Zara said, trying again to move past her.

"This is important." Tommi frowned. "We have to do something about that horse."

"Yeah," Kate put in softly. "We feel really guilty for not telling Jamie what happened. Ford's suspensory is really messed up—he might never jump again."

Tommi nodded. "You need to come clean with Jamie," she said. "Otherwise we will."

"No way!" Zara blurted out. "If you tell Jamie what I did, he'll kick me out for sure. And I don't want to leave!"

She took a step backward, realizing she'd just done it. Let them know how much she actually liked this stupid place. How much she cared about staying. Did they even realize what a big deal that was for her?

Tommi and Kate exchanged a look. Neither of them said anything for a few seconds.

"Look . . . ," Tommi began at last.

Then they all heard footsteps coming and turned around. Jamie and Fitz had just entered together. Fitz was grinning, which Zara guessed meant he'd done well in his round right after hers.

But Jamie instantly clued in to the tense mood. "What's going on here?" he asked cautiously.

🐎

Tommi's mind swirled as Jamie stared at them, waiting for an answer. For a second she wasn't sure what to say. She shot a look at Zara, whose expression was closed and stormy. Then she glanced at Kate. Her face had gone pale the moment Fitz had entered. She was staring fixedly at the toes of her Blundstones.

Yeah. Tommi could see that it was going to be up to her.

"I'm glad you're here," she told Jamie. "We want to talk to you about what happened to Ford."

"Oh?" Jamie's eyebrows shot up.

Tommi looked over at Zara again. Some of the anger had drained out of her face; now she just looked strained and kind of sad.

Could she really do it? Everyone thought Tommi had nerves of steel. But could she actually rat someone out right to her face? Get her kicked out of a barn that seemed to mean something to her already? She could see Fitz's eyes widen as he realized what she was about to do; hear Zara's sharp intake of breath.

"Um," Tommi said, her nerve flagging, "I, I meant w-we just wanted to say how sorry we were to hear about his stall accident."

"Hold on," Zara spoke up, her voice shaking a little. "That's not all *I* want to say. There's something you need to know . . ."

Kate snapped out of her daze at Zara's words. She'd been completely focused on Fitz since the moment he'd entered. She'd kept her eyes averted, but the rest of her was tingling with shame and confusion. Had she been wrong to refuse to listen to his apology earlier? Or was she being a sucker now for thinking—hoping?—it might possibly have been for real?

She forgot about all that now as she realized what was happening. Was Zara really about to confess what she'd done? Kate hadn't been sure she had it in her, and couldn't help being a little impressed.

"I—I know we aren't really supposed to be on the showgrounds after hours, but I didn't think anything bad would happen," Zara was saying. "I mean, I just wanted to celebrate, you know? Ellie did so great, and a party seemed like a fun idea, and . . ." Seeming to realize she was rambling, she took a deep breath and turned to face Jamie. "Anyway, the point is—"

"No!" Kate whispered, suddenly realizing what this meant. As soon as Jamie knew the truth, that was the end of the road for Zara at his barn. He was generous with second chances, but not thirds.

"Wait," Fitz blurted out, cutting off Zara's next words. He spun to face Jamie. "I'm sorry, dude," he went on. "I know I should've told you right away. It was me—I'm the reason Ford got hurt."

"What?" Jamie exclaimed.

Kate gasped.

"Yeah," Fitz said. "I was trying to impress this cute girl from Fair Fields, and since you let me ride Ford in a couple of lessons I just grabbed him because he was handy." He shook his head. "Anyway, I was way too drunk last night to really realize what I'd done. But I'm totally sorry. I'll make sure my parents make it up to you."

Jamie's face had gone hard. "I see," he said in a tone that made Kate shiver, glad that she wasn't on the receiving end.

"Like I said, I'm sorry." Fitz shrugged. "But I didn't want to take the easy way out by not confessing. Or, you know, letting someone else take the fall and sacrifice on my behalf."

As he said the word "sacrifice," he shot Kate a quick look. She breathed in sharply.

"Come with me," Jamie told Fitz, his words clipped and angry. "I think we'd better continue this conversation in private."

He stomped off. Before following, Fitz sought out Kate

with his eyes again. They held a hopeful, pleading look, and that was when she knew for sure. He'd done this for her.

After Fitz and Jamie were gone, the others just stood there for a moment. Zara was the first to speak.

"Wow," she said. "What just happened?"

Tommi shook her head. "I have no idea. Why would Fitz do something like that?" She shot Zara a look. "I mean, even if you two have been—"

"We haven't," Zara interrupted. "I mean, yeah, it would make some kind of sense if he was trying to get into my breeches or whatever. But I don't think he's into me, so . . ."

Kate didn't say a word. She still couldn't believe he'd done it. But there was no other explanation. This was his big, dramatic gesture. His way of proving he was willing to sacrifice for the chance to be with her. It was kind of demented, sort of like Fitz himself. But weirdly sweet at the same time.

"So what now?" Zara demanded. "Are you guys going to tell Jamie the truth?"

There was a moment of silence after Zara's question. Tommi wasn't sure what to say; she was still trying to process what had just happened. It didn't seem fair that Zara would get away with this, or that Fitz would be punished for something he hadn't done.

"You don't think Jamie will kick him out, do you?" Kate asked, turning to Tommi.

"Doubtful." Tommi shook her head. "He'll be pretty hard on him for a while, though. Guaranteed."

"Look." Zara took a deep breath. "This isn't right. I don't want to feel guilty every time I come to the stupid barn. Maybe I should go talk to Jamie after all. And apologize to Javier, too. I never would've ratted him out even if my wild guess turns out to be true."

Tommi could see that she meant it—all of it—and just like that, it didn't seem to matter anymore. "Talk to Javier if you want, but don't bother confessing to Jamie," she told her. "Fitz may not have crashed that horse, but he's done plenty of other stuff he could stand a little payback for."

She shot a look at Kate, who didn't meet her eye. She looked like she was spacing out a little, probably still trying to process all this. Or maybe trying to stop herself from hyperventilating over being that close to Fitz. But Tommi could deal with that later.

"Anyway," she went on, turning her attention back to Zara, "if he's so eager to take the fall, maybe we should just let him. His parents can afford to rehab that horse, or buy the owners another one, or whatever it takes."

"Okay," Zara said. "But I—"

Tommi didn't let her finish. "Look, I know how easy it is to make a mistake. Especially when everyone's always watching you, just waiting for you to screw up." She shrugged. "I'm willing to give you another shot if you're really sorry about what happened. But only one more. Third strike and all that."

Zara almost rolled her eyes at Tommi's comment. She still wasn't thrilled with the idea that Fitz was throwing himself on his sword or whatever, especially since she wasn't sure why he'd done it. But this was all starting to feel a little too after-school special.

She almost said something sarcastic, but stopped herself as she met Tommi's eye. Maybe she *did* understand, at least a little. She'd grown up in the same fishbowl as Zara had—sort of, anyway. Could she really trust her to keep a secret this huge? Could she trust any of them?

What choice did she have?

"I think Tommi's right," Kate said in her wimpy little voice. But now, for the first time, Zara noticed it had an edge of strength to it. Or something like that. "Fitz decided to do this. Even if he did it without thinking it through, he needs to deal with it." She glanced over at Tommi. "*Especially* if he did it without thinking."

Tommi's eyes widened for a second. Then she nodded.

Zara had no idea what that was about. But she didn't really care. It had just really sunk in what this meant. She was okay. She wasn't going to get kicked out of the barn, at least not right now. And maybe she'd even just found a couple of new friends here. Or at least people she might want to have as friends. She had a feeling she was going to have to work pretty hard to earn their trust after what had happened—as hard as she'd always expected everyone to work to earn hers. Was it worth it?

Just then Tommi gasped. "Oh my God!" she cried, staring at her watch. "I need to get moving. I told the guys I wanted to tack up Legs myself for our class today, but he needs a really good warm-up, and . . ."

"Say no more," Kate said. "I'll help you get him ready."

"Me, too," Zara put in.

The other two glanced at her with surprise. But then Tommi nodded.

"Thanks," she said, shooting her a small smile.

Zara followed as the other two girls hurried toward the tack room. Yeah, maybe it was worth it. At least it was worth sticking around long enough to find out.

What's up next for Zara, Tommi, and Kate?

Read on for sneak peeks of the next

A CIRCUIT *novel*

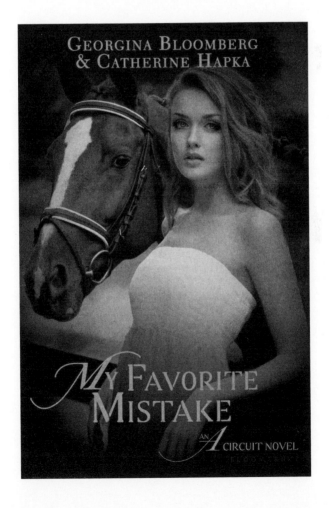

ZARA

— — — — —

"Zara! Hi!" Summer was in the aisle watching Max sweep when Zara entered the barn. "I was hoping you'd come out today. Did you get my text?" She hurried toward Zara, her obnoxious little brat of a dog leaping at her heels.

Great. Just what Zara needed to make her foul mood even worse. Summer was like the ugly chin zit you assumed would go away if you ignored it long enough. Only it didn't. Just kept getting bigger and more disgusting.

"Nope, didn't get any text from you," Zara lied. "Your phone must be screwed up or something."

Summer's pale blue eyes widened with alarm. "Do you really think so?" she exclaimed, fishing a shiny new pink cell phone out of the pocket of her Tailored Sportsmans. "But I just got it! It's exactly like the one Tommi has—well, except hers is boring black—so I figured it was probably, like, really good . . ."

Zara hardly heard her. Her mind was already wandering back to her father's big news. Yeah, leave it to Zac to think she'd actually be okay with having a babysitter while he was in Europe. Clueless didn't even begin to cover it.

But whatever. It looked like she'd just be spending even more time at the barn than usual. At least for the rest of the summer.

As she wandered off down the aisle, she realized Summer was tagging along at her heel as obsessively as her stupid mutt might do. And yapping nonstop just like him, too. Did she even notice that Zara wasn't listening?

"... and anyway, I heard Fitz is, like, totally grounded from the next show," Summer was saying as Zara tuned back in. "I wonder if—"

"That's nice," Zara cut her off. "Got to run. Ellie's probably waiting for me. And she hates to wait."

Both those things were true, at least. Zara had called ahead from the car to ask the grooms to get the mare ready. And Ellie tended to get testy if left in the cross-ties for half a second longer than she felt was necessary.

Zara couldn't help smiling as she thought about her new horse. Yeah, so maybe it hadn't all been smooth sailing so far. But that was part of the fun, right? At least Ellie had a mind of her own. Zara was already looking forward to the next show when the two of them could show everyone what they could *really* do.

"Oh, you mean you're going for a ride right now?" Summer asked eagerly.

"Um, duh," Zara said. "Why do you think I came to the barn? To get a mani-pedi?"

Summer appeared totally unfazed by the sarcasm. "Cool, I was thinking about riding soon, too. I'll join you."

Zara bit her tongue—literally—to stop herself from snapping out a rude reply. Sure, Summer was a pain in the ass. But she wasn't really the one who was making Zara feel like crap. Nope, that honor belonged to her own father, the guy who barely noticed when she stayed out until dawn or came home wasted three nights in a row—and yet suddenly seemed to think she needed to be treated like a five-year-old.

"Whatever," she muttered as Summer hurried off down the barn aisle shouting for Miguel.

Zara turned toward Ellie's stall. The mare was cross-tied in the aisle with Zara's saddle already neatly positioned atop a spotless Mattes pad. Javier was bent over the horse's front legs, fiddling with her sheepskin-lined Eskadron boots.

When she saw the young groom, Zara's stomach twisted as she instantly flashed back to the Hounds Hollow showgrounds. The drunken crash. The injured horse. Her desperate threat to turn in Javier, to tell Jamie he was illegal. How long had it taken for someone to tell Javier about that? Whatever, he had to know all about it by now. All about how she'd almost ruined his life.

One of the barn dogs, Hugo, was sitting nearby chewing on a stray bit of hoof the farrier must've tossed him. The dog wagged his tail and jumped to his feet when he noticed Zara coming, which made Javier look up as well.

"Hi, Miss Trask," the groom said politely, his dark eyes unreadable behind their long lashes. "She's almost ready for you."

"Thanks," Zara muttered, not quite meeting his gaze.

He finished adjusting the boot and stood. "Are you ready?" he asked. "I'll bridle her for you now if you like."

"Sure, thanks."

Javier hurried off toward the tack room with Hugo right behind him, leaving Zara standing there feeling guilty and unsettled as she wondered what the young groom was thinking about her right now. Ugh. And this was supposed to be her refuge from the annoyances of home?

Just then Fitz wandered into view at the end of the aisle. Great. Another person she definitely didn't feel like dealing with right now. She'd barely seen him since the end of the show, mostly because his parents had banned him from the barn for a week once they heard what had happened. Well, what had *supposedly* happened.

Zara still couldn't believe he'd jumped in to cover for her. The weirdest part was that he hadn't even done it to try to get in her pants. That would have been better, actually. She would've known how to handle that.

This? Not so much. She didn't like owing anyone anything.

"Hey, good lookin'. What's cookin'?" Fitz quipped when he got closer. "Didn't know you were here today."

"Sorry, guess I forgot to alert the media," she muttered.

It came out sounding more sour than funny, but Fitz laughed anyway. "How's Ellie today?" he asked, stepping over to give Ellie a scratch on the withers. The mare turned her head as far as the cross-ties would allow, nuzzling him in obvious hope of scoring a treat.

Zara didn't answer. Javier had just returned with her bridle. He expertly slipped it on, then handed over the reins.

"Do you need anything else, Miss Trask?" he asked in his soft voice.

"No, I'm good." Zara forced a smile. "Thanks."

"See you, Javier," Fitz said. As soon as the groom disappeared around the corner, he glanced at Zara. "Hey, guess what?"

"Do I have to?" Zara jammed her helmet on and clicked the throat snap shut.

"What? No, seriously." Fitz lowered his voice. "I was talking to Max, and he said nobody ever told Javier what happened that night. You know—what you said about him."

Zara spun around to face him. "Wait, for real?" she said. "Come on. This place is gossip central. How could he not know?"

Fitz lifted one shoulder, then let it drop. "Guess the other guys didn't want to freak him out. I told Max you were never going to actually rat out Javier to Jamie, anyway. So no harm, no foul. At least for that part."

Zara wasn't sure how to respond, so she didn't. Just turned and lifted the saddle flap, pretending to check her girth.

After a moment of silence, Fitz cleared his throat. "Anyway, I just thought you'd like to know," he said. "Gotta go. Have a good ride, okay?"

"Thanks," Zara muttered without taking her eyes off the girth.

She wasn't going to let Fitz know it, but her mood had just ticked up a notch thanks to his news. Okay, so all the other juniors still knew exactly what she'd done, plus now she had this new garbage at home to deal with. But at least she wouldn't have to feel guilty every time she looked at Javier from now on.

At least there was that.

TOMMI

— — — — —

"Easy, big guy," Tommi said as Legs shifted restlessly at the end of the lead. "Come on, just one more time up and back, okay?"

The sound of the show's loudspeaker system crackled in the distance, but the shed row was deserted except for the two of them. Jamie was still out at the eq ring, Elliot had just left to take an adult client's horse to the warm-up, and the other grooms were busy elsewhere. Tommi was glad. She needed some time alone with Legs to figure out what was going on with him.

Just then Legs pricked his ears and lifted his head, staring toward the end of the aisle. Turning that way, Tommi saw Kate entering, still dressed in her tidy navy show jacket and tall boots.

Tommi felt a flash of guilt. Oops. She'd meant to try to get over to the ring to watch Kate's eq trip.

"Hey," she called. "Did you already ride? How'd it go?"

Kate frowned, a dark look flashing through her eyes. "Could've been better."

Uh-oh. Tommi knew better than to ask. Kate would tell her about it when she was ready.

Meanwhile Kate was looking at Legs, who was pawing at the sawdust footing. "He any better today?" she asked.

"I'm not sure. Actually, do you have a sec? I could really use someone to jog him while I watch."

"Sure." Kate took the lead, giving the lanky gelding a pat. "Come on, Legs. Let's go."

She clucked and wriggled the lead, urging Legs into a trot. Tommi kept her eyes trained on the horse's legs, watching for any sign of a bobble, any shortness of stride—anything at all that wasn't what it should be. But whatever it was that she'd felt, she couldn't see it now. She sighed as Kate and Legs stopped.

"Anything?" Kate asked.

Tommi shook her head. "I'm starting to think that bitchy hotshot trainer chick was right yesterday," she muttered. "Maybe I did choke—maybe I imagined the whole thing."

"No way," Kate said. "Trust your gut. If you thought he felt off, it was better not to push him, right?"

Tommi didn't answer. Just stared at the horse, who was standing there nudging at Kate's shoulder with his muzzle, looking bored and impatient. With no clue that he held her entire future in those long, slender, oh-so-fragile legs of his.

Just then Zara wandered into view. "Hi," she said. "What are you guys doing?"

"Trying to figure out if Legs is lame or if I'm crazy," Tommi said with a loud sigh.

Zara wrinkled her nose. "You mean because of that thing yesterday? You're still obsessing over that?" She grinned. "Come on—we all know you punked out of that class because you knew you couldn't compete with my awesome ride!"

Tommi shot her a look. "Whatever. This isn't a joke. If he's not sound enough to hold up to the show lifestyle . . ."

"Don't panic, Tommi," Kate put in softly. "It could just be an abscess or some other minor thing like that."

Zara didn't look too interested. "Hey, so did you already finish your eq class?" she asked Kate. "I meant to come over and watch, but I got, um, distracted." She smirked and licked her lips.

Even though she was still distracted by her own problems, Tommi couldn't help noticing the little gesture and wondering what it meant. Could it have something to do with Grant?

"So I got there a little too late—Jamie said you'd already finished," Zara was saying. "Anyway, how'd it go?"

"It went," Kate said tightly.

"Ooookay." Zara raised an eyebrow. "Guess that means no ribbon this time, huh?"

Kate shook her head, staring at the ground. Tommi winced on her behalf. Why did she always have to be so damn hard on herself? So she'd blown a class. It happened to the best of them. Kate needed to shrug it off and move on, not eat herself alive over it.

"So what happened?" Zara asked. "I thought you guys were, like, the new barn superstars or whatever."

"Maybe Fable is," Kate said quietly.

Zara shrugged and returned her attention to Legs. "So what's wrong with him, anyway?" she asked, giving the gelding a pat.

"Good question," Tommi replied grimly. "I could feel he wasn't quite right when I rode him. But I can't see anything from the ground, so I'm not sure what to do about it."

"Well, that's why we have vets, I guess." Zara didn't sound too concerned. "It's not like you don't have other horses to ride."

Tommi didn't know why she'd bothered to say anything. Why she'd expected Zara to understand. How could she? She'd never taken anything seriously in her life, at least as far as Tommi could tell.

"Whatever," she said. "If he doesn't get better, my pro career could be over before it begins."

"Lighten up, chica," Zara said. "This is supposed to be fun, right?" She stared from Tommi to Kate and back again. "Right?"

Kate shrugged, keeping her gaze on the floor. Tommi just rolled her eyes. In her opinion, Zara was a little too much about the fun. But what was the point of saying so?

The buzz of her cell phone interrupted her thoughts. It was a text from Alex:

Hi Tommi—hope ur having a good show! Can't wait 2 c u when u get back on Sun. Maybe we can get 2gether then if ur not 2 tired from winning all those blue ribbons & stuff?

Tommi smiled as she scanned the message. He was so sweet—and hearing from him was exactly what she needed right now. It was a reminder that there was more to life than horses.

She texted him back quickly:

Sun night sounds like a plan. Will let u know 2morrow what time I'll b home, ok? ttyt!

After sending the text, Tommi stuck her phone back in her pocket. Kate handed her Legs's lead.

"I'd better go," Kate said. "Javier offered to cool Fable out for me, but I know he's got other stuff to do, so . . ."

Letting her voice trail off, she took off down the aisle. "Wow," Zara commented. "She seems even more stressed than usual. And that's saying something."

"She's fine. Just busy, that's all." But as Tommi watched Kate disappear around the corner, she couldn't help feeling a flash of concern. Kate *did* seem extra tense lately. Was it because Fitz wasn't at the show? Tommi wondered if maybe having him around was good for Kate after all.

Then Legs shoved at her with his head, and she gave him a pat.

"Okay, mister," she told him. "We're not accomplishing anything here. Let's get you back to your stall."

KATE

▬ ▬ ▬ ▬ ▬

Elliot paused in the middle of grooming Marissa's horse, sniffing at the air. "Smells like the pizza's here," he said. "You'd better go before that pack of wolves eats it all."

Kate glanced up from rubbing down the dark bay gelding's legs. "What? Oh, um, that's okay, I'm not that hungry. And I know Miguel was hoping to leave early tonight . . ."

"Shoo," the groom said firmly, plucking the liniment bottle out of her hand. "You've barely stopped moving since we got home from the show, girl. You deserve a break."

Kate was tempted to protest. She wasn't really in the mood to hang out listening to the other juniors gossip over their post-lesson pizza. Then her stomach let out a hollow grumble, and she realized she was ravenous.

"Okay," she told Elliot. "Maybe I'll just grab one slice and then come back and help you guys finish up."

Halfway to the tack room, she could already hear the others laughing and talking. The scents of hot tomato sauce, cheese, and garlic drifting down the aisle made her feel a little weak in the knees. When had she eaten last? She couldn't remember, but her stomach was telling her it had been way too long.

Fitz waved when she came in. He was lounging against an empty saddle rack shoving pizza into his mouth. Everyone else was already there, too. Tommi, Marissa, and Zara were sitting on the bench. Summer was standing nearby, waving her hands around as she talked to them. Dani had just grabbed another slice, stepping over Jamie's bulldog to get it. As usual, Chaucer was planted right in front of the boxes on the bandage trunk, while the younger dogs worked the room begging for scraps.

"Hi," Kate said to Fitz, bending over to grab a slice of plain cheese from one of the boxes. "What's all the excitement?"

Fitz smirked. "Summer's just whining because she got shut out in the eq. Again."

Summer heard him and looked over. "Shut up," she said. "You know I'm totally right. That girl only pinned higher than me because her mother's head trainer at that big barn on Long Island and the judge obviously knew it."

"Get over it, Summer," Dani said. "That girl beat you because she's ridden like ten horses a day since she was in diapers."

Marissa picked a gob of gooey cheese off her pizza and fed it to one of the dogs. "Yeah. Or if anything gives her an edge, it's that she's even taller and skinnier than Kate." She glanced down at herself with a rueful smile. "Which pretty much explains why *I* never pin in the eq."

Dani, Tommi, and Fitz laughed, but Summer shot Kate an

irritated glance. "Being tall and skinny didn't help Kate much this time, did it?" she snapped. "Even *I* beat her. And I'm not tall, or a trainer's kid, or even a working student who gets fancy horses to ride for free anytime she wants. So there!" She flounced over and grabbed another slice of pepperoni.

Kate froze in midbite, suddenly feeling like some kind of gangly eight-foot-tall beanpole freak. Was that really what Summer and the others thought of her? That she only won because Jamie gave her horses to ride for free? What did any of these people know about her, anyway? What did they know about all the work she had to put in to earn those rides?

Tommi frowned. "Shut the hell up, Summer," she said. "Don't take it out on Kate just because you're feeling pissy about your own riding."

"Yeah." Marissa giggled. "Look on the bright side—at least you didn't do a face-plant over the first jump like that poor kid from Maple Mount whose horse tripped . . ."

Kate didn't hear the rest. Fitz had just stepped around the trunk and sidled up next to her. She was so distracted she almost choked on the big bite of pizza in her mouth. Swallowing it down in a loud gulp, she smiled up at him uncertainly.

"Don't pay any attention to Summer, gorgeous," he whispered, slipping an arm around her shoulders. "She's just jealous because you're hotter *and* more talented than she is."

Kate just shrugged, shooting the other girls a glance. She still felt self-conscious, as if everyone in the room was judging everything about her, even though the others had already moved on to gossiping about someone else. She set down her pizza, suddenly not in the mood for this.

"I should go help the guys finish up," she said.

"I've got a better idea. Let's go for a walk—just the two of us." Fitz gave her arm a squeeze. "What do you say?"

Kate hesitated, glancing up into his playful hazel eyes. Seeing the way he was looking at her made her shiver without really knowing why. She flashed back to that night in the hay stall. He'd been so sweet since then, so eager to make it up to her. Was he for real?

Whatever. Tommi and the others might think she was naive, but Kate couldn't help believing—or was it hoping?—that Fitz was sincere. That he actually thought she was something special. Not that she quite understood why, but still, it was nice.

"Okay, I guess," she said.

He smiled, grabbed her hand, and pulled her out of the room. Kate was pretty sure she saw Tommi glance at them as they left, but the others didn't seem to notice their departure. Good.

Fitz led her down the aisle and around the corner into the feed room. Then he dropped her hand, took her by the shoulders, and gently turned her to face him.

"This is more like it," he said. "Come here."

He pulled her in for a kiss. Kate sank into him, feeling the tension seep out of her body for the first time in days. For a second she forgot about everything else as their mouths explored each other.

Then she felt his hands start to wander. "Hey," she said softly, pulling away and pushing his hands back where they belonged.

"Sorry," he said in a low, husky voice, a sheepish smile playing on his lips as he pulled her close again. "Force of habit. I'll be good—I swear."

To her surprise, he was. At least mostly. A couple of times things started to get more intense, but he always pulled back before it got uncomfortable. For a while Kate drifted along in a pleasant haze, letting what was happening between them happen, not thinking, just feeling.

Then some small part of her mind started to wonder: Why? Why was Fitz trying so hard, changing his usual hound-dog habits just to be with her? Was she really worth it? What exactly did he see in her?

She started to get that sour feeling in the pit of her stomach again. The same one she'd had the other night while talking to her dad after the big blowup. The same one that had attacked her at the show when she'd seen Jamie waiting at the gate for her after that eq round. Why did they all keep trying so hard, believing she could be what they wanted her to be, when she couldn't seem to live up to any of it?

Her body tensed. Fitz felt it and pulled back. He put one finger under her chin, tilting up her face so he could look into her eyes.

"What?" he whispered. "You seem kind of—I don't know, like a million miles away all of a sudden. You getting tired of me already?"

His words were light, but she saw real doubt in his eyes. She shook her head.

"Sorry," she said. "It's not you at all. Guess I'm just distracted."

"By what?"

She shrugged, not sure what to say.

"Come on, Kate." He caressed her cheekbone lightly with one finger. "You can trust me."

She hesitated. Could she? She felt really close to him right now—as close as she'd felt to anyone in a long time. But that didn't mean she'd forgotten what had happened the last time she'd let herself trust him. No, she wasn't ready to risk something like that again. Not quite yet.

Besides, how could someone like him ever understand what she was going through? Fitz sailed through life like he owned the world. Which his family pretty much did, come to think of it. He couldn't know what it was like to be her, to have her family, her problems. Her life.

He was still staring at her. Waiting. She had to tell him something.

"It's just—uh, my friend Natalie," she blurted out without really thinking, just latching on to the first thing she could think of that didn't directly involve him or the barn. "Um, we've been, you know, kind of drifting apart lately, and now she invited me out to her barn on Saturday."

"Wait. You mean that lesson barn where you first learned to ride?" he asked. "Happy something, right?"

She nodded, a little surprised that he remembered. "Yeah. Happy Acres. They're having a show, and Nat's all excited about some new project horse she's working with, and, well, I guess I'm just a little nervous about going back there."

Fitz smiled, his finger tracing the outline of her chin. "Dr. Hall's got the perfect solution to your problem," he said. "I'll come with. You know, like for moral support."

"What?" Kate blurted out in surprise. "Wait, you don't have to do that. It's just a dinky little beginner-type schooling show, and I'm sure you have better stuff to do on Saturday."

"Nothing better than spending the day with my favorite girl." Fitz shrugged. "Besides, it'll be fun. Jamie's always telling us to observe other riders and stuff, right?"

Kate wasn't sure the Happy Acres show was quite what Jamie had in mind. Still, what could she say?

"Um, okay, if you're sure . . . ," she began.

"Sure I'm sure." Fitz grinned down at her. "It's a date."

Kate smiled back weakly, trying not to imagine what Nat was going to say when she showed up with Fitz. Talk about worlds colliding . . .

ACKNOWLEDGMENTS

Thank you to both of my parents for getting up early to take me to horse shows, spending endless hours in the freezing cold and scorching heat to watch me show, clapping when I win, and cheering me up when I lose. But most important, thank you for always supporting my dreams and making me believe in myself. Thank you to Robin Greenwood, Siobhan Latchford, Scott Stewart and Ken Berkeley, Jeffrey Welles, Tracy Brindle, Barbara Jaques, and Jimmy Doyle. Without you I would have never made it to where I am today. Most of all, thank you to my friends who have stuck with me through the years and who always have my back, tell me when I am wrong, and support me no matter what choices I make. Growing up with you guys around horses made for the best memories a girl could ask for, and having you still by my side to look back on it has made the sacrifice and hard work bearable. What I have won in the ring and accomplished outside of it would mean nothing without you.

Georgina Bloomberg

Kathy Russel

GEORGINA BLOOMBERG is the younger daughter of New York City mayor Michael Bloomberg. An accomplished equestrian, Georgina is on the board of directors of the Equestrian Aid Foundation, is an ASPCA Equine Welfare Ambassador, and is the founder of the charity The Rider's Closet, which collects used riding clothes for collegiate riding teams that are unable to afford them. She also sits on the boards of the Bloomberg Sisters and Bloomberg Family foundations. Georgina is a graduate of New York University's Gallatin School of Individualized Study.

Georgina is donating a portion of her proceeds from this book to the Equestrian Aid Foundation.

CATHERINE HAPKA has published many books for children and young adults, including several about horses. A lifelong horse lover, she rides several times per week and keeps three horses on her small farm in Chester County, Pennsylvania. In addition to writing and riding, she enjoys animals of all kinds, reading, gardening, music, and travel.

BONUS ROUND
A NOTE FROM GEORGINA BLOOMBERG

I have always loved that all kinds of people are attracted to and involved in the show circuit. It doesn't matter where you come from or how you grew up, showing horses brings people together and gives them something to share. When I was younger, I was blessed to ride at a barn with a large group of other riders my age. We came from different towns, different financial backgrounds, and different kinds of families, but none of that mattered. We were all riders who shared the common bond of love for horses and being at the barn. We spent as much time as we could together—riding, planning sleepovers, and scheming about the trouble we could get into. Playing pranks on each other, hanging out in the office and giving the secretaries a hard time, and running off on trail rides when we were supposed to be cleaning tack or schooling a horse for a show were part of a normal day for us. The barn was like a second home—our escape from whatever pressures we had at school or with our family, and we loved it. A number of the kids I learned to ride with (and got into trouble with!) are still great friends of mine, and the days we spent showing together provided us with a bond that will never fade away.

Many people have asked which character I see as the most like myself in this story. On the surface, it would be Tommi, but the truth is that I can relate to each main character. I know what it's like to question your talent, like Kate, or feel conflicted about balancing your social life with the pressures of competing on the circuit, like Zara. And most important, I can relate to the way they support one another. That is truly based on my own friends. No matter how poorly a class went or what was going on in our lives away from the barn, we were always there to cheer for one another—or cheer one another up. Riding may be an individual sport, but my friends and I made ourselves into a team.

Now that I am older and have my own operation, I think of my barn as my team. We have many members who each contribute a vital part to our efforts at the shows and at home. From the vet to the grooms to my trainer, each person is crucial to what I can accomplish in the ring. It's reassuring and inspiring to know that I have so much support behind me. No successful rider gets to the top on her own!

I know firsthand that life on the show circuit can be hard, but when you learn to appreciate the good days, brush off the bad ones as learning experiences, and draw support from your fellow riders, it can also be great! The show circuit has started to change Zara's attitude, given Tommi the ability to prove herself, and helped Kate feel comfortable and confident. Now, the question is, will they use what they've learned in the show ring or get into more trouble? Only time will tell!